Praise for Unlimited

A fast-paced, gripping thriller. Rich not only with adventure, but also with visual details and dramatic snapshot insights into the Middle East.

—Phyllis Tickle, Contributing Editor, *Publishers Weekly*

This book delves into a series of crucial issues with a sensitivity that left me literally stunned. Bunn tells a story that grips the reader and refuses to let go.

—Keith Hazard, Deputy Director (ret), CIA

Written with remarkable sensitivity, Bunn masterly accomplishes a feat that would leave the State Department in awe. The nonstop action and suspense demand to be met by fast-paced reading. I highly recommend this powerful masterpiece.

—Christianbooks.com

Bunn does for readers what keeps them coming back. Descriptions so vivid you can smell the food and choke on the desert sand. Bunn breaks the mold. Fans will leap for this precise and intricate tale.

—*Publishers Weekly* (starred review)

Bunn's exciting, action-packed writing features a strong sense of place. It is sure to please his fans and win him new ones.

—*Library Journal* (starred review)

An entertaining, suspenseful, hopeful adventure. Bunn's writing is taut, his message clear.

—*Christian Retailing* (top pick of the month, July 2012)

A must-have for every inspirational reader.

—*Booklist* (top ten book of the year, 2011)

UNLIMITED
DAVIS
BUNN
B&H
PUBLISHING GROUP
NASHVILLE, TENNESSEE

Printed in the United States of America

978-1-4336-7940-7

Published by B&H Publishing Group,
Nashville, Tennessee

Dewey Decimal Classification: F
Subject Heading: MYSTERY FICTION \ ORPHANAGES—FICTION \ RENEWABLE ENERGY RESOURCES—FICTION

Scripture quotations are taken from the Holy Bible, King James Version.

Publisher's Note: The persons and events in this book are fictitious with the exception of Harold Finch and certain references to his accomplishments and career. Any other similarity to actual persons, living or dead, or actual events is purely coincidental and unintentional.

1 2 3 4 5 6 7 8 • 16 15 14 13

This novel is dedicated to
Dr. Harold Finch
"What is impossible with men is possible with God."

Acknowledgments

My involvement with a project called *Unlimited* began a few years ago, when a film producer called with a quick question about a story line in a screenplay. This led to longer conversations, which led to personal meetings, which led to my being invited to join the project as one of the writers and executive producers. Crafting a novel tied to the film's release—the book you are holding in your hands—soon became part of the vision.

Vision is truly the right word. Through this project I have come to know some of the most inspired—and inspirational—individuals I have ever encountered. They exemplify the big idea behind this work: how to unleash the God-given forces of success that live in every one of us. Like most film projects, this one had its share of explosive possibilities and unforeseen disappointments. But the integrity and perseverance of the team carried us through—toward the silver screen and unto the page. So I want to begin these pages by expressing my thanks.

First of all, to film producer Chad Gundersen, whose latest project at that time was *Like Dandelion Dust*, based on the best-selling novel by Karen Kingsbury. He had another project in development, one based upon the life and teachings of Dr. Harold Finch—an inventor and educator who achieved exceptional results in business. For decades, Harold had devoted his resources to fund missionary projects and orphanages. He had lectured around the world on the dynamics of success from a biblical perspective, and wanted to capture that legacy in a film. I had enjoyed an international business career prior to becoming a novelist, so the concept—and the man—seized my attention.

I soon met Harold Finch, a day I will never forget. He is difficult to thank on this acknowledgments page, because he has made such an unexpectedly deep impact on various aspects of my life. His teachings on setting and achieving goals have enhanced my spiritual and professional growth. His friendship, and the example he sets in matters large and small, will stay with me forever. So thank you, Harold.

I was then drawn into the *Unlimited* team, with Chad making introductions to Nathan Frankowski, a writer and director, and Jon Stone, a cowriter. The main setting for the story is an orphanage in the Mexican borderlands. After months of behind-the-scenes work, the film went into production in Texas. I spent time on the set getting to know the crew and actors. Interacting with these highly talented and dedicated artists was a great privilege. I learned much about the beauty and sorrows which mark today's Mexico.

From the professionals behind the camera, I would especially like to thank Michael Charske (Location Manager), Elise Graham

(Line Producer), and Jacob Cena (Assistant Cinematographer). Notably, Jacob shared his ordeals as a survivor of the gang warfare that has overwhelmed the city of Juarez.

From the actors I gained insights into the back-story of the roles they played. I then applied these character lessons in the development of this novel. My profound thanks go to Robert Amaya, Fred Thompson, Emilio Roso, Oscar Avila, Crystal Martinez, and Daniel Ross Owens. Unusually, rather than the film being based on a novel, this novel is essentially based on a film. I was encouraged when someone pointed out a winning precedent—the 1970s movie *Love Story* was only later adapted into a best-selling book.

Vital assistance—both creative and practical—was provided by many others. Vinnie and Jodie Carafano direct the orphanage where the filming took place. Mary Beth Maifield is Director of the Youth-with-a-Mission orphanage in Juarez; she brought the plight of these children into vivid clarity. Brenda Luna-Bravo, who was raised in the YWAM orphanage and is now studying at the university in El Paso, shared many hardships and the value of hope. David Mullens is a pastor who runs a missionary church. For three generations, his family has farmed two thousand acres in Mexico. This has all been jeopardized by the violence that has swept the country. David introduced me to life in the border regions, and the meaning of not only surviving but thriving through a steadfast faith. Julio Marin is youth pastor at the Calvary Chapel of Melbourne, Florida, familiar with leading mission trips to Mexico. Even before I left for the filming, this dear friend helped me build the platform that supported this story. And speaking of stories—another word of thanks to Julie Gwinn for her early enthusiasm for this novel.

I need to return to Chad Gundersen, and the multifaceted talents he deploys in making an idea into a reality. He brought me into this world of film production, and these experiences have made *Unlimited* one of the most singular projects of my career. Chad, for your partnership and friendship I will always be grateful.

Finally, my final heartfelt thanks go to Isabella, my wife and dearest friend. Thank you, darling, for the gifts of wisdom and strength and love.

Prologue

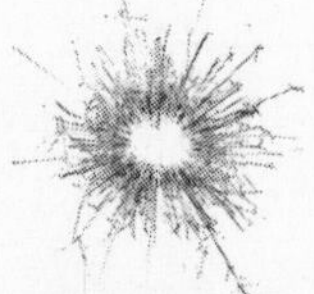

Simon crawled away from his burning car, amazed that he was still alive. He stayed low in the shallow trench running alongside the Mexican highway. His brain was still scrambled from the wreck. He was not entirely sure why he needed to remain out of sight. Only that it was important. Vital.

He clambered over the loose rubble, dragging his canvas duffel along with him. He halted for a moment, willing strength back into his limbs and clarity into his brain. As he gasped for breath, Simon glanced back. His beloved car, his last remaining connection to the life he had once assumed was his to claim, lay on the passenger side in a ditch. The Mustang's tires were all blown out and shredded. The sun descended behind the rim of the western hills and cast the scene in deep shadows, as though ashamed over what had been done to him.

He gripped the duffel and lifted his head a fraction of an inch above the trench's lip. On the other side of the road, a man stood waiting for a break in the traffic. The man whistled a cheery tune as he watched the road.

Simon realized he had seen the man before, smirking as Simon had driven away from the border post. Which meant that, unless Simon was very fast and very lucky, he was going to die.

His best hope was to make it to the *maquiladora*, the industrial zone. The first buildings were less than a mile away. Even as bruised and shaken as he was, he could do that easily. But not with the pack.

The pack contained far more than eleven months of research. The apparatus and the diagrams were his last hope of returning to the university as a physicist. It was his lone chance at the star he had always assumed would one day be his. Saving him from a lifetime of bars and empty chatter and the easy downward slide to oblivion.

He had to find somewhere to hide it.

The duffel bag was too heavy for him to carry very fast. The apparatus it contained had to weigh forty pounds, and there were another ten pounds of graphs and diagrams and spreadsheets and pages from his proposal. But he could at least balance himself better.

Simon fit one arm and then the other through the duffel's two canvas straps, then slung the bag across his back. He took a hard breath, willing himself forward. When a pair of lumbering trucks hid him from sight, Simon slithered over the trench's opposite ledge. Then he launched himself up and away.

The bag struck his back with every step. A sharp edge poked his neck. He assumed it was the control panel. Simon would be badly bruised when this was over. If he survived.

The ground was so rough and the light so dim, Simon found the second ditch by falling into it. He was desperate not to roll and damage the apparatus further. He crouched and skidded his way down the side. And at its bottom, he found the hiding place.

A cracked and pitted concrete pipe ran along the culvert's base. A jagged hole gaped five feet down from where he landed, just large enough to take the duffel. Simon lay on the filthy pipe and shoved the bag up as far as he could manage, getting it well out of sight. Unless they came looking with a flashlight. Unless they guessed he had hidden it here.

He scrambled up the other side and headed into the desert. He was tempted to try for the highway. But the hunter still had his SUV, and there was too much risk of Simon being caught in the open. So he aimed for the fence surrounding the industrial zone.

Simon glanced back and saw the bearded stranger loping toward him. Then the man barked. Like a lone coyote on the scent of prey. A sharp sound, hard and merciless as the terrain.

Simon ran faster still.

Chapter 1

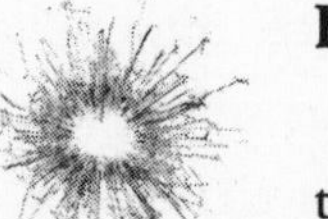

Five Hours Earlier

A hot, dusty wind buffeted Simon through the Mustang's open top. He started to pull over and close up the car. But the convertible's electric motor did not work, and he would have to fight the top by hand. When he had started off that morning, the predawn air had carried a frigid bite. Now his sweatshirt lay in the empty passenger seat, covering the remaining water bottle and his iPod.

The car's radio worked, but one of the speakers was blown. The iPod's headphones were hidden beneath the sweatshirt as well. Simon doubted the border authorities cared whether he listened to music on an in-ear system. But he didn't want to give them any reason to make trouble.

He didn't know what he had been expecting for a small-town border crossing, but it definitely was not this. An American flag flew over a fortified concrete building. The flag snapped and rippled as Simon pulled forward. In front of him were three trucks and a few vans. One car had Texas plates, one produce truck was from Oklahoma, and the other half-dozen vehicles were Mexican. That was it. The crossing was four lanes in each direction, and all but two were blocked off with yellow traffic cones. The border crossing looked ready to handle an armada. The empty lanes heightened the sense of desolation.

As he waited his turn, a harvest truck rumbled past, bringing sacks of vegetables to the United States. The driver shot Simon a gold-toothed grin through his open window. As though the two of them shared a secret. They were passing through the only hassle-free crossing between Mexico and the USA.

Or so Simon hoped.

To either side of the crossing grew the fence. Simon had heard about the border fence for years. But it was still a jarring sight. Narrow steel girders marched in brutal regularity out of sight in both directions. The pillars were thirty feet high, maybe more, and spaced so the wind whistled between them in a constant piercing whine, like a siren, urging Simon to turn back while he still could.

Only he didn't have a choice. Or he would not have made this journey in the first place.

Simon passed the U.S. checkpoint and drove across the bridge. Below flowed the silted gray waters of the Rio Grande.

The Mexican border officer took in the dusty car and Simon's disheveled appearance and directed him to pull over. Simon heaved a silent sigh and did as he was ordered.

The Mexican customs official was dressed in blue—navy trousers, shirt, hat. He circled Simon's car slowly before saying,

"Your passport." He examined it carefully. "What is the purpose of your visit to Mexico, señor?"

"I'm making a presentation to the Ojinaga city council."

The officer glanced at Simon, then the car, and finally the black duffel bag that filled the rear seat. "What kind of presentation?"

"My advisor at MIT retired down here last year. We've been working on a project together." He plucked the letter from his shirt pocket and unfolded it along the well-creased lines.

The officer studied it. "Do you read Spanish, Dr. . . . ?"

He started to correct the man, then decided it didn't matter. The officer had no need to know Simon had dropped out. "Dr. Vasquez, my professor, he translated it."

"You have cut this very close, señor." The officer checked his watch. "It says your appointment is in less than two hours."

"I expected the trip from Boston to take two days. It's taken four. My car broke down. Twice."

The officer pointed to the duffel. "What is in the bag?"

"Scientific instrumentation." Simon reached back and unzipped the top.

The Mexican officer frowned over the complicated apparatus. "It looks like a bomb."

"I know. Or a vacuum cleaner." He swallowed against a dry throat. "I get that a lot."

The officer handed back Simon's passport and letter. "Welcome to Mexico, señor."

Simon restarted the motor and drove away. He kept his hands tight on the wheel and his eyes on the empty road ahead. There was no need to be afraid. He was not carrying drugs. He was not breaking any law. This time. But the memory of other border crossings kept his heart rate amped to redline as he drove slowly past the snapping flags and the dark *federales'* cars.

His attention was caught by a man leaning against a dusty SUV. The Mexican looked odd from every angle. He was not so much round as bulky, like an aging middleweight boxer. Despite the heat, he was dressed in a beige leather jacket that hung on him like a sweaty robe. The man had a fringe of unkempt dark hair and a scraggly beard. He leaned against the black Tahoe with the ease of someone out for a morning stroll. He caught Simon's eye and grinned, then made a gun of his hand and shot Simon. Welcome to Mexico.

A hundred meters beyond the border, the screen to his iPod map went blank, then a single word appeared: *searching.* Simon did not care. He could see his destination up ahead. The city of Ojinaga hovered in the yellow dust. He crossed Highway 10, the east-west artery that ran from the Atlantic to the Pacific. He drove past an industrial zone carved from the surrounding desert, then joined the city traffic.

Ojinaga grew up around him, a distinctly Mexican blend of poverty and high concrete walls. The city was pretty much as Vasquez had described. Simon's former professor had dearly loved his hometown. Vasquez had spent his final two years at MIT yearning to return. The mountains he had hiked as a boy rose to Simon's right, razor peaks that had never been softened by rain. Vasquez had bought a home where he could sit in his backyard and watch the sunset turn them into molten gold. But they looked very ominous to Simon. Like they barred his way forward. Hemming him in with careless brutality.

Between the border and downtown, Simon checked his phone six times. Just as Vasquez had often complained, there was no connection. Landline phone service wasn't much better. Skype was impossible. Vasquez had maintained contact by e-mailing in the predawn hours. He had claimed to enjoy the isolation. Simon would have gone nuts.

The last time they had spoken had been almost two weeks earlier, when Vasquez declared he was on the verge of a breakthrough. After months of frustrating dead ends, Vasquez had finally managed to make their apparatus work. Since then, Simon had received a series of increasingly frantic e-mails, imploring him to come to Mexico to present the device to the city council.

What neither of them ever mentioned was the real reason why Vasquez had taken early retirement and returned to his hometown in the first place. Which was also the reason why Simon had made this trip at all. To apologize for the role he had played in the demise of Vasquez's career. That was something that had to be done face-to-face.

Simon found a parking spot on the main plaza. Downtown Ojinaga was dominated by a massive central square, big as three football fields. Simon imagined it must have really been something when it was first built. Now it held the same run-down air as the rest of the town. A huge Catholic church anchored the opposite side of the plaza. The trees and grass strips lining the square were parched and brown. Skinny dogs flitted about, snarling at one another. Drunks occupied the concrete benches. Old cars creaked and complained as they drove over *topes,* the speed bumps lining the roads. In a nearby shop-front window, two women made dough and fed it into a tortilla machine.

The city office building looked ready for demolition. Several windows were cracked. Blinds hung at haphazard angles, giving the facade a sleepy expression. A bored policeman slumped in the shaded entrance. Simon entered just as the church bells tolled the hour.

The guard ran his duffel back through the metal detector three times, while another officer pored over the letter from the city council. Finally they gestured him inside and pointed him down a long corridor.

The door to the council meeting hall was closed. Simon heard voices inside. He debated knocking, but Vasquez had still not arrived. Simon visited the restroom and changed into a clean shirt. He stuffed his dirty one down under the apparatus. He shaved and combed his hair. His eyes looked like they had become imprinted with GPS road maps, so he dug out his eye-drops. Then he took a moment and inspected his reflection.

Simon was tall enough that he had to stoop to fit his face in the mirror. His hair was brownish-blond and worn rakishly long, which went with his strong features and green eyes and pirate's grin. Only he wasn't smiling now. There was nothing he could do to repay Vasquez for what happened, except help him get the city's funding so they could complete the project. Then Simon would flee this poverty-stricken town and try to rebuild his own shattered life.

He returned to the hall, settled onto a hard wooden bench,

and pulled out his phone. For once, the phone registered a two-bar signal.

Simon dialed Vasquez and listened to the phone ring. The linoleum floor by his feet was pitted with age. The hallway smelled slightly of cheap disinfectant and a woman's perfume. Sunlight spilled through tall windows at the end of the corridor, forming a backdrop of brilliance and impenetrable shadows.

When the professor's voice mail answered, he said, "It's Simon again. I'm here in the council building. Growing more desperate by the moment." The door beside him opened, and Simon turned away from the voices that spilled out. "Professor Vasquez, I really hope you're on your way, because—"

"Excuse me, señor. You are Simon Orwell, the professor's great friend?"

Simon shut his phone and rose to his feet. "Is he here?"

The two men facing him could not have been more different. One was tall, not as tall as Simon, but he towered over most Mexicans. And handsome. And extremely well groomed. The other was the product of a hard life, stubby and tough as nails. The only thing they shared was a somber expression.

Even before the elegant man said the words, Simon knew.

"I am very sorry to have to tell you, Señor Simon. But Professor Vasquez is dead."

"No, that's . . . What?"

"Allow me to introduce myself. Enrique Morales, I am the mayor of Ojinaga. And this is Pedro Marin, the assistant town manager and my trusted ally."

"Vasquez is dead?"

"A heart attack. Very sudden."

"He thought the world of you, Señor Simon." Pedro spoke remarkably clear English.

The mayor was graceful even when expressing condolences. "*Nos lamentanos mucho.* We lament with you, Señor Simon, in this dark hour."

For some reason, Simon found it easier to focus upon the smaller man. "You knew the professor?"

"He was a dear friend. My sister and I and Dr. Harold, perhaps you have heard of him? The professor was very close to us all."

"You're sure about Vasquez?"

"Such a tragedy." The mayor was around his midthirties and had a politician's desire to remain the center of attention. "You came all the way from Boston, is that not so? We are glad you made it safely. And we regret this news is here to greet you."

"I . . . we're scheduled to meet the city council."

A look flashed between the two men. "I believe they have completed their other business, yes? Pedro will escort you. I must hurry to the city's outskirts. We are dedicating a new water treatment facility. Long in coming. But so very needed. It is our attempt to aid the poorest citizens of our community. Like the professor's bold project, no? So very noble." Enrique was clearly adept at filling uncomfortable vacuums. "Please join me for dinner tonight. Yes? Splendid. We will meet and we will talk and I will see what I can do to assist you through this dark hour. The restaurant by the church. Nine o'clock."

Enrique turned and spoke a lightning-swift sentence to Pedro, whose nod of acceptance shaped a half bow. The mayor's footsteps clipped rapidly down the hall. He tossed quick greetings to several people as he departed, clapped the senior guard on the shoulder, thanked the second guard who opened the door for him, and was gone.

Simon stared into the empty sunlight at the corridor's end, wishing the floor would just open up and swallow him whole.

Then he realized Pedro was waiting for him. "This way, señor. The council will see you now."

Chapter 2

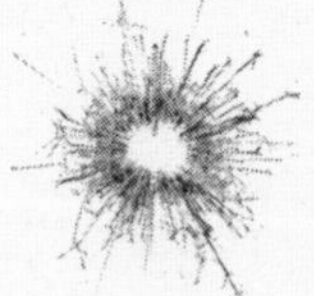

Entering the council chamber, Simon felt as though he was being ushered through a waking nightmare. He could not force the world back into place. He saw tiny fragments, little shards that remained jumbled together like a puzzle he could not fit together.

Not even when his professional life depended on it.

Three city officials were seated across the conference table from Simon. The woman who led the city council meeting introduced herself as Dr. Clara. The two men wore cheap three-piece suits, one blue, the other a shade between gray and green. Simon dismissed them in a matter of seconds. It was instantly clear that Dr. Clara was the only person who mattered. Simon thought of the name applied by field researchers to the dominant animal in a pack. Dr. Clara was most definitely the alpha dog. This meeting was really between Simon and her.

Dr. Clara was a heavyset woman poured into a too-small dress. Her hair was clenched into a tight bun, just like the dress squeezed her body. She listened to Simon's presentation without expression, her gaze flat and measuring. Then she broke in with, "What you are telling us, Señor Simon, we have already heard from Professor Vasquez. You seek to harvest power that is currently wasted in the transmission process and transform it into usable electricity. Is that not correct?"

"Basically, yes. Like I was saying, more than a third of all power is currently lost between the generating station and the end user. Our device—"

"We can offer you a thousand dollars American."

Simon gaped across the polished table. "You expect me to turn over the apparatus and years of research for a *thousand bucks*?"

"We are offering to buy your machine, yes, that is correct."

"What about the offer for two hundred thousand dollars in research funding you made to Professor Vasquez?"

Dr. Clara spoke English without accent or emotion. "I recall making no such offer."

Simon unfolded the letter and passed it over. The two men leaned in to read with her. Dr. Clara scanned it swiftly and slid it back. "I did not write this letter. I did not sign it."

"Vasquez wouldn't have urged me to come help with this presentation over a forged letter." Simon took a hard breath. Yelling would get him nowhere. "Look. This is a revolutionary device. Professor Vasquez was convinced it would change your region's future."

He had so much more he wanted to say. How Vasquez had never been in this for the money. How he had intended to place his share in a trust. One that would help the poorest children of Chihuahua, the state in which Ojinaga was located. Vasquez yearned to help those who had not been given the same gifts as himself, the same opportunities, the same great life. He had accepted that Simon had been in it for the money and the fame. Vasquez was a man who seldom criticized. He had lived with his faith as a silent beacon, waiting for Simon to ask the unspoken questions.

The woman broke into his thoughts with, "Your device does not work, señor."

"*Yet.* My device does not work *yet.*"

"And your associate, Dr. Vasquez, is dead."

Simon felt the noose tightening around his professional neck. Cutting off his air and any hope of recovering his career. "We are *this close* to a major breakthrough. That is why the research funding is so critical."

"We are a poor city. Even if your device worked, we could not pay you what you claim was promised."

Simon caught something in her gaze. For an instant, she separated herself from the two men who enjoyed watching him squirm. Her dark gaze opened in a remarkable manner, as though she was struggling not to weep. Simon had a fleeting vision of a very different woman. One trapped in sorrow and something more. Before he could fathom what message she was trying to send him, the instant was gone. The blank-faced councilwoman said, "Our offer stands. One thousand dollars for your machine and these drawings."

He rose to his feet and began cramming his documents and the apparatus back in the duffel. "Your offer isn't enough to get me home."

The two men smiled, as though this had been their intention all along. Dr. Clara continued to lean forward, so as to mask her expression from her associates, and shared with him another secret look. Only this time it was full of warning.

He zipped his duffel shut. "What aren't you telling me?"

She shook her head, clearly disappointed with his question. "I hope you enjoy your stay in Mexico, señor."

Simon walked down the corridor and passed the guards and stepped through the main doors. It felt as though the building expelled him. The late afternoon sun blasted directly into his eyes. Behind him he heard loud voices and laughter. The duffel bag weighed a thousand pounds. The apparatus anchored him to a billion broken dreams. The heat was a burden that threatened to drive him onto his knees. To his left, the church bells began ringing, hammering at him with musical nails.

Simon was midway across the square when he halted. He set the apparatus on the ground by his feet. He stared at the battered Mustang, willing himself to get back behind the wheel and drive. Head north, cross the border, get back to Boston.

But for what? Get another bartending job? Make another futile attempt to be reinstated at MIT? Try to convince the school he had finally turned his life around?

The bells finally stopped ringing. A doorway in a yellow stucco wall beside the church opened, and young children spilled out. They all wore uniforms of white and pale blue. They chattered gaily as they crossed the square toward a waiting bus. So many shining faces, so much young hope.

Simon picked up his duffel and walked to his car. He dumped the apparatus in the rear seat, climbed in, started the car, put it into gear, and pulled away. Behind him, the children chased a pair of doves and shrieked their carefree laughter.

He traveled the same road he had driven south, filled with bitter regret. He had no idea where Vasquez was buried and would not have gone to the grave site if he did. He had not been to a cemetery since the day after his ninth birthday, when he had been dragged by his new foster family to his parents' funeral. The apologies he had carried south, the four days of words he had spoken to the empty car, were lost to the blistering heat.

As the city faded into poverty, Simon's rage finally erupted. He shouted at the westering sun and pressed the pedal to the floor. The Mustang's engine bellowed a manic note, as though giving voice to all his bitter tumult. Simon blasted out of town and flew into the desert. The industrial zone and border station were masked by the dusty sunset. And beyond that lay two thousand miles of road and the cold, hard reality of nothing to lose.

He was already over the bump before he realized what he had hit.

The dusty wooden plank had been dragged across his lane just as he approached. Ten-inch nails studded the plank, dozens of them. They glimmered in the light like teeth. A man squatted in the trench beside the road, almost hidden by the SUV's shadow.

All four of the Mustang's tires banged, tight sounds like gunshots. The Mustang had been traveling at over seventy miles an hour. The wheels deflated in a split second. The rims hit the pavement and began throwing up sparks higher than his windscreen. The car shrieked like an animal caught in a trap.

Simon wrenched the wheel, but the car did not respond. The Mustang spun in a lazy circle, the sparks rising like fireworks. He heard a blaring horn and spotted a massive truck's front fender come racing toward him. For the first time he genuinely thought he was about to die.

The left front tire rim caught a rock or groove or something, and the car jerked as though yanked by an unseen hand. The Mustang veered off the road just as the truck blasted by.

The car tumbled into the trench and gnashed down the rocky slope. Rocks and shrubs screeched against the right side. The trench was about fifteen feet deep and grew steeper the closer they came to the bottom. The Mustang swooped down the final drop and hammered its nose into the concrete trough lining the base. The car rocked once, twice, and then creaked and groaned and came to rest at a steep angle. The trench's narrow dimensions kept the Mustang from turning completely over.

Simon huffed a series of very hard breaths. The loudest sound he could hear was the boom of his heart. Rocks scattered and slid down the ledge beside him. Somewhere in the distance a truck's horn continued to blare as it drove away.

Simon forced his hands to unclench the wheel. His thoughts formed a rambling noise, but one thing was vividly clear. He was still in danger. He was certain he had to move. Get out of the car. And flee.

He unhooked his safety belt and eased himself down to the earth. He clambered out of the car, scaling his seat and searching for handholds in the dirt. Everything hurt. Then he remembered the apparatus and crouched down to where he could look into the rear seat.

The black duffel bag was gone.

Instantly his life and the world came into sharp focus. The final remnant of his former world was inside that duffel bag. The last remaining vestige of his life as a scientist.

Gone.

Then he saw it. Hidden in the scar his car had plowed in the yellow dirt, melded into the trench's shadows.

His legs were trembly and his fear was very real. But he managed to clamber around the side of the car, hop across the concrete base, and scale the raw earth. The duffel was twisted at an odd angle, which suggested that the apparatus inside was badly damaged. But now was not the time to worry about such things. Because his mind was clearing enough to realize that the danger was not over.

In fact, if he was right, it was only just beginning.

Chapter 3

As Simon raced across the desert, he heard a faint noise behind him. Simon had trouble identifying it. It was a faint beeping, like a radar gun, or . . .

He risked a glance back. Silhouetted against the last shard of daylight was the hunter. He used both hands to steady his aim and hummed a bizarre beeping noise, almost like he was playing a video fighter, bringing Simon into the target-circle.

The hunter treated Simon's death as a game.

Simon scaled a steep-sided ledge, using all four limbs to fight for holds in the loose earth. A bang sounded behind him. The bullet whined off a rock to the right of his face, then something smacked him in the forehead. Simon lost his footing and tumbled over the ledge.

He fell and rolled and came up running, though his mind felt disconnected and his legs were wobbly. Even so, he ran. His vision blurred and then cleared, his limbs refused to follow the scattered directions from his brain, then snapped back into rhythm. Still, he ran.

The maquiladora, or industrial zone, was made up of three distinct components. A cluster of brand-new structures rose to his right. Their prefab siding gleamed in the guard lights. They were surrounded by new fencing topped with barbed wire. A generator rumbled loudly somewhere out of sight. Simon searched for a way through the fence and found none.

The wound on his forehead drummed in time with the generator. Each breath punched a new hole in his pain. He swiped at the blood that trailed across his left eye and glanced back. The hunter had returned to his SUV. He spun in a dusty circle and flew across the scrubland, taking aim at Simon.

Directly ahead of Simon were a cluster of perhaps two dozen older buildings. They formed an industrial slum, with pitted walls and broken windows and empty parking areas. Beyond the farthest structures, traffic rumbled down the highway connecting Ojinaga to the border. Simon resisted the urge to try for the cultivated area connecting the newer zone to the highway. The angle of the hunter's approach suggested this was what he wanted. He knew the terrain and Simon did not. The hunter intended to herd him into the dead zone between the desert and the fence.

Simon veered toward the zone's third section: a vast workers' compound. Bordering the apartment blocks were tiny garage-style operations servicing the newer industrial structures to his right. The housing was as grim as anything he had ever seen.

Beyond the dwellings Simon glimpsed what appeared to be a dusty market square. This entire section was fenced, of course.

Everything of value in Mexico was fenced. But Simon ran toward it anyway, hoping against hope that he would find a hole or a break or at least a tree that would give him a lever on which he could scale his way to safety.

The hunter must have seen what he intended, because the SUV's motor roared angrily. The change spurred Simon to a speed he had not thought possible. He was not being chased by a man. He was fleeing death itself.

He could not find a way through. The fence was rusting, but the holes were all covered with black-mesh nylon. Simon didn't slow, he didn't hesitate. He leapt as high as he could and smashed into the fence, full force.

To his left, the stanchion holding up the fence snapped clean off.

Simon clung grimly to the fencing as it bent forward like a fan. He clung to it like a limpet on a branch. The stanchion to his right groaned and cracked and gently laid him onto the earth.

Moving on all fours, he gingerly picked his way across the coiled barbed wire. Soon as he was across he scrambled like a football player coming out of the crouch.

"Help!"

The closest structures were 150 yards ahead, separated from him by scrubland that had been parceled into tight little farm plots. Chickens clucked nervously as he scrambled between the waist-high fences. From one of the nearest structures he heard the whine of a saw cutting metal. But he saw no one.

"Help! Please! Somebody!"

The race took on a nightmare quality. His legs trembled with the fear that safety would remain just out of reach. He clawed ahead, his hands outstretched, willing someone to appear from one of the buildings and do something, anything to end this horror.

"Help me, somebody—"

Gunfire sounded behind him. Dusty furrows were dug from the earth to his right. Simon ran harder still.

His lungs sawed for a breath in the hot air. He could feel the hot wetness drip down his face. The pain was almost blinding. But the buildings were closer now, the shadows longer.

Simon lanced between two tall dormitories. He raced down an alley that felt choked with despair. He bounded out the other side, scrambled down another weed-strewn lane, tripped over an unseen ledge, and tumbled into the dusty plaza.

Most of the stalls were locked for the night. The plaza was almost empty. A few stragglers wandered away from him. The departing stallholders either did not hear or chose to ignore him. One woman's face showed vague alarm as she locked her stall and hurried away.

Then he spotted lights belonging to a slightly larger stall, one with a screened-in front section. Simon did not shout because he no longer had the air to form a word. He could scarcely carry himself across the plaza. He had no idea how close the hunter was. He could no longer hear the SUV. His ears were filled with the sawing rasp of his own breaths and a faint buzzing sound, like the drone of a thousand angry insects.

He slammed through the screened door and spilled onto the raw wood floor. Even then he kept moving. He crawled on his knees around the plywood counter. A lone customer occupied the last stool. This man looked vaguely familiar, but Simon's pounding head refused to form a coherent thought. The customer and the lone cook both gaped as Simon crawled into the space beneath the counter. The cook said something in high-pitched Spanish. Then the sound of shouts and footsteps rang out, and the cook went silent.

The customer bolted into action. He leapt around the counter and hefted a boiling pot off the stove. He backed up two paces, so he was clear of the counter, and slung the contents onto the floor.

Simon's foggy brain finally recognized the man. He managed to croak, "Pedro."

"Hush, for your life." As the city manager poured the steaming pot over the bloodstains, he spoke in a staccato undertone to the man behind the counter. The cook responded with a fearful whine. Pedro spoke again, just one or two words.

The cook grabbed the broom propped in the corner by the portable gas stove and walked around the counter. Simon heard feet thump against the counter wall by his head and realized Pedro had returned to his seat.

The cook pushed the screen door open and swept the water outside. A third voice yelled in protest, probably because the water splashed over his boots. This new voice was hard, sharp. The Spanish coming from this man was knife-edged. Simon gripped his knees and scrunched in tighter. He shivered uncontrollably.

The third man entered, pushing the cook back with his voice. Simon heard the broom skitter across the floor. Heavy footsteps creaked the floorboards. The hunter's voice grew louder, angrier. The cook responded with the same fearful whine.

Then Pedro added his own words, his tone subservient. Respectful. But not afraid. The hunter growled once more, then stomped from the place.

Then silence gripped them all. Simon's brain registered everything through the dual veils of terror and pain. Outside, the hunter snarled in frustration as he moved away.

Pedro murmured softly, "Stay where you are."

Simon shut his eyes. His head stabbed with every racing heartbeat. He could feel blood from his forehead leak onto the floor. His shivers were growing stronger now.

But he was safe.

The knowledge was exquisite.

Pedro's voice remained very steady. "My truck is parked outside. I will back it around so the passenger door is by the exit. When you come out, stay low." He spoke to the cook in Spanish, who handed Simon a clean dish towel. Pedro told him, "Press the cloth to your forehead."

"It hurts."

"You have been shot, yes? It's supposed to hurt. Press hard."

Simon did as he was told. Pedro pulled out his keys and pushed open the cantina's screen door. Simon heard him whistling a little tune.

The pickup's door creaked open and shut. When the engine fired, Simon crawled from his hiding place. His head and neck and shoulders had stiffened, which caused him to groan aloud. The cook responded with a fearful tirade. Simon crept around the counter as the truck pulled in tight. Simon slipped out the door just as Pedro reached over and opened the passenger door.

The pickup was moving before Simon settled into the seat. Pedro said, "I will take you to the border."

"Great. Thanks." Then Simon paused. "Wait, that won't work."

"There is no waiting. The men who seek you, they are still out there."

Simon's tongue felt too thick for the confines of his mouth. "My car was forced off the road. My passport is locked in the trunk."

Pedro gave a heavy sigh. He scouted in all directions, then crossed over the highway and headed into the rough terrain. "They will still be out there, the people who hunt you."

"It was just one man."

"One man that you saw." The truck jounced hard over a rocky outcropping. "Where is your car?"

"In a ditch." The fringes of his vision began to blur. "They put a board across the road. Blew out the tires."

"That is a common tactic of the drug cartels. You are involved in drugs?"

"I'm down here to meet with your town council, remember?"

"If this was the cartel, they will have allies among the border agents. They might hold you until your hunters arrive." Pedro lightly drummed the wheel. Then he spun the wheel and drove back in the direction they had come. As he pulled onto the road, he checked carefully in all directions. "Slide down into the foot well."

"Where are you taking me?"

Pedro drove slowly into the ever-deepening night. "Somewhere safe."

Chapter 4

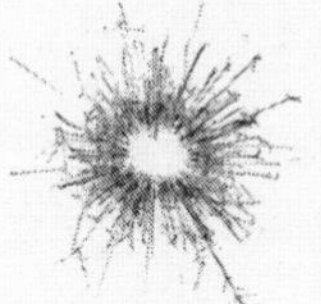

Sofia Marin did not want to enter that room. She knew who was waiting for her. Though they had never met, she knew Simon Orwell, and she knew his faults. Sofia knew how bad he could be. She knew all too well. "Why did you bring him here?"

Pedro continued to tug on her hand. "You want to stand and discuss this now? While he bleeds?"

"He was shot. You said it yourself. He was chased. The gangs want him."

"You don't know that."

"If it wasn't the cartel, then who? What if he brings the gangs here? What if you were followed?"

Her brother tightened the grip on her hand and pulled her forward. "Enough with the what-ifs. You could question a donkey to death."

"What if his being here endangers the children?"

"We were not followed."

The closer she came to that door, the more she held back. "You know this how?"

"For one thing, the gunman was behind the tenements when I put Simon in the truck. I saw his SUV drive away." Impatiently Pedro dragged her through the doorway. "For another, I cut across the desert. If anyone had followed, I would have seen them for miles. But I wasn't followed. Now come and help."

Simon lay upon the bed. He was just like the photographs Vasquez had shown her. Even with the blood soaking his head and shirt, he was just as handsome. Just as appealing. Just as dangerous. "He should not be here."

"Then help to get him ready to leave!" Pedro let go of her, so he could flap his arms in exasperation. "You have to fight me at every turn. You can never just do what you are going to do anyway. First you have to argue. Then you have to run away."

It was a familiar refrain, and it bit especially deep because that was exactly what she wanted to do. Turn and run from this man.

Instead she pulled over the room's one chair and seated herself by the bed. "Juan."

The young boy stood in the doorway, as Sofia knew he would be. He knew everything that happened around the orphanage before it happened. "Yes?"

"Run to the infirmary for my kit."

The boy, all overlong limbs and angles, entered the room. "I have it here already."

"Of course you do." She accepted the leather satchel with a

smile she did not feel. "Now go find Harold and tell him he has to come. Immediately."

Simon swam up through deep, dark waters. He came to the surface gradually and opened his eyes to a soft light and very harsh pain.

A beautiful woman was seated beside his bed. She had just finished sewing his forehead. She clipped the thread and set her utensils in a metal plate. The fingers of her gloved hands were stained with his blood. He probably should have felt a little queasy at the sight, but just then all he could think about was that he was safe. The place, wherever it was, radiated a sense of calm.

His vision expanded to where he could take in the room. Four people watched him, all with very somber expressions. One was Pedro, the mayor's assistant. Beside the lady's chair stood an older man, very erect, with knowing eyes. He studied Simon with a severe intensity.

The fourth figure stood to his right, over in the doorway. Simon could have shifted his head around and looked more closely, but just then he could not be bothered. The half-seen person was no threat. Of this he was certain. Besides, if he moved his head he would not be able to look at the woman.

She had the most perfect skin he had ever seen. Her complexion was a dusky gold. Her hair was a bit longer than shoulder length and swept in two careless curves about her face, like the fall of waves on a windless night. Her features shone with a vibrant intelligence.

She was also very angry. With him. Every time she met his gaze, she blistered him with all the words she kept trapped behind her tightly compressed lips. Simon knew the expression. He should. He had angered far too many women in his life.

But it usually took a little longer to get them this upset.

It was the older man who spoke. "You're Simon Orwell, the friend of Professor Vasquez?"

He nodded. "He's dead, right?"

"Yes. We lost our friend eleven days ago."

"Twelve days." The beautiful woman corrected him. "It's after midnight."

"That's impossible," Simon declared.

"Why do you say that?"

"Because his last e-mail was four days ago."

Their response surprised him. No one protested that what he said was absurd. If anything, his words seemed almost expected. As though what he told them heightened some deep concern.

The woman peeled the back off a pressure bandage. Her gestures were tight. She said to the man who had saved him, "You see? You do not bring the friend of Vasquez to this place. You bring danger."

Pedro said, "What was I supposed to do, Sofia, stand by and let him die?"

"Better that than . . ." She glared at him and mashed the bandage down hard.

"Ow!"

"You hush. You should not be here." She stripped off the gloves and rose from her seat. "You are nothing but trouble. Vasquez always said that. Now we know why."

Sofia looked at the key that hung around his neck. Her expression said it all. She knew about the key. And she knew about what Simon had done with it. Even so, he could not look away. When her gaze returned to his face, angry and pained and worried, all Simon could think was, *Guilty.*

The old man said softly, "Vasquez also said many other things about him."

"I know this one. I know his type better than any of you. Better you dump him on the street."

Pedro frowned. "Sofia, how you talk."

"You mark my words." She lifted the metal plate in one hand and a black leather case in the other. She stomped across the floor, pausing in the doorway only long enough to say, "When the children are in danger, you remember what I tell you this night."

The two men stared at the empty doorway. Simon had the impression they had stood and stared like this on many other occasions.

Finally the older man asked, "Do you have someone you want us to call and tell you are all right?"

Simon felt the burn of old familiar shame. "No. It can wait."

"Get some rest. We will talk in the morning."

"Where am I?"

"Everything can wait until tomorrow."

The old man cut off the light as he left the room. As they clumped down unseen stairs, Simon heard Pedro murmur something, but he could not catch the words.

But he did hear the old man's response. That came through with a piercing quality. It was precisely what Vasquez had said on another dark night, perhaps the darkest hour Simon had ever known.

The old man said, "It is all in God's hands."

Chapter 5

Simon woke thinking of his first best friend.

When he was seven, his parents had spent weeks worrying about a solitary man who had moved into the house across the street and never spoke to any of his neighbors. The next morning Simon had rung the man's doorbell and demanded to know who he was and why he was bothering Simon's parents. The man had proven to be alone because he had recently lost his wife. He had taken a new job in a new city as an attempt to restart his life. His wife had always been the one to meet people. The man was an electrical engineer who became a dear friend to them all and steered Simon into science.

Nearly two years later, Simon had rewarded the man by mixing together household chemicals and blowing the roof off his garage. A month after that, Simon's parents had been killed in an auto accident. Simon had entered foster care and never saw the man again. He had not thought of the man in years.

Simon rolled over and discovered he had slept holding the key Vasquez had given him. He had no idea why he still wore it on the chain around his neck. The professor was dead, and the reason why Simon had been given the key in the first place had died with him.

But he had never taken it off. He wore it like a talisman that had lost all purpose. Or a reminder of who he could once have been. As though maybe he could still remake the broken components of his former life and regain what he could no longer even name. Hope, perhaps. Or a purpose beyond the next good time. The professor had never stopped believing in Simon's potential. Not even when everyone else at MIT had written him off.

Not even when Simon had betrayed him.

Simon opened his eyes and discovered an imp standing in the doorway.

The kid was brown and skinny and possessed a grin too big for his body. Simon rubbed his face. "Where am I?"

"Three Keys Orphanage!" He spoke like he was making a double-barreled announcement of pure, unbridled joy. "I am Juan!"

Simon eased himself up to a sitting position on the narrow wooden cot. He must have jammed his neck when the car slid off the road because it gave off a sharp pain as he twisted his head back and forth. His forehead throbbed, but the pain was subdued now, like a wound that had already started the healing process. He gingerly reached up and touched the bandage. It seemed to be professional work.

"Your wound, it was nothing," Juan announced. "A graze.

Three stitches. You are fine. But Sofia wants you to take the antibiotics with your breakfast. You are hungry?"

"Starving."

"Sofia, she says that is the best sign that you will soon be well. Wait here!" The kid bolted out of the room.

Simon rose to his feet in gradual stages. The bedroom was spare in the extreme—wooden cot, the straight-backed chair where Sofia had been seated the previous night, a narrow table, a stool. A cross hung on the wall by the bathroom door. The floors and walls were all bare plywood, scarred from use and cleaning. The odor of a cheap industrial cleanser clung to the still air.

Simon limped to the narrow window and unlatched the hook. Soon as the window opened, the sound of children spilled through. Laughter, happy shouting, and in the distance a piano and someone singing.

He overlooked a dusty courtyard rimmed by whitewashed structures. The buildings were flanked by broad verandas with overhanging roofs. The courtyard was perhaps 150 feet long and half as wide. Stubborn clumps of grass grew in several places, but it was mostly hard-packed earth.

Children played a rowdy game of soccer. There were perhaps a dozen kids on one team and thirty or maybe even forty on the other. The dozen kids were bigger and older and knew what they were doing. The younger kids were getting hammered, so they threw the rule book aside and did everything but actually tackle the bigger kids. The laughter was infectious.

Juan scampered through the soccer match like it wasn't even there, tin plate in one hand, tin cup in the other. Simon heard footsteps race up the stairs, then the kid appeared in his doorway. "Breakfast!"

Simon grinned as he took the food. The kid accented everything with a shout of pure joy.

He ate standing at the window. The tin plate held beans and yellow rice and a limp tortilla. The sun felt good on his face. The food was bland but fresh and filling. The sensations meant he was alive. Even if his safety was temporary, that felt good as well. The place was both active and calm, a remarkable and jarring combination. Simon felt as though he had been deposited in a place he would never understand.

Then the bell began ringing.

The kids scampered over to an outside pair of faucets. They crowded about, washing their hands and faces and bare feet. Then they lined up, littlest in front and tallest behind. All aimed at the door directly below the tolling bell.

"It is time for morning chapel," Juan declared. "You will come?"

"You go ahead." Simon kept his face to the window as the kid scampered down the stairs. Juan's invitation and the ringing bell brought the professor's absence a great deal closer. Faith had remained a vital component of Vasquez's life.

A clutch of villagers entered through the orphanage's main gate and headed for the chapel. The beautiful woman, Sofia, was the last through the portal. She shooed Juan ahead of her, her voice a musical chant even when scolding. After she climbed the three steps, she turned back. Sofia looked straight at him, a blistering moment of silent communication.

Simon raised his cup in a mock salute. She snapped her head

back around. Her hair shimmered like a wave of liquid onyx. Then she was gone.

The bell went silent. Simon stared at the open doorway and listened as the kids began to sing. He could still feel Sofia's gaze. And he understood her silent message. All too well.

He had to get out of here. Before he got one of those kids killed.

Sofia sat in her customary seat, near the back of the chapel. And tried hard to stop thinking about Simon.

Her brother was in his normal place, up front leading the children's choir. Because of Pedro's responsibilities as assistant town manager, he could not attend morning chapel more than once or twice a week. The children treated his appearances as causes for celebration. The orphanage choir stood in a semicircle around him. Pedro pretended to pull on a massive rope, struggling to make them sing on tempo. They sang and they laughed at the same time.

As she observed her brother, she recalled the day she and Pedro had arrived here. She had been six, her brother scarcely three. A woman had come to their home and shown a paper to the weeping nanny. The woman had then driven them here to the Three Keys. Pedro had cried for their parents on the way. The woman had smiled and said they would come soon and bring them candy. But Sofia had sensed a dark secret hidden in the woman's smile.

Three weeks after they had arrived, Harold brought her into his office and spoke to her about how the cartel had mistaken her parents for enemies and sent them home to Jesus. Sofia had not moved or scarcely even breathed because she did not want to cry in front of him. Pedro still wept at night for their mother and father, Sofia could hear him in the boy's dorm next door, his wails piercing the dark. She had to be strong for them both.

Harold spoke to her in his heavily accented Spanish, his face suffused with the love and compassion he carried with him everywhere. He asked if she would like him to pray with her. When she nodded, he settled his hand upon her head and asked for a special blessing upon her heart and her life as a result of this change, and that God's healing grace would restore Pedro and her. He asked for God to help them both through this transition.

Sofia did not understand much of what Harold prayed, but she felt a stillness fill her, the first such calm she had known since their life had been taken away.

Sometime before her seventh birthday, she felt as though her parents stopped really existing. She never spoke about this with Pedro. She feared that saying the words would bring back his cries in the night. But for her, Harold became her father and her mother.

Despite herself, she glanced at the chapel's open doorway. Hoping Simon would appear. But it was not going to happen. Though she had never set eyes on him before last night, she knew him inside and out. And she knew this chapel was the last place on earth he would ever come.

When Harold stepped to the podium, Sofia forced herself to turn back around. Simon was not of this place. He did not belong. And today he would leave.

Before it was too late.

Chapter 6

Simon showered and dressed in a T-shirt and cotton drawstring trousers that had been left for him. He returned to the window as children spilled through the chapel doors in a chattering flood. They were all dressed the same, in shorts and white T-shirts stamped with the orphanage logo of three interlocked keys.

Simon watched Sofia cross the courtyard with Harold and Juan. The kid looked gangly from this angle, all skinny limbs and barely contained energy. Simon wished the beautiful lady would glance his way. But she remained deep in conversation with Harold. If she even noticed him there in the window, she gave no sign.

Simon left his dusty shoes under the bed and padded down the stairs in his bare feet. Juan stood just inside the open doorway at the foot of the steps. Simon had the impression this was the kid's favorite pose, hovering at the perimeter, absorbing everything.

The doorway opened into Harold's office. His was a simple room holding a battered desk, an upright piano, stacks of papers, and a slowly revolving ceiling fan. Directly opposite where Simon stood was an old-fashioned wall clock, the white enamel face pitted with rust. The second hand ticked in slow cadence around the circle. Simon heard the soft drumbeat of passing time and felt the pressure grow.

Sofia was talking softly on the phone. She stood at Harold's desk with her back to Simon. Her index finger traced a line down an old-fashioned ledger that lay open on the desk. Her voice in Spanish sounded lovely. Harold stood beside her, his arms crossed, his face creased in worry. Juan aped Harold's stance, arms crossed, head cocked to one side, watching and listening with tight focus.

Finally Sofia hung up the phone. "Why didn't you tell me you had missed four payments?"

"Because I don't want you giving us any more of your money," Harold replied. "You already do too much."

"You can't run an orphanage without electricity."

"Tell me what the power company said."

"They agreed to give us two days."

"What?"

"It's the best I could do."

"When is the next delivery due from America?"

"Any time now." Sofia pulled over a calendar. "The Marathon churches are a week late in their donations."

"I'll call them."

"No, Harold. I will make the call. You are too soft. They need to understand how urgent things are." She tapped the ledger. "What the orphanage needs is an income of its own. In the meantime, I'll speak with Enrique—"

"No. I won't have it."

"Which would you prefer, that I speak with Enrique or the children lose their home?"

"Don't say such things." Harold kneaded the place over his heart. "God will provide. He always has."

Sofia's only response was to cross her arms. The fabric of her blouse tightened as she clenched herself. "What about Simon, when is he leaving?"

"I for one would like to see him stay."

"Here? But the gang might have tracked him!"

"Pedro doesn't think so. And you know how much the professor thought of him."

"I know *exactly* what Vasquez thought of Simon. And so do you!"

Harold stood in partial silhouette, with the morning sun blazing through the window beside him, casting him in shadow. He was a tall man, slightly bowed by age and responsibility. His voice carried great strength even when speaking softly. Like now. "I see great things in that young man. So did the professor."

"He ruined the professor's life!"

"He also was the professor's last great hope." Harold stopped her response with an upraised hand. "What if God has brought him here for a divine purpose?"

Simon found himself flooded with bitter regret. The professor had posed the same question the last time they had spoken.

What if God intended something great? Would that not make it worth their while to forgive and move on?

A handbell clanged through the open window. The sound turned Sofia around to where she spotted Simon hovering in the doorway. Her gaze tightened even further. Her full lips clamped down hard on what she was about to say. She gathered up her purse and started for the door. "I'm late for my first appointment. I will stop by this afternoon."

Harold moved toward Simon. "Welcome, son. Good to see you up. How's the head?"

"Sore, but healing. Thanks again for letting me stay."

"Don't mention it." Harold swept up Juan in one outstretched arm and then reached forward with his free hand and clapped Simon on the shoulder. "Let's go grab us a cup of coffee."

As they crossed the courtyard, a gaggle of kids tried to crowd in, but Juan halted them with a word. They giggled and stared at Simon but did as Juan ordered.

The mess hall floor and walls were raw concrete. Harold poured two heavy ceramic mugs of coffee, handed one over, then pointed to a battered refrigerator. "Help yourself to milk and sugar. We keep it in there to try to hold the ants at bay."

As they returned to Harold's office, Pedro joined them and ruffled Juan's hair and asked about Simon's wound. Simon's response was accepted with a casual nod. Clearly gunfire and wounds were not new to this crowd. Which only added another item to the growing list of reasons why Simon wanted to get back across the border.

Harold slipped around his desk and pointed Simon and Pedro into the room's two chairs. Harold said, "In addition to his job with the mayor, Pedro helps me keep this place running. Juan is my number-one assistant."

The kid stationed by the entrance beamed.

Pedro asked, "Who was after you yesterday?"

"No idea," Simon replied.

"Are you sure? Ojinaga is normally a safe place."

"The town's isolation has been our friend." Harold waved at the map on his back wall. "We are surrounded by desert and mountains. The violence has stayed away."

Simon had heard the same words from Vasquez. Many times. "Yesterday was the first time I've ever visited Mexico. I arrived, I heard about Vasquez, I got cheated by the council, I left. I was headed back to the border. Then some thug pulled a board studded with nails across the highway, wrecked my car, and chased me to the restaurant."

"It's a common form of ambush in other areas of Mexico," Harold said.

Pedro asked Simon, "So you have no idea who they were?"

"All I can tell you is, I saw the guy who chased me when I crossed the border. I think he was waiting for me." Simon remembered the dangerous clown's grin, the hand made into the gun, and shivered despite the heat.

"Which means they could be hunting you." Pedro frowned. "Sofia was right. We need to return you to America."

"There's still that little problem," Simon said. "My passport is back in my car."

"Which is where, exactly?"

"In a ditch beside the highway. Close to where I slipped into the industrial zone." He hesitated, then asked, "You said the professor died almost two weeks ago?"

Harold nodded. "He was a dear friend to me and the orphanage."

"But Vasquez e-mailed me right up to when I left for Ojinaga."

"Worse and worse," Pedro muttered. "What were the messages about?"

Simon caught sight of Harold's shrewd gaze and realized the man already knew. "A project we were working on together. He said the city council had promised us a grant to finish our work."

"So what is it about the project that would interest the cartels?"

"We don't know the cartels are behind this," Harold pointed out.

"Who else could it be?" Pedro rose from his chair. "We need to go get your passport and take you to the border."

"Go bring the truck around, I'd like to have a word with our new friend." When Pedro had left, Harold asked, "Have you ever thought that God might have brought you here for a reason?"

"Not really. No."

"This is a safe place, son. From the sounds of things, you need one. Here at the orphanage, the Lord is our refuge and our strength."

"You want me to stay? Why?"

"It's not about what I want," Harold replied. "It's about what God intends."

"You heard Pedro. I was duped by the city council. They

lured me down here. Every minute I spend south of the border is a risk."

"We have allies who might be able to help you."

"To do what?" Simon struggled to comprehend what the orphanage director was saying. "Stay here? In Mexico? Work on the project without Vasquez? Risk my life and the lives of everyone here?"

"What do you have waiting for you back in Boston?"

Harold looked at him with a compassion born on having heard it all, and seen even more. Simon's face burned with a shame that bordered on fury. He rose from his chair. "Thanks for everything. But no thanks."

Harold called after him, "Think on what I said, son."

Simon headed for the truck idling by the orphanage gates. The kids were back playing soccer again. They raced around him like he was just another obstacle. Simon felt eyes on him but did not turn around. He'd have enough trouble as it was, leaving the old man's words behind.

Chapter 7

Pedro took the road headed away from the industrial zone. He waited for a protest, then realized Simon had been unconscious when they had arrived at the orphanage. Pedro glanced over. Simon frowned at the sunlight and tapped his fingers on the side window. He appeared oblivious to the outside world. Pedro had no idea why Sofia was so tense and worried around Simon. He did not need to know. He just needed to get the man his passport and send him back to America where he belonged.

Which brought Pedro back to Harold's attitude. Why he felt drawn to this young man was a mystery. Especially when Sofia was so adamant that Simon's presence could only mean trouble for them. Trouble was one thing they did not need more of. Especially now with their mounting money problems.

Pedro knew what Simon was going to say before the gringo even opened his mouth.

"So . . ." Simon glanced over.

Pedro shot him a warning look. Pedro hoped the man would keep the words bottled up and save them both the hassle.

"So, what's the story with your sister?"

As subtle as a car wreck, this one. "Sofia is a very special lady."

"Yeah, I caught that much. You were both orphaned, right?"

"When I was three and Sofia six. She cared for me. Now she cares for everybody. She lives in an apartment just beyond the orphanage gates. Harold owns the place, and she rents it back and pays too much. Harold won't take money from her, so this is her way of helping."

"What does she do?"

Pedro wanted to ask, what did it matter? Simon was on his way out of Mexico in a matter of minutes. "She trained as a pharmacist. She runs a small company supplying pharmacies and *supermercados* with medical supplies and medicines through all Chihuahua." Before Simon could ask the next question, Pedro whipped the wheel and said, "Hang on."

The truck bounced hard as they turned off the road. They headed across the desert, holding to a rutted track that led in a vast semicircle around the town's outskirts. If Ojinaga continued to grow, this was slated to become the city's ring road, rimmed by low-cost housing. Right now, though, such plans were meaningless. OJ, as the town was known among locals, was barely holding on. If the new plants had not recently opened up in the maquiladora, they would be losing population every day.

Pedro disliked how OJ was profiting from the violence in Juárez. He hated watching the news these days, seeing what was happening so close to OJ, all the families struck by the violence, all the lives wasted. In his town, there had only been one shooting in the past twelve months, and no murders at all. Pedro could not help but glance over again. Simon's wound would double that statistic.

He turned his attention back to the road, then felt the American's gaze on him and expected him to whine about the rough ride. "I am sorry for the bouncing. It must hurt your head."

"Hey, no problem. If it helps us get there safely, bring it on."

Perhaps this gringo was not quite as soft as he first appeared. "Hold on, Señor Simon. We will be there soon."

They returned to the highway by a billboard showing the mayor, Enrique, flashing his brilliant smile. Pedro parked in the same lot where he had been the previous day. It may have been the exact same space. Simon had been too woozy to remember clearly. Pedro cut the motor. "Wait here, please."

So polite, this guy. As if Simon had any choice but to do what he was told. Simon watched through the scratched and dirty windscreen as Pedro walked across the lot and entered the same little restaurant. The place had *El Bandito* painted in a rainbow of letters across the front window. A long, low roof shaded the outdoor sitting area that was framed by a one-pole fence, like a hitching post. Pedro greeted the diners on the veranda before entering the restaurant.

He was not inside long. When he came out, he was eating a burrito and carried another wrapped in wax paper. He motioned with the burrito for Simon to join him, then turned the motion into a wave at the other diners.

As they crossed the dusty plaza, Simon unwrapped his burrito and took a bite. The taste was astonishing. Eggs and white cheese and spinach and chopped tomatoes and salsa. "Wow."

"You like?"

"This is great."

Pedro grinned. "You are thinking maybe I went to that restaurant for the ambience? The romantic atmosphere, perhaps? The fine linen tablecloth and candles?"

"Can we stop by for another on the way out?"

Pedro stowed his smile away. "First we must survive what comes next."

They meandered through the stalls surrounding the plaza. Pedro greeted a few of the locals and received soft words in reply. Instead of heading for the fence, Pedro took a well-beaten path toward the factories. Simon felt his hackles rise as they approached the run-down buildings farthest from the highway. He could almost hear the gunshot. His forehead pulsed hard.

Pedro searched the empty area and asked softly, "Where did you cross the fence?"

"About fifty feet back."

"You are certain?"

"See where the pole is broken and the fence dips down almost to the earth? That's where I came through." In the distance, a machine whined a very high note. It was probably a sander polishing a metal surface, but to Simon it sounded like an alarm. "Are we going or not?"

In reply, Pedro headed for the fence.

The surrounding desert was littered with refuse and cactus. Dark-winged birds circled lazily far overhead. Given his current run of luck, Simon assumed they were vultures. "What happened to Vasquez?"

Pedro picked his way carefully around a clump of rocks. "They say it was a heart attack."

"Who is 'they'?"

Pedro gave him that sour look Simon had been seeing a lot of lately. Like his questions revealed a myriad of issues these people would rather not think about. "In Mexico, there is always a 'they.'"

"Great. That explains everything."

Pedro's footsteps were a delicate dance as his eyes scoured the way ahead. "The police have not released the body."

"Why not?"

"They will not say. We have asked. Many times."

Simon realized the man's subtle way of moving was probably because of snakes. He stepped farther away from the next rocky shadow. "So the police think it could be murder?"

Pedro was clearly reluctant to answer. "Or the police are involved. Or someone the police answer to."

Which made no sense at all. "The professor didn't have an enemy to his name."

"You must ask your questions to Harold. And Sofia. I saw Vasquez, of course. He was often by the orphanage. But he was their particular friend." Pedro pointed off to their right. "The highway is over there."

"I need to make a stop." Simon was having trouble getting his bearings. He struggled to fix his position based upon memories laced with panic. Then he saw the long vein of shade running in too straight a line to be anything but man-made. "Over here."

Simon scampered to the trench and dropped over the ledge. He ran down its length until he spotted the crack in the concrete pipe. He knelt in the dirt and fished around in the dark. It was hard to say what scared him more—finding snakes or finding nothing at all.

But the duffel was there. As he dragged it out, though, he heard a dismal clank. "Oh no."

"What is that?"

"The apparatus. Why I came to Mexico." The clank turned into a hundred clatters as he slung it over his shoulder. Like he was carrying a sack filled with loose coins. "The wreck and my run must have damaged it."

"We can worry about that later." Pedro kept squinting at the distance. "Right now we must hurry."

Long before they arrived at the highway, Simon was fairly certain there was nothing to recover. They followed a lone plume of smoke to the burned-out hulk, all that remained of Simon's car. The destruction was total. The trunk lid lay some twenty feet away, blackened and crumpled, obviously blown there when the gas tank exploded. The few cars that passed slowed, but no one stopped. His entire life was exactly like the car. A wrecked and ruined hulk. His one remaining friend, gone. His ticket back across the border, lost. His chance at resurrecting his career, over. He murmured, "It's all gone now. Everything."

He turned away. As destroyed as his car.

Then he saw the man.

The hunter walked away from them, headed into the sun.

Which meant Simon could only see his silhouette. Just like the day before.

He hissed to Pedro, "Hide!"

Without hesitation, Pedro dropped behind the rock pile alongside Simon. The man knew enough to hide first and wait to ask, "What is it?"

"That's the guy who attacked me."

Pedro peeked over the ledge. "How can you be certain?"

Simon didn't need another look, but he eased up anyway. "Same build. Short, stocky. And that coat."

"I remember the coat." Pedro risked a quick glance. "What is he carrying?"

"What's left of my suitcase. If he's going to steal my things, why did he wait until now?"

Pedro crawled away, holding as long as possible to the shadows. "We need to get out of here before we're spotted."

Pedro did not speak again until they were back across the fence and into the industrial zone. "There can only be one answer to what he was doing."

"Well, if you've got one that makes sense, you're way ahead of me."

"Give me your duffel bag."

"Why?" But he unslung the sack and handed it over.

"Go hide somewhere. Back in the shadows. Keep an eye out for me. I'll signal when you should come."

Simon wanted to argue. The hunter most likely had his passport. But something about the tension Pedro placed into every quiet word pushed him to move. He stepped behind the nearest stall and headed back the way they had come.

When Simon arrived at the first decrepit building, he slipped into the shadows and moved around to where he could see across the plaza. He watched Pedro carry the duffel bag to his truck. The assistant town manager stowed it in a locked compartment in the rear, then resettled his load of cleaning gear and chemicals so the compartment's lid was hidden. Then he sauntered back toward the restaurant.

Soon after Pedro entered through the screen door, a dark SUV pulled into the space alongside the pickup. The driver's door opened up and the stocky man stepped out. The same close-trimmed beard, the same absurd leather coat.

In a flash of insight, Simon understood the reason behind the hunter's timing. The man stretched his back and dry-scrubbed his face, the acts of an extremely tired man. The man had left the Mustang as it had been because he had been waiting for Simon to return.

The thought left him chilled and sweating at the same time. They were still looking for him. And he was trapped. Without his passport, he had no chance of escape.

The attacker combed his beard with his fingers and dragged back the lingering remnants of his hair. He studied Pedro's pickup, then entered the restaurant. Simon scarcely breathed until the hunter reappeared. The man turned in a slow circle, taking in the silent plaza and the stalls that had closed for the afternoon siesta. His gaze lingered on the shadows where Simon hid. Then he kicked at a rock and walked back to his SUV. The motor roared, echoing the man's frustration. He pulled from the space and burned rubber out of the lot.

Simon remained exactly where he was until Pedro emerged.

The town manager walked to his pickup, opened the door, slid behind the wheel, and started the motor. Simon knew he was scouting the area, searching carefully for danger. Finally Pedro's hand extended from the pickup's side window. He waved.

Simon scrambled across the plaza.

Chapter 8

When they arrived back at the orphanage, Sofia was in Harold's office. She stood at a side table, reading from a ledger and making notes in her little book. She did not notice them in the doorway, or if she did, she chose to ignore them. She said to Harold, "You have to pay the power company everything you owe them."

Harold was seated behind his desk in an old-fashioned wooden office chair. He had swiveled around so he was facing in the opposite direction. He had a Bible open and supported by one hand, so it was up close to his face. "God has always provided."

"I will ask Enrique for help."

"The mayor has bigger fish to fry." Slowly, deliberately, Harold turned a page. Simon had the impression they spent many hours like this. Sofia prodding, Harold doing his best to deflect. "Like running for governor of Chihuahua."

"You are speaking at his Ojinaga fund-raiser. He is indebted to you." She glanced at the old man. "You can't run an orphanage without power."

"Or without faith. Isn't that right?" He looked up and spotted Simon in the doorway. "How did it go?"

From behind him, Pedro replied, "We found nothing but trouble."

"Come in and tell us about it."

Pedro gave it to them fast and low. Sofia remained where she was, standing by the narrow side table, with her arms wrapped around her middle. Her fingers were white from clenching her arms. Like she was trying to shield herself and the orphanage from whatever it was Simon had brought with him.

Harold's response was very different. He clearly did not like the news that Simon's attacker had staked out the car. But he also was not troubled by it. In fact, he seemed grimly satisfied. As though it confirmed something he had already expected. When Pedro went silent, Harold said, "So his passport is lost to us."

"All he retrieved was the black duffel bag. Simon had hidden that away in the desert."

"Where is the bag?"

"In my pickup."

"Did you recognize the man chasing him?"

"I may have seen him around. But I don't think so."

Sofia spoke to the bare wood floor. "It has to be the cartel."

Pedro protested, "Enrique has pushed the cartel's men out of Ojinaga and he will soon do the same for all Chihuahua."

Harold said, "The man is probably a local thief hired to steal the device. He may even be linked to what happened to Vasquez."

Sofia gave him a swift look, then dropped her gaze back to the floor. As though doing her best not to allow Simon to enter her field of vision. "Do you even hear what you are saying?"

"I hear very well. I remember hearing Vasquez talk about this brilliant student. He was certain Simon would take his research further in weeks than he had done in years."

"Vasquez is dead," Sofia said, her voice flat. "So is the project."

"Perhaps Simon could bring it back to life."

"Simon is not even at MIT anymore. He is a bartender." She looked at him for the first time. "Is that not so?"

Harold saved him from responding. "Call Enrique. See if he can help us."

"With the power company or with getting Simon a passport?"

Harold simply smiled at her. "Give him my best."

After Sofia slipped from the room and Pedro left for work, Harold opened a drawer in his desk and drew out a gaily colored box. Juan was halfway across the room before Harold opened the lid. "You want one?"

"What is it?"

"Red Rope." He handed a licorice ribbon to Juan, took another for himself, then offered the box to Simon. "It was my vice during smoke breaks at NASA. Red Rope won't kill you as fast as cigarettes."

"You worked in the space program?"

"During Apollo. Back then, pretty much the whole crew lit up every chance they got. That's how I met Armando. He worked for a contractor we used for the Houston control systems."

"I remember him mentioning that." Simon found it odd to hear the professor referred to by his first name. To all of MIT, he had always been known simply as Vasquez. "So you moved from NASA to an orphanage."

"I've done a lot of things since then. Started a few businesses, then gave seminars for Fortune 500 companies. Helping people identify the right tools to grow their firms."

Simon knew what was coming. He felt the same thing he always had when people started to tell him what he should do with his life. He had heard the words so often they might as well have been tattooed on his brain. Too much, too soon, too easy. That was his problem, so they said. "You were a motivation guy. Be all you can be, right?"

A steely glint appeared and vanished in the old man's gaze. Which meant Harold had caught the attitude behind the words. Simon had the impression very little got past him. Harold said, "There's a lot more to it than that. The world is full of motivated people going nowhere."

Simon liked that. "I believe I've met a few of those."

"Which is your excuse for not doing more with your own life?"

"I've never felt a need for excuses."

Harold smiled. "Good answer. Not the best, but not bad."

Simon found himself drawn to the man. "So you gave up a successful training business to come here?"

"After NASA, I spent years helping good companies become great. Satisfying work, but not world changing. Then I got a letter from a young man, an orphan I'd met in India." Harold used the remnant of his Red Rope to point at a framed letter hanging on the wall beside his map. "Nabeel attended a seminar I gave. Three years later, he wrote thanking me for changing his life. He'd taken the tools I'd offered and started a business, and now he's employing a lot of other orphans. What's more, he helped over a dozen start businesses of their own."

Harold's gaze wandered to where Juan stood by the window, chewing happily on the licorice. "The letter was from Nabeel, but the message was from God. The world sees these Mexican orphans as hopeless cases. Born into violence, left without family, lost. But God has planted hope in them. Hope and gifts and a boiling desire to grow beyond where they are. My aim is to help them achieve this."

The bitter longing surged with a vengeance. Simon had not felt it in quite a while, but he instantly knew what it was. A desire to do more. Take the risk. Invest it all in the one big chance. Only there were no chances left. They died with Vasquez. "So you've found the secret to instant success."

"No, son. There's no secret, and success is never instant." He tore a page from his notepad, laid a pencil on top, and slid it across the desk. "Usually I start with this. I ask my students to write down three goals they want to achieve in life."

Simon stared at the empty page. It was easier than meeting the man's gaze. Harold did not threaten. He was soft spoken and very polite and Simon had yet to see him become angry. But there was something about the man that probed, that *challenged.* "What is this, fifth grade?"

"A lot of companies have paid a lot of money for this little bit of wisdom. So what is your first goal?"

He said the first thing that came to mind. "Find my passport."

Harold laughed but pulled the page back and wrote it down. "And number two?"

"Get across the border." Simon raised his hand. "That's it. There is no number three."

"Well, it's a start. Not much of one, but still, a start." Harold turned to Juan. "Give us a moment alone, would you, son."

But the kid had no interest in leaving. He asked Simon, "The device you and Vasquez worked on. I hear Sofia and Harold speak of this, but still I don't understand. What does it do?"

"If we could get it to work, it would convert raw wasted energy into useable power."

"Energy like electricity?"

"That's it."

"If you need electricity, why don't you just plug it into the wall?"

Simon grinned. "You sound like my ex-girlfriend."

"She must be brilliant!"

"Juan," Harold said. "Shut the door on your way out."

When they were alone, Harold pulled a laptop from the shelves behind his desk and opened the top. "There's something I want to show you."

The screen showed the silhouette of a face rimmed by ceiling lights. The only clear feature were his smiling teeth. It also gauged the strongest light and dimmed everything else to outlines. But Simon knew the silhouette belonged to Armando Vasquez.

Simon felt the lump grow in his throat. He tried to tell himself it was due to fatigue—the drive from Boston, the council meeting, the wreck, the trek back across the desert, the stress. His head throbbed. What he wanted most just then was to crawl in a hole and pull the lid back over him. But he could not draw his gaze away from the screen.

Vasquez leaned over his apparatus, which was perched on the tailgate of a decrepit pickup truck. The device's central lid was open and he was making adjustments while watching an oscilloscope. Planted in the earth at his feet were several dozen lightbulbs. The computer at Vasquez's end was angled so the oscilloscope's screen was clearly shown. The lines were all over the place, as they always had been with Simon's own attempts. In the background was a faint humming.

Simon asked, "What is that noise?"

"I have no idea," Harold replied. "Watch closely."

Simon muttered, "He never gives up."

"He never gave up on you," Harold replied, without taking his gaze from the screen.

Simon found it impossible to give his standard sharp comeback. For there on the screen was another lost chance. Simon had not come to Mexico for the apparatus or for the grant. He had come down to apologize. It was an alien act, something he had never done before. Everything in his life said apologies were for the weak, a futile gesture for people who had not learned how to walk away. But the incident that had taken Vasquez from Boston had driven a wedge deep into Simon's life. He needed to say the words. For both their sakes. Only now he would never have a chance.

Then something happened that shocked Simon so hard, the past was forgotten. The lines on the oscilloscope started moving in regular tandem.

Up to this point, their calculations had all pointed to finding a single rhythm, one vibratory pattern that could be used to convert the wasted energy into usable power. But every attempt they had made at isolating the proper frequency had proven a failure.

The calculations had haunted them both. They were so clean. So *right.*

Then five weeks earlier, Vasquez had traveled to Sofia's office in the maquiladora. The industrial zone often had service when the city's phone service was down. Vasquez had called to announce that their goal was not, in fact, one frequency. It was a *harmonious multitude.*

Which was impossible, of course. The calculations became unmanageably huge. They had been through all this before.

But Vasquez had applied a new derivative, one drawn from recent developments in quantum physics and based upon the same principles now used to forecast weather. Vasquez had claimed a breakthrough was within their grasp and begged Simon to come.

Simon asked Harold, "When did he make this video?"

"The night before he died."

On the computer, Vasquez moved in close to the laptop. His weary features came into vivid clarity, and he offered the camera his famous grin. It was impossible one person could possess so many teeth. Or look so purely happy.

"I hope," Vasquez said, "that you are watching carefully." He leaned away and hit the switch.

All the lightbulbs at his feet lit up. The light was dim, but unmistakable.

"What . . . ?" Simon shifted Harold's laptop around so the screen faced him directly. "He did it?"

Harold merely smiled.

The lightbulbs grew brighter and brighter. The light became so strong, the laptop could not handle it. The entire screen turned white.

"Armando called the device *Ilimitado*." Harold's features glowed from more than the screen's light. "Unlimited."

The camera revealed a portly man humming to himself and dancing in unbridled joy. Then there was a series of bangs, fast as popcorn in the microwave. Then the image vanished, and the computer screen went dark.

"What just happened?"

"All I can tell you is, there was a power outage that struck all of Ojinaga. Possibly all of north Chihuahua state."

"Because of this machine? Come on."

"The timing is too coincidental. And you know what scientists say about coincidence."

"Okay, first of all, the machine was not plugged into the mains. And second, the laptop camera has a backup battery. But it went blank too."

"I'm only telling you what happened," Harold replied. "Phones, televisions, computers—everything went down."

"Impossible."

Harold shrugged. "You're missing the most important issue here, son."

"Which is?"

"Armando could have reached out to anyone with this invention."

Simon pretended to study the blank screen. "He was *so close.*"

"Listen to what I am saying. You are his last great hope. He reached out to you. *Don't let him down.*"

The knock on the door startled them both. Juan poked his head inside. For once, the kid's happiness was extinguished. "Dr. Harold, the van is here. The police, they have brought us another one."

Chapter 9

Sofia drove her van along the Texas highway. As they approached the Presidio border crossing, the U-Haul truck filled with donations moved in tight to her bumper. These days, she often served as unofficial guide and hostess to the orphanage's American sponsors. Newcomers often looked askance at her, asking themselves how this beautiful woman survived as an orphan in Mexico. And why she went back at all.

The answer was, she lived for the orphanage.

In her rearview mirror she saw hands point out the truck's windows. The church group gaped at the border fence. The line of black steel girders marched off in both directions and disappeared into the wavering heat. The tall girders were spaced so tightly that not even a large dog could fit between them. They were prison bars for a country.

Fifteen miles to the west and nineteen to the east, the fence ended. To have extended it farther in either direction would have cost more than a four-lane interstate. To the west rose three mountain ranges, one after the other, desert peaks scarred by eons of harsh winds and temperatures that hit a hundred and forty degrees at noon. The Chinati Mountains, the Cuesta del Burro, and the Sierra Vieja were no respecters of borders. They raked the sky with defiant glee. There were no roads, nor towns, nor water, nor any chance of crossing the border and surviving.

To the east stretched the region known as the Big Bend, two hundred miles of caverns and forest and some of the wildest territory either country still possessed. Every now and then a wildcat wandered into Ojinaga, usually in the high drought of summer, on the prowl for a stray pet.

Not even the human traffickers would dare risk becoming lost in those harsh terrains. Which was why Ojinaga remained an island of relative safety, a haven in the middle of Mexico's lost decade.

The people of Chihuahua state were very humble. It was their nature to be respectful of their giant neighbor to the north. Life in much of Chihuahua was backdated twenty years. Many families still did not have cars. There was none of the cross-border hostility that marred relations in other areas. Before the troubles, if one of their kids decided to leave town, north was where they went. North to a better life.

Back when the fence went up, most OJ locals had been baffled. What was their big neighbor to the north so afraid of? It was not like Mexicans were going to walk across the Rio Grande and start a war.

But no one asked those questions anymore.

Until just six or seven years ago, drugs remained a problem north of the border. This was what fueled the resentment, how the Americans blamed Mexico when the Ojinaga locals were innocent bystanders. But this was no longer true. Now, the drug problem was everywhere. Kids as young as nine were using. In towns like Ojinaga, previously the worst trouble a teenager might find was drinking mescal. Today, the tragedy scarred far too many families and cost too many young lives.

Sofia recognized the American officer on duty in her lane. When she had started her business five years earlier, she had known some of the men and women by name. She could ask about their families. She had spoken at several of their churches in Presidio, seeking sponsorship for the orphanage. All this was gone now. The border guards were governed by new rules of engagement. All foreigners were treated as potential hostiles. Sofia endured the border inspections because she had to.

Sofia crossed the Rio Grande, followed by the church group. The drought had reduced the river to a narrow stream. The mudflats on both banks were bone white. A flank of high cane rustled in the hot wind.

She pulled into the inspection bay and opened all of her van's doors and handed over the manifests. She purchased many of the surgical supplies in the U.S. because she could be more certain of sterility. She supplied hospitals and private clinics that were willing to pay almost three times the cost of the same equipment from a Mexican distributor. Sofia did not survive because she was the cheapest. Her business was built on trust.

The church's rented truck pulled into the next bay. The driver ran a moving company in Odessa and used a corner of his warehouse as a staging area for local donations. Friends like these formed the orphanage's last remaining lifeline. Harold had started the orphanage with money from selling his business. But twenty years and a recession later, The Three Keys clung to life by the slimmest of margins.

When the inspection ended, they linked up and headed south. Eight miles later, she turned off the highway and took the rutted road toward the orphanage. Sofia sent up a silent prayer that Simon was already gone. Erasing the dread and the longing. Clearing away one more obstacle from her path.

Then she saw the police car parked in front of the gates.

Sofia leapt from her van and raced through the gates. She crossed the silent courtyard to where Simon stood on the broad porch fronting Harold's office. Simon's haughty demeanor was gone, his armor shredded by what he observed.

The agent's name was Consuela Martinez. Officially she was part of the Mexican drug task force. But she also served in a number of informal capacities. One of which was rounding up young survivors of *la violenza*. She and Harold spoke softly. A little girl stood between them. Martinez held the girl's hand. In the agent's other hand was a sheaf of documents.

Simon's gaze looked haunted. "The little girl is an orphan?"

"I assume so," Sofia replied.

The child looked shattered and so weary she could scarcely hold herself erect. She was probably nine or ten years old. She was also extremely beautiful. Her features looked sculpted from alabaster. Not even her exhaustion or tragic shock could erase the magnetic quality of her loveliness.

Simon said, "I thought Pedro said the violence does not touch here."

"No place in Mexico is totally safe. But OJ is so isolated, it escapes the worst. So far."

"OJ?"

"Ojinaga. It's how we call it." Sofia watched Harold stoop down in front of the child and pull a strand of Red Rope from his pocket. Sofia's eyes burned at the memory of other times. Red Rope was Harold's favorite remedy for childhood traumas. "Agent Martinez is based a hundred miles to the west in Juárez. Such a beautiful girl should not be placed in the state orphanage system. They can disappear, you understand? So she brings them here. When she can."

The shadow in Simon's gaze defied the sunlight. "Is this what happened to you?"

"We were younger than this one. I was six, Pedro three. Our parents were mistaken for members of a rival gang. Or so we heard later. At the time all we knew was, they were gone. Without Harold . . ." She could not keep the desperation from her voice. "Do you see how important it is not to bring danger to this place?"

Simon watched Harold rise and sign the documents held by the agent. "Why does he want me to stay?"

"That is *not* the question you need to be asking. Whatever Harold is thinking, you need to look at that little child and realize what you could bring down on this place."

Simon's shoulders slumped further. "Soon as I get my passport, I'm out of here."

"I spoke with Enrique. He is on his way over. Hopefully he can help."

"Okay. Great."

Sofia studied the man standing beside her. Something about Simon left her wondering if he, too, was an orphan. Vasquez had never spoken about Simon's family. Sofia resisted the urge to ask him. She did not need to know anything further about this one.

Relief flooded her at the prospect that Simon would soon leave them for good. But Sofia was too honest not to admit that she also felt regret. Which was absurd, really. She knew all his bad habits. And yet, standing here and observing him at his weakest, she could not help but feel a sense of the *other* side, the one that Vasquez had talked about endlessly. The intelligence, the promise, the fire in Simon that had almost been extinguished and yet might still burn brightly again. If only . . .

If only she could banish those thoughts. She said the first thing that came to mind. "When I was seventeen, I ran away."

He jerked out of his own sorrowful cave. "From here?"

"From here, from Harold. I was in full teenage rebellion. And this place has *so* many rules. I argued with everyone."

"I can't imagine that ever happening," Simon said dryly.

"Harold wanted me to grow up and take over the orphanage. He had it all planned out. And some days I was content with that. Other days, I could have screamed with the frustration of feeling so trapped."

She stopped, surprised at herself. She seldom spoke of these issues, even with Pedro. She had not even told Enrique. Why would she reveal such secrets to this man?

"You loved it and you hated it," he said softly, his gaze distant. "You wanted it and you wanted nothing more than to get away."

She felt the exact same sense of conflict now. She was thrilled by his ability to understand, to connect. And yet repelled by him and the risk he represented. And still she continued, "For the first time in my life, I saw beyond this place and yearned for a different future. What precisely, I had no idea. If I had been certain about what I wanted, Harold would not have pressed me. And when I was younger, I had told him I would run the orphanage. Harold did not realize I was changing. Or perhaps he did but assumed it was just a teenage phase. In the end, I ran away. A missionary couple I had known for years helped me obtain a scholarship to the university in El Paso. I studied biology and pharmacology on a church scholarship."

He was watching her intently now. "Why did you come back?"

"This is my home. I never wanted to leave permanently. I just wanted to live here on my terms." She pointed to the little girl who now held Harold's hand. "I wanted to help other little girls hope and dream and grow up safely."

Simon nodded slowly. "I don't want to do anything to harm these kids, Sofia."

"Then you must leave. Now. Today. Forget what Harold said about this big dream of yours. This apparatus. Go back to *el norte* and finish it there."

Simon's voice grew sadder still. "I didn't come to Ojinaga to complete this device. Not really."

"Then why else did you—?" Her question was cut off by the sound of an all-too-familiar siren. "Wait here."

Chapter 10

As the dark SUV pulled up by the front gates, Simon felt a faint rush of fear. Other than the siren and the flashing red light attached to the roof beside the driver's window, it could have belonged to the hunter. Then the passenger door opened, and a smiling Enrique stepped into view.

He entered the orphanage like he owned the place.

The kids pretty much erupted from their hiding places. They scampered over and danced around him. Enrique smiled and he talked, and the kids answered with a single unified shout. He accepted a plastic bag from his driver and started doling out handfuls of hard candy. The kids shrieked and laughed and raced about, their hands full of sweets.

The mayor of Ojinaga was every inch a winner. He wore a starched long-sleeve shirt, white with broad chalk-blue stripes that matched his silk tie. His suit pants were a rich tan. His tasseled loafers defied the dust. Simon imagined the man had them polished twice a day.

Simon realized he did not like the mayor. Enrique had done nothing to justify such feelings. But his gut said this guy was too used to having it all. And Sofia was part of that plan.

At Sofia's approach, Enrique separated himself from the kids so he could give her a kiss. The children shrieked with laughter. Simon had the distinct impression that Sofia merely endured his attentions. When she was free, she pointed to Simon, then started over to where the little girl stood with Harold and Agent Martinez.

Juan skipped over to stand beside Simon. "That is Mayor Morales."

Simon watched Sofia take the little girl's hand and lead her into the dormitory. "We've met."

"He lets me call him Enrique. He is a very good man."

Enrique started toward Simon, then changed course when the agent approached and saluted him. Simon said, "Sure is a popular guy."

"Enrique is running for governor of Chihuahua. He will win. He must. He has stood up to the drug cartels here in Ojinaga. He has arrested many of their men."

Then from the girl's dormitory there came a soft wail.

Instantly the kids went silent. Many children slipped into the shadows. Harold crossed the courtyard and entered the dorm. From inside came another soft cry, a wordless lament against a hot and uncaring world.

Agent Martinez spoke to Enrique, gesturing back toward the girl's dormitory. Even the mayor's nod carried a sense of imperial smoothness, turning the gesture into a half bow. Simon could not understand what he said, but the man's tone carried power. The agent softened enough to smile briefly.

Then she noticed Simon and said something that turned the mayor around. Enrique waved him over. "Señor Simon, come and meet one of the good guys!"

Simon had no interest in talking with the cops, any cop, north or south of the border. But he had no choice. He hated how he recoiled inside, as though guilty of some crime rather than being the victim this time. Old habits died hard.

Agent Martinez had a cop's gaze, hard and tight and measuring. She showed no expression as Enrique said, "Señor Simon Orwell, honored guest of our fair city, was brutally attacked yesterday. How is your wound, señor?"

"Healing."

"The bullet missed our guest," Enrique said cheerfully. "The rock ricochet did not."

"Guns are much less common in this country," Martinez said. "Where did this happen, señor?"

"I was run off the highway by the industrial zone and chased through the desert."

Enrique set a hand on Simon's shoulder. "Señor Orwell came to visit Professor Vasquez, formerly of MIT, perhaps you have heard of him?"

Agent Martinez hesitated a fraction of a second, then said, "Perhaps. The name sounds familiar. What was your business with the professor?"

"We're working on a project to transform wasted power into usable electricity." Simon stopped and amended, "Rather, we were."

"There was a discussion with our city council," Enrique went on. "Or perhaps I should say, a misunderstanding. With Dr. Clara."

"Ah." The agent nodded slowly. "Of her I have most certainly heard."

"Señor Orwell was on his way back to the border. A man pulled a board studded with nails across the highway. The attacker chased him into the maquiladora, where Señor Simon was rescued by my assistant town manager. Very fortunate, yes? They returned to his car this morning, only to discover it had been burned out."

"You were carrying drugs, señor? Or large amounts of cash?"

"Do I look to you like a courier?"

"What you look like, señor, is a man who has had other discussions with the police."

"Look, *I* was the one attacked here."

"Of course, señor. And my job as agent in the national task force is to determine whether drugs or drug money was involved."

"There were no drugs," Enrique said smoothly. "There was no money."

"You are certain of this how?"

"Because Señor Orwell came seeking a grant to continue his scientific research that he started with Professor Vasquez. The professor has recently died. We are told it was a heart attack."

The agent's phone rang. She slipped it from her belt and checked the readout. "I must take this. If you will excuse me, Mayor Morales. I am sorry for your troubles, Señor Orwell. Good day."

Enrique's gaze followed the agent back through the orphanage gates. "There are too few such people in Mexican law enforcement these days. Agent Martinez is a true friend of the people. She has had numerous death threats. Her family lives in Mexico City under an assumed name."

Simon watched the unmarked car pull away and did not respond.

"Is it true what she said, that you have had other run-ins with the law?"

Simon remained silent.

"Excuse me. It is none of my business." The hand dropped from Simon's shoulder. "Only, it appears you will need to apply for a new passport. I can certainly expedite matters. But this will be more difficult if you have a record."

Simon said carefully, "I have no priors."

"Excellent. In that case, it will only be a matter of a few days. A week at most."

"A week?"

"Perhaps less. You could, of course, travel to your nearest consulate or the embassy in Mexico City."

"I'm broke. Everything I brought with me is gone."

"Then leave it with me." Enrique started toward Sofia, then turned back. "Is it true what they say, that you can complete the professor's work?"

Perhaps it was just how everything the mayor did and said carried this polished edge. But Simon had the feeling that Enrique's question was not so casual as it appeared. Or that the question had just popped into the mayor's head. "Maybe. With time. And money."

Enrique flashed the smile made for billboards. "Then let us hope you are successful upon your return to your country, Señor Simon."

The mayor crossed the courtyard to where Harold stood in the dormitory doorway. The orphanage director turned and greeted Enrique as an old friend. They talked for a few moments, then Enrique patted Harold's shoulder, called softly into the dorm, and walked back to his car. He waved at Simon before the driver closed his door.

As the car pulled away, Simon thought, *there goes a man who has everything.*

Which was bitterly ironic, as it was exactly what they used to say about him.

Chapter 11

Carlos was on the hunt. It was his favorite part of the job. And his job was anything his *jefe* told him to do.

Carlos was lucky to be alive. Of the kids he ran with in his youth, he was the only one still drawing breath. And it was all because of his boss.

When he was eleven, the war had come to his village.

In Mexico, there was only one war these days. The gangs that controlled the drug trade were in the middle of a civil war, fighting each other for control and power. And the civil war gave no thought to innocents. In this war, there were only winners and losers. That was what the cartel men had said when they came to his village. Did Carlos and the other children want to win? Or did they want to die?

The gang needed the village's kids. That was why they came. To recruit every child over nine years of age. The gang loved hitting villages like his, close to major cities and familiar with the war and the violence. Everyone in his village knew a family who had suffered. They heard the tales from cities like Juárez or Chihuahua. So when the gang came to their village, the locals already knew the consequences if they refused to cooperate.

The gang gathered all the kids in a dusty lot beyond the empty factory that once had employed half the village making pottery. They showed off their guns—the military-grade automatic rifles, the pistols, the Tasers, the machetes. They made the children hold them and handle them. They then gave the children a choice. The kids could join the gang and each receive five hundred American dollars to take home to their families. Or they could watch their families die. All of them. Even the animals. A lesson to be remembered by all who joined the gang. That there was no escape. That hope was a myth imported from north of the border, from the *Yanquis* who consumed the drugs and fueled the violence that had come to their village. Here, there was no hope. Only this choice. Join or die.

Carlos had known there was no choice at all. Not for him. Only for his family. If he joined the gang, he would die an early death. Almost all the soldiers in every gang were dead before their twenty-fifth birthday. It was a tragic statistic that played on television and filled the newspapers. Mexico's youth were being wiped from the face of the earth.

But at least he could save his family. So Carlos had said yes and joined the gang.

He spent four years as a mule, ferrying drugs across the American border. He traveled with the *coyotes*, pretending to be the son of some other family. So his own family would survive.

All the money he earned he gave to his mother. He was the

oldest of five children, and his family was now secure. They bought land. They prospered. His photograph was placed upon the altar in the corner of his mother's bedroom. Every six months she pleaded with him for a new photograph. Carlos hated these photographs for two reasons. First, each photograph was a reminder to him of just how close death remained. Second, in each photograph he could see the change. Carlos had always been known for his smile. And it was still there, the teeth shining through his beard. But inside, where it mattered, there was nothing left. The photograph did not lie.

Then when Carlos was fifteen, a marvel had come to his village.

The jefe had managed to sweep away the gang. How he had done this was a matter of much debate. But no one questioned that it was the boss who had done this thing. And not just from his small village. Across the entire north of Chihuahua state, the cartels vanished.

The jefe's family had owned much of Chihuahua's finest farmland for generations beyond count. They now owned hotels in resorts like Acapulco and inside the capital city. They could have slipped across the border and lived an easy life in the safety of America, where people walked the streets without fear of death. Though most of his family now lived elsewhere, el jefe had remained and fought for the little people. And made life safe once more for the family of Carlos.

When the gang left their region, Carlos returned home and opened a small business repairing cars. He was too young to own the business outright. So his mother and his uncle, his late father's brother, cosigned as partners. His mother arranged this. She was the smart one in the family and Carlos agreed with everything she suggested. He tried to tell himself he was content with his life, living in the small village and eating in his mother's kitchen and repairing cars. He even started seeing a young woman.

Then when Carlos was twenty, the jefe had called and asked to see him.

The boss did not actually come himself, of course. He sent a car. The driver was very respectful. The boss did not order Carlos to come. He asked it. As a favor.

When Carlos arrived, the boss came out of his fine office and personally shook Carlos's hand and ushered him inside and offered him coffee and made sure he was comfortable. Then the boss ordered everyone out and told his secretary there were to be no interruptions. Then he asked, "Are you happy with your life?"

Carlos shrugged. The drive from his village to this office had taken almost two hours, long enough to decide why the boss had called. "I am alive. Thanks to you. And my brothers and sisters will not be forced to do what I have done. Thanks to you."

The boss nodded slowly, accepting both the gratitude and the fact that Carlos had acknowledged the debt. "I have a problem. I was wondering if you could help me."

"If I can, I will do this thing."

"Do you not want to know what my problem is?"

"If you want to tell me, I will listen. But it does not matter."

"What precisely are you saying?"

"I will do whatever you ask."

The words hung in the cool, still air. Then the boss smiled. It was a beautiful thing, this smile. Huge and uncomplicated and full of power. It was as fine a reward as Carlos had ever known. "I have a man who is troubling me greatly."

"Give me his name," Carlos replied instantly. "He will never bother you again."

Again the smile appeared. No words of thanks could possibly have matched the quality of this reward. "I seek to do everything I can to help lift up our little corner of Mexico."

"This I know," Carlos said.

"Unfortunately, to do this, I am sometimes forced to take actions that are outside the law."

Carlos wore a leather jacket that creaked as he shrugged. "This is Mexico. It is to be expected."

"If I am to be successful, no connection can ever be made between these actions and myself."

"I understand."

"For this reason, I regret that we shall not be able to meet together very often. Perhaps never again."

Carlos nodded his acceptance. The prospect of never being in this man's presence again was bitterly disappointing. But he had found a purpose in life. He would do what was required of him.

The boss rose to his feet. He was a young man, tall and strong and handsome. The power radiated from him like heat from the sun. "Know that you have my undying gratitude. Your family will want for nothing."

Carlos spoke the words he knew the boss wanted to hear. "Whatever you require. Tell me and it will be done."

Carlos was seated in his car, watching the orphanage's front gates. He had tracked his quarry back to their lair. The attack was to be secret this time. His orders were clear. No fuss, no witnesses, no sign. Just make the Yanqui disappear.

So far, this American had not been alone for an instant. The police had come and gone, the mayor, the woman Sofia. Now the town manager was poking around. But it was only a matter of time.

Carlos had scouted twice around the orphanage exterior. Despite his size, he could join with the shadows and move in utter stealth. It was his gift, this silent passage. He took pride in his work, as he did the trust his boss placed in his abilities.

Because cell-phone service was spotty in north Chihuahua, Carlos carried a satellite phone. It meant he could be reached anywhere, instantly. The phone was very cumbersome. But it was also virtually impossible to have a call over a satellite phone traced. When his phone buzzed, he picked it from the seat beside him, saw who called, and pressed the receive button. "Jefe."

"You are on him?"

"He is two hundred meters away. The orphanage has only one entrance. If I move to where I can observe him, I will be seen."

"No, no. Stay where you are. In fact, I want you to pull farther back."

"I can take this one. Now, if you like. The others, they can be frightened into silence. Or erased as well. You know I can do this."

"No. The orphanage is not to be touched. And this man, I must rescind my order."

"You do not want him killed, even in secret?"

"For the moment, he must live."

Carlos did not object to the change in orders. It was not his nature to object. Not with this man. "As you say, Jefe."

"Stay on him. Report back to me any movement. And be ready to move upon my command. His stay of execution is only temporary."

Carlos cut the connection and settled back into his seat. He did not move his car. There was no need. It was a perfect position for unseen observation. The orphanage gates opened onto a small village plaza. There were hundreds of such places in Mexico, thousands. Tiny hamlets that had been swallowed by growing towns and cities, yet which maintained their individual nature.

There was a whitewashed church, and a small grocery, and a pair of cafés, and seven little shops that somehow managed to eke out an existence. Old men sat on weathered benches beneath dusty trees. Another man sat behind the wheel of a truck, waiting with the eternal patience of a Mexican peasant. No one paid Carlos any mind.

He stared at the gates, content to wait and observe. He understood the boss. There was no need to trouble him with discussions or further questions. The American would be kept on a long leash. He would be allowed to breathe the air another day. Perhaps two. But the orders remained in place.

The American would never be allowed to cross the border alive.

Chapter 12

Simon went upstairs and took a long shower, trying to wash off the morning and the sweat and the emotions. Occasionally he heard Sofia's voice in the office below him. She sounded upset. Simon assumed she had just heard it would take a week to get him a new passport. Through the guestroom's open window, he saw that Pedro's truck was parked by the front gates. Which was a good thing. He had an idea and he needed Pedro's help.

A fresh bandage had been laid out on the bed, alongside a tube of antibiotic cream and another T-shirt and drawstring trousers. Juan, no doubt. The kid was incredible. As Simon peeled off the wet bandage, Sofia's voice rose momentarily, long enough for him to catch one word. *Reckless.* Simon sat on the stool and toyed with the key strung around his neck. Reckless had been Vasquez's favorite way of describing him.

The last time Simon had seen the professor, Vasquez entered the bar during Simon's shift and ordered him to stop wasting time and get back to his real work. By that point, Vasquez was the only person at MIT who hadn't written him off.

Simon started to offer his standard response, that he spent so much time in the bar, he might as well get paid for his troubles. But something in the professor's gaze stopped him. Vasquez had barely been able to contain his excitement. He was working on a new method of generating power. For years the professor had searched for a means to break the Mexican power company's stranglehold over the poor. Vasquez was never more passionate than when he was defending the oppressed of Mexico.

In Mexico, electricity was controlled by a government monopoly called Comisión Federal de Electricidad, or CFE. Vasquez accused the CFE of fostering an attitude of corruption. Nothing was done without kickbacks. The senior bureaucrats running CFE had fought and schemed all their lives to arrive at the point where they could line their pockets. Supplying power was the least of their concerns. CFE had the highest cost per kilowatt of any major power company in the entire world. CFE was so inefficient, over half of all power generated was lost between the station and the end user. The professor could go on for hours about CFE.

That night the professor had revealed to Simon the project that had consumed his every free hour for years. He made a major breakthrough, but more was needed. Much more. And Simon was the answer. Of that the professor was absolutely certain. He spoke with a believer's fervor. Vasquez was *convinced* of this.

Simon leaned over the bar and watched as Vasquez described his work, using bar napkins and a pen that blurred and stained over the wet spots. Simon was totally captivated, rushing back from filling orders. Amazed at the man's vision. Jealous of the professor's ability to dream. And frightened of letting him down.

When Simon descended the orphanage stairs, Harold played a piano while Juan stood and sang beside him. Simon was surprised at the quality of the boy's voice. It broke a couple of times, as Juan struggled to work through the change to manhood. It bothered Juan a lot more than it did Harold, who beamed approval and said several times, "Good, that is excellent. You are ready!"

Pedro stood on the shaded stoop outside Harold's office. Simon knew there was more at work than the town's assistant manager holding up a post in his former home. Pedro was waiting for him. Bearing the weight of his sister's words.

"I know you took a risk bringing me here. I appreciate that," Simon said, then repeated the same words he had told Sofia. "I don't want to do anything that might harm these kids."

Pedro swiped his face with a hand broad as a shovel, as though a hard life had expanded and flattened it. "This is south of the border. Very few things are the way any of us want them."

Simon nodded, more in respect to what the guy had lived through than an acceptance of his words. "I need two things. First, a passport."

"Enrique is handling this."

"He also said it was going to take a week."

"Maybe less. Four days, he hopes."

"Still, do I stay here for another four days?"

"Harold says you are our guest." Pedro did not speak so much as sigh the words.

Simon tried to keep the relief from his face. He had virtually no money and nowhere else to go. And this place did seem to offer a basic level of comfort and safety. "Okay. Great. Thanks."

Pedro shrugged. Clearly the decision was not his, and the gratitude was misdirected. "And the second thing?"

"Harold showed me a video of Vasquez in his lab making the apparatus work. I need his data."

"What are you saying?"

He took a breath. "I need to get into his lab."

"You are as Sofia describes. Reckless. A threat."

"You heard what Harold said. This machine could be a big deal. And I need to find out what Vasquez was closing in on."

"Harold would also say we should not take this risk."

Simon saw the man fish his keys from his pocket and knew he had won. "Then I guess we better not tell him where we're going."

Carlos was confused. Which for him was a dangerous condition. He responded to confusion with an icy rage. When he became bewildered, people were hurt. It was inevitable.

And this day, the American was to blame.

Carlos had never disobeyed a direct order from the jefe. But today might be an exception.

He had followed the town assistant manager's decrepit pickup from the orphanage. Carlos saw the American in the passenger seat. So long as they had remained on the main road circling to the west of Ojinaga's downtown, Carlos could hang back. Pedro's pickup had a tall frame holding a stepladder and cleaning equipment. Carlos could see it even with six cars between them.

When Pedro turned off the main road and started up the hill known as Boys' Town, following them had grown more difficult. But Carlos was not worried. They could only be headed toward the professor's house. There was nothing else in Boys' Town that could possibly interest them. The former houses with the women were mostly shut down. And the people around the orphanage were all religious. Carlos assumed that included the American. It meant nothing to him. It changed nothing. A job was a job. Duty was everything.

But now he had failed the boss. He had lost them.

Carlos could not risk keeping the truck within view. There was almost no traffic on the road that climbed the Boys' Town ridge. When he had first come to Ojinaga, driving this road had been entirely different. After dark the traffic had been so bad, most people parked along the main road and hiked in. The visitors had been almost all men. *Vaqueros* in from the surrounding farms climbed the ridge, laughing against their nerves, their high-heeled boots clicking on the stones. They shared the road with loud-mouthed tourists from across the border.

From almost every house had come music and the clink of glasses and the raucous laughter. Carlos had known Boys' Town intimately, for it was from this place that many of the coyotes operated. The violence and the danger had lurked just beyond the reach of the gaiety, and many dawns revealed fresh corpses.

Then the change had come to Ojinaga and all the north Chihuahua cities. Through the jefe's actions, the brothels had been banished with the gangs and the coyotes. All these illegal activities had been tightly linked. Carlos had heard that many of the houses had simply moved into the surrounding scrublands, taking over ranches and setting up their businesses out of sight. Carlos did not care. His job was not to rid the world of badness. To do this would have meant putting a bullet in his own head. His job was to serve his family and his jefe.

But today he had failed. Carlos hated nothing more than failure. His rage took on an icy calm, so powerful he remained untouched by the heat. Carlos pulled down the road leading to the professor's home. The house was silent, the lane empty.

Carlos left the car and headed inside. He would check the house, just to be certain.

Then he would find the American. And he would try to keep his control.

But there was no telling what might happen next.

Chapter 13

Simon had seen places like this on television. But he was still not prepared for what he faced. They crossed the main road and started up a road that was barely more than a steep alley. The hill they climbed was separated from Ojinaga's other districts by the north-south highway and a narrow gorge. The cone-shaped hill was carved into a series of uneven steps, each lined by a circular lane. Houses of every size and description lined these roads, everything from brightly painted mansions to windowless hovels.

The road grew worse the higher they climbed. The pavement was rutted, the potholes deep. They passed a couple of cars descending the grade in slow motion, dipping and rocking over the pitted surface. They climbed at such an angle Simon was pressed back into his seat.

At a particularly steep juncture Pedro stopped, which entailed pressing both feet on the brakes and pulling out the hand brake as well. He squinted around, muttering to himself. Then he put the truck back in gear, raced the engine, and took a right. The roads circling the hill were not paved at all. The truck's engine emitted a trickle of steam from either side of the hood.

Simon asked, "Do you know where we're going?"

"Maybe."

"Should we ask someone?"

"They will not tell us. The professor is dead. We are strangers. This is Mexico."

"Why didn't we ask Sofia?"

Pedro took his eye off the road long enough to cast Simon a scornful look. "She has never been to this place."

"I thought you said she was the professor's friend."

"She was. But this hill is Boys' Town."

Simon waited. When Pedro said nothing more, he pressed. "That means what exactly?"

"It is where the bad women worked. Before. Some say there are still a few houses. But I do not think this is true. Enrique has shut down all the ones we know of." Pedro spun the wheel and turned the truck as far as he could manage. "It is not this street. We must go up another level."

All Simon could see were blank walls, most of rusting metal. A few were solid concrete-block topped with barbed wire. Inside the fences, skinny dogs tracked their progress and barked. "How can you tell?"

"The professor, he bought this home because he loved his view of the mountains." Pedro waved at the cracked and grimy front windshield. "We have gone too far around the hill. You cannot see the mountains from here."

Reversing the car took nine tight maneuvers. Pedro retraced

his route, then turned up the hill. He took another left, and this time Simon understood why. A hundred meters after they turned, the mountains emerged in all their glory. From this height, the view was stupendous, a rich array of desert tones and jagged peaks that laced the far horizon.

Then Simon's attention was drawn to the lane ahead. "Stop!"

Pedro hit the brakes. "What's the matter?"

"Back up!"

"But the professor's house—"

"That's the attacker's car!"

Pedro clearly did not believe him, but he reversed the truck back around the bend. "Señor Simon, the town is full of dark SUVs."

"I've seen that one often enough to be certain." He opened his door. "Turn your truck around and park where he won't see you if he leaves."

Pedro's face showed rising alarm. "What are you doing?"

Simon shut his door. "I'll be right back."

Pedro watched Simon move away from the pickup. The man was everything Sofia feared. He was a threat to the orphanage. He did not belong. He was a wastrel. Yet in spite of it all, Pedro agreed with Harold. He liked Simon. He liked him very much.

The gringo had been hunted by a very bad man. This bad man was still out there somewhere. Why the hunter was so intent on Simon, Pedro had no idea. Many things in the border country made no sense. But Pedro knew one thing with absolute certainty. People had been afraid for too long. And Simon was not ruled by fear.

Back at the orphanage, Simon had thought Pedro was angry with him. But this was simply not true. Pedro always left an argument with his sister feeling exhausted. He could work all day in the sun and still not be nearly as weary as he felt after five minutes with Sofia. When she started on one of those tirades, he felt like a wet dishrag being twisted in her strong hands, until every drop of energy was wrenched out.

But nothing would have come from telling Sofia what he felt. Which was this: Simon's coming was an act of God.

The orphanage was in serious trouble. For weeks, Pedro and Harold had been praying for a miracle. And Harold thought Simon Orwell was the miracle they had been waiting for. Why Harold felt this way, Pedro had no idea. And he did not need to know. He trusted Harold's judgment. For him, that was enough.

Pedro spent a great deal of his time observing from the periphery. Especially when he was in the company of Enrique. Around the mayor, Pedro went unnoticed. He used such times to observe the life from which he had been excluded. He saw how families had to rely upon each other. How Mexican parents were the only real authority that mattered. Most schools were abysmal failures. Parents were the main educators of their children. They were the source of their children's identity. And for most Mexicans, success was just another word for survival.

Most Mexican families did not seek to raise their children up to positions beyond their own. That was a confusing trait they observed north of the border. What good came of this, when the children were pushed away, never to return? Here in Mexico, family was everything. The children's first responsibility was to be there when it mattered most and take care of their own. When their parents grew old, the children saw to their parents' needs.

Pedro felt his orphan status every day. It was a weight he had learned to carry and live with. But he never forgot his heritage. And he never stopped giving thanks for Harold. That one blessing made up for all the misfortune and the sorrow Pedro had known.

He knew the situation within most state orphanages. He had visited several with Enrique. Those encounters had given him terrible nightmares. How close he had come to enduring the same tragic fate as these children. How vital it was that Harold's orphanage find the resources necessary to survive.

Harold had done far more for Pedro than give him a sense of identity. Harold had *inspired* him.

Many of the visiting missionaries saw Pedro as a glorified janitor for a grimy border town. But thanks to Harold, Pedro knew different.

His goal in life was to continue Harold's dream and take over running the orphanage when it was time. For now, he protected the orphanage from his position within the city government. He needed no thanks. He desired no recognition. He knew, Harold knew, God knew. For Pedro, that was enough.

He backed the pickup into an alley where shadows from the neighboring wall masked it from the sight of any passing vehicle. Then he slipped from the pickup and followed Simon. The young man might indeed be the answer to their prayers. But only if Pedro could keep him alive.

And something else. Something vital. Pedro needed to be certain, absolutely positive, that God was behind Simon's arrival. After all, Sofia could in fact be right. Simon could be nothing more than a threat. Pedro considered it his responsibility to be certain. One way or the other.

So as he left the alley, he sent a swift plea up toward heaven. *God, please give me a sign. If Simon is indeed the answer we have been praying for, please show me this clearly.* The lives of the children depended upon Pedro getting this one right.

He knew Simon carried a huge weight. Pedro had heard from his sister how Simon had wasted his life. But what man was free from wrongful deeds? And Pedro had learned from Harold that no man was a failure as long as he continued to draw breath. Simon might have given up on himself. But God had not given up on Simon. Of this Pedro was certain.

And one other thing he knew. One thing that Sofia in her agitated fear either did not see or chose to ignore. Harold was only getting started with this one. Pedro had seen Harold's impact on too many people to question his ability to change a life's course.

Pedro ran across the dusty road. Simon had no idea what was in store, just around the next bend.

Chapter 14

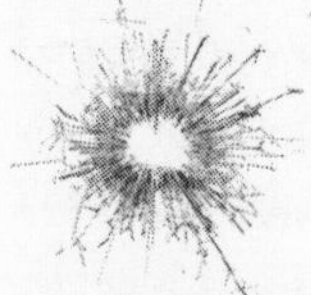

Simon moved down the silent street, slipping from shadow to shadow. From the other side of the wire fence he heard a noise inside the professor's house. He assumed it was the hunter. Simon knew what he was doing was borderline insane. He also knew his actions were drawn from a lot more than just getting his passport back.

He had always been attracted by danger. It was the lure he could not resist. Whenever most people started screaming and running away, Simon was at his calmest. His senses were on full alert, his mind crystal clear. He could literally count every dust mote, give a name to each blade of sunlight. The blood sang in his veins.

The SUV's passenger window was rolled down. Simon opened the door and slipped inside. The interior was blisteringly hot. Sunlight glared through the darkened front windshield. His ability to see was cut down by the tinted glass, but it appeared to have no impact whatsoever on the heat. Simon could not understand why anyone would want to darken the view ahead. All this sped through his brain as he rifled the dash, then did the same to the compartment between the seats and the pockets in each door. Nothing.

He spied a briefcase on the backseat. It was one of those fancy slipcovers, without handles, to be carried like a pouch. The gold label on the front flap was carved with the word, *Dunhill*. A fancy container for a bad guy. He unzipped the compartment and found a few papers, all in Spanish.

Then he heard a hiss from the other side of the street. This was followed by the slam of a door.

Simon jammed the papers back into the briefcase and slipped out the passenger door. He could not risk shutting the door completely because just then the gate squeaked and clicked shut. He knew Pedro was across the street and petrified by the sight of the hunter approaching the car. Simon squatted in the road, tracking the hunter's boots from underneath the SUV.

Then the hunter started around the car.

Simon couldn't run for the other side of the street. To do so would expose them both. He kept his head down, still tracking the hunter's feet, moving as soundlessly as he could manage, keeping the SUV between them.

The hunter came around to the passenger side and halted. He examined the door, opened it, then slammed it tight. He did not move.

Simon's fear mixed with the adrenaline rush, and he was ready to bolt if the man saw tracks in the road-dust and started toward him. There was little chance he could make it to safety.

This was the hunter's world. Simon's only haven was a universe away. He had no idea how to even find the orphanage.

The hunter stood like that, staring across the street, motionless. It felt to Simon as though hours passed. Then the man turned and walked back the way he had come. He climbed into the SUV and started the motor.

Simon scrambled backward, crablike, until a space opened between two houses. He wedged himself inside and crouched as the SUV rocked back and forth, turning around in the tight lane. The dark vehicle had a massive motor that roared as the hunter finally managed the turn and raced away.

When the motor's noise faded, Simon rose from the shadow. Across the street, Pedro did the same. Simon walked over, expecting rage, fear, anything but how Pedro greeted him.

Pedro smiled. His grin was infectious. "Do you do this often? Scare people half to death?"

Only then did Simon realize his legs were weak and shaking. He gripped the side wall. "I thought you'd be furious."

"*Amigo,* I am too scared to be angry. But give me a few minutes. Maybe I will recover."

Simon had to fight down a case of the giggles. He was afraid if he started laughing, he wouldn't be able to stop. "Let's go check it out."

The giddy feeling did not last. The professor's front door was solid wood, very thick, with iron bars crosshatched over a small portal at head height. The door was locked. Simon used the key on the chain around his neck and unlocked the door. He was instantly confronted by all he had lost.

The first thing that met him was the smell of cherry-flavored pipe tobacco. Vasquez did not often light up. The occasional pipe was his way of marking a truly good day. And by the strength of this cold odor, Vasquez had known many good moments recently.

Pedro asked, "How do you have a key to this house around your neck?"

"Vasquez made every lock work to just one key. Lab, filing cabinets, clean room, home. The works."

"But how is it . . . ?"

"Later, okay?" Simon moved deeper into the house. There was no way he was going to be drawn into that discussion.

The place was an utter wreck. Vasquez had never been neat and tidy. On the best days, his office resembled a tsunami zone. Which was hardly surprising. Many great scientists were abysmal housekeepers. What made Vasquez unique was how precise and methodical he was when it came to records. Which was why Simon was here. Vasquez would have been keeping records to the last possible moment, to his dying breath.

If Simon was going to make any headway, he needed to find out not just the professor's final entry, but the last established pattern.

Vasquez's latest research had undoubtedly taken a different turn. Simon had no idea what that was. In order to continue, he first had to determine which course of action to follow. Hundreds of possible variances existed. Thousands. Simon kept tossing up different potential avenues of research, unexplored directions that could have potentially resulted in success. But he had no idea which one Vasquez had identified. That was why he came. To find out.

Pedro walked through the foyer and whistled softly. "Who did this?"

"Your friend and mine, most likely. The guy in the leather jacket."

"But why? The professor did not have an enemy in the world."

"Apparently Vasquez had at least one." Simon continued down the narrow hall that led into a living-dining area. The L-shaped room had an array of windows fronting a back porch. All the windows framed spectacular views of the mountains.

The room had not merely been searched. It had been completely torn apart. Holes were banged in all four walls at odd intervals. The sofa and padded chair had been ripped open. The carpet had been peeled off the concrete floor. The wallpaper fell in ragged strips. The ceiling was gouged like the walls. Every light was shattered.

"I have a bad feeling about this," Pedro said but did not retreat. Instead he turned to the right off the front foyer rather than following Simon into the living room. Pedro's feet scrunched over glass. "Simon."

"What."

"Come take a look."

Through a side door, Simon spotted what looked like Vasquez's office. "In a minute."

"Simon. Now."

Reluctantly he retraced his steps down the central hall and entered the kitchen. "Whoa."

The cabinets and fridge and stove and tiled floor were all porcelain white. Every cupboard was smashed beyond repair. The fridge door hung on one hinge. Again, every light was shattered.

The door leading from the kitchen to the rear veranda had an upper portion of glass. The smoked glass was impact resistant, two panes with thin wire crisscrossed through the central seam. The glass on the floor came from the ceiling lights and a second window, narrow and long and set above the stove.

The second window was framed by iron bars. No doubt the hunter had tried this one first, then realized he could not pry back the bars so he turned his attention to the door. What made the scene almost ludicrous was how the door was now shut. No doubt the hunter still had some childhood habit of closing the door behind him. Under different circumstances, Simon would have laughed out loud.

Pedro looked aghast at a red stain that swept like an evil rainbow over the wall and the stove and the sink and the fridge. "They said Vasquez had a heart attack."

"Who told you that?"

"The police, soon after it happened. I work for the mayor. I asked, they told me. His heart." He tracked the stain's broad arc. "Why would they lie?"

Simon backed out of the room. "You're asking the wrong question."

"What do you mean?"

He did not answer. That discussion needed to wait. Simon

retraced his steps back through the living room and entered the study. Here the professor's imprint was most visible and the damage most total.

The professor had taken out the rear wall and extended the home. His office had once been the garage. The concrete floor remained, but the roof had been perforated by two sparkling new skylights. The office area contained a desk and shelves and a faded Oriental carpet that Simon remembered from Cambridge. The new extension held a pair of lab tables, an industrial generator, high-speed ventilators, compressors, and strip lighting connected to adjustable chains. The lighting was shattered and the shelves beneath the lab tables smashed open.

Simon's attention was held by the one item in the entire house that remained intact. The professor's laptop sat in the middle of the desk. It stood out like a jewel on a ruined stage. Every side of the desk had been hammered open, no doubt searching for hidden compartments. But there on the top was the laptop. Undamaged. Waiting.

Simon opened the laptop. It hummed out of sleep mode and the screen lit up. The first thing that popped up was the last e-mail. The one that had invited him to Mexico. The e-mail was dated three days ago. Telling Simon to hurry. Repeating the confirmation of the city council's funding but warning that their patience was wearing thin, and they needed to hear from the American scientist who was working with Vasquez.

Someone who spoke precise enough English to mimic the professor's way of writing had lured him to Mexico. Simon slapped the laptop shut. He would go through the files later. He scouted around, trying to see beyond the mess.

As Simon surveyed the demolished chamber, Pedro stepped toward the left-hand wall. The floor-to-ceiling bookshelves were torn out. Holes had been punched in the wall behind. The floor was littered with books and manuals and sheaves of printed data and the sort of debris that every successful scientist gathered over a lifetime. Pedro gingerly picked up a broken picture frame and shook away the glass before extracting a photograph.

Simon stepped to where he could look over Pedro's shoulder. "I know that woman!"

Pedro said nothing.

"She's the woman who ran the city council meeting. She lied to my face!"

"That sounds like her." Pedro's voice had gone flat. Toneless.

"Who is she?"

"Her name is Dr. Clara. She is the dark face of Mexico. The public figure who will do anything, say anything, for those who remain hidden. Enrique fights against her a great deal." Pedro shook his head slightly, little more than a twitch. "Professor Vasquez saw something in her. He claimed she was the most misunderstood woman in all of Ojinaga. In this, the professor was very wrong."

"You think she was behind the attack on the highway?" When Pedro did not respond, Simon added, "She was behind the professor's death?"

Pedro sighed. "We may never know. But yes. I think it is possible."

"What was Vasquez doing with someone like that?"

"The professor knew Dr. Clara since childhood. We heard they had been seeing each other. Sofia tried to warn him, but it was too late. Vasquez was growing very close to Dr. Clara. I heard a rumor they were engaged."

Simon shot him a look. There had never been a woman in Vasquez's life. Simon had asked him about it once, and the professor stared sadly into the distance and spoke about a woman he had left behind when he came to America. Simon had never mentioned it again. The thought that Dr. Clara, who had cheated them both and possibly caused the professor's death, was who he had spent years pining over left Simon queasy. "Is that a joke?"

"No joke." Pedro folded the photograph lengthwise and stowed it in his pocket. "Can we go?"

"Not yet." Simon started to turn away when he spotted a second photograph. He slid it out from underneath a pair of textbooks, brushed away the glass, and lifted it free of the frame. The picture was of the professor and him, taken on a snowy morning in front of the main physics lab. The professor had his arm around Simon's shoulders. They both were laughing. "I remember when that was taken."

"He would like you to have it. Come. We should go."

"In a minute."

"Every instant we stay here is a risk. To everyone."

Simon nodded but did not speak. He had not found what he came for. It had to be here. It *had* to.

Then he saw the globe.

"What is it?"

"The professor kept this in his office." Vasquez had found it in a Boston flea market. The hand-painted surface was battered and deeply dented. But Simon knew the antique globe held a very special secret.

For the second time that afternoon, Simon slipped the key from around his neck.

The lock was hidden under Antarctica. The continent had to be pressed in a special manner or else the spring didn't give. The professor had reworked the lock so it opened to the same key. The professor had been obsessed by this notion. Vasquez was always losing everything. Especially keys. He had made a joke of it as he handed Simon the key. The only other person in the world who had a duplicate. It was as great a gift as Simon had ever received.

Which was why Simon's vision was none too clear as he unlocked the globe.

The secret compartment was not large and held only two items. One was his personal Bible. The other was a set of lab papers containing long lists of numbers. At the top of the first page, two lines were scrawled in Vasquez's almost illegible script.

Don't let me down.

I wish you every success.

Simon knew exactly what he held. He whispered, "Bingo."

Which was the moment when everything changed.

Chapter 15

The front gate squeaked.

A shadow crossed the narrow window facing the street. The glass was milky white, intended to let in light but not permit passers-by to see into the professor's office and lab.

As the shadow swept by, Simon recognized the man's profile. The bulky jacket, the round head, the scraggly contour of a closely trimmed beard. Pedro stared at Simon, helpless in his fear.

Simon's response could not have been more different. He felt the familiar wash of adrenaline, the heightened awareness, the sudden ability to pierce the moment and see things most people remained blind to. He knew the hunter had not tried the front door, which could only mean one thing. The hunter often came here and assumed the front door was still locked. Which was why the upper glass in the kitchen door had been broken out. This was where the hunter was headed now. Back along a path that had become familiar. The hunter did not yet know they were inside.

There was only one logical course of action. Simon ran for the kitchen.

As he raced across the lab's concrete floor, he scooped up a black cable. The hunter had probably used it to shift the generator, moving it far enough to ensure nothing had been hidden underneath. And had torn it out in the process. The cord was supple and covered in woven cloth.

Simon reached the kitchen before the hunter. He quietly slipped the door's dead bolt into place. The hunter's footsteps moved down the side of the house. The man whistled softly, a pair of notes, up and down. Simon doubted the man was even aware of the sound he made.

Simon fashioned a noose from the cable. He had always been good with knots. It had been his one merit badge as a Boy Scout, before he had been kicked out for fighting. He then tied the cable's other end around the copper gas pipe where it ran out of the wall. And waited.

The hunter tried the door, found it locked, and grunted softly. He reached inside and fumbled blindly.

Simon crammed the noose over the hand and hauled back.

The hunter's arm and shoulder came through the broken upper door and his head slammed against the shattered door frame. Simon lashed the cable down tight, trapping the man halfway inside the door. The man's astonished face was inches from his own.

He scrambled away from the hunter. "Give me back my passport!"

The hunter grinned back at him. There was no humor in those glittering black eyes. No life. Nothing.

Then he barked. Like an animal's bark. A predator in sight of prey.

From outside the door there was the snick of metal-on-metal. The hunter's other hand came into view, holding an open switchblade.

Simon raced from the kitchen. Pedro stood by the front door, eyes round, mouth gaping like he was struggling to draw breath in a vacuum.

They fled.

"What were you thinking?" Harold demanded.

Simon watched Pedro hang his head as though he was being punished. But there was no criticism in Harold's voice that Simon could hear. Instead the man seemed genuinely curious. As though he was seeking to understand before passing judgment.

"Did you even give a thought to the orphanage? Or the children?"

"Of course I did," Pedro replied to Harold. "I hardly ever think of anything else."

"Then how could you take such a risk?"

"You said it yourself. Because of what Simon might be."

Simon was certain the hunter took his orders from someone else. The man's gaze had held a predatory gleam but no deep intelligence. He was probably very good at his job. It was doubtful he had any scruples whatsoever. Simon couldn't understand how a man would serve another person so slavishly. He could still taste the man's breath, the foul odor of beef and chili spices. He remembered those eyes and knew the man would not give up. It was only a matter of time before he attacked again.

Harold said, "That did not give you permission to endanger our young charges."

"I did not do this thing to endanger anyone. I did it to save us."

Simon liked Pedro. The man held a quiet strength, a quality he hid away most of the time. As though he preferred people to underestimate him.

"I can understand Simon taking a risk like that. But you?"

"Every day holds risk. Every breath we draw in these days. Life itself is a risk."

Harold stopped then. And waited. Like he knew Pedro was not going to give and there was nothing to be gained by pushing. Two men who had known each other for a lifetime and knew how the other thought. They trusted one another, at a level far beyond words, beyond any quarrel or worry. Simon wondered what it would be like to know another person so intimately. He had spent a lifetime keeping people at arm's length.

Then he noticed the new paper on Harold's board.

The side wall was covered by an oversized corkboard. Upon it were dozens of paintings and drawings and stories. The words were written on wide-ruled paper used by very young children learning to write. Many contained letters of love to Harold. The paintings were cheerful and bright and happy.

There in the center of the board hung Simon's two goals. They held pride of position, right at the heart of the community.

The words were so tawdry, the wishes so cynical. As empty as his life.

"Simon."

Reluctantly he turned back around. And faced the man on the other side of the battered desk.

"Did you find something that justified taking such a risk?"

"Maybe."

"What are you going to do with it?"

"I'm not sure. Yet. Can I be excused?"

Harold cocked his head to one side. Inspecting him carefully. Then he nodded. "Yes, Simon. You can go."

He rose from his chair and reached to the board. He took down the page that contained his two empty goals. And walked from the room.

At the doorway he could not help but glance back. Harold was seated there, his head still cocked slightly. Only now he was smiling. As though Simon had done the right thing. For once.

Simon heard the bell ring through his room's open window. The sound pulled on him like a magnet. He resisted the urge. He remained where he was, sitting at his table on his little stool. Studying the two pages Vasquez had left for him. The scrawled words at the top of the first page branded themselves into his brain. *"Don't let me down. I wish you every success."*

The children erupted from the chapel. A few minutes later, the dinner bell clanged. Simon went outside and joined the line snaking out the mess hall door. The kids giggled and pointed. But when he did not respond, they left him alone. Juan slipped over and asked if he wanted anything. Simon thanked him and said no. Juan must have seen he was more than simply distracted, for the kid didn't say anything more.

Simon took his metal plate and mug to the table by the far window and sat by himself. Even when all the other places became filled, he remained alone. Lost in thought, the lines of numbers danced in the golden light spilling through the western window.

When he was finished eating, he took his plate and mug and utensils to the plastic trays by the dishwasher's portal. Then he walked back to the doorway leading to Harold's room and the orphanage guestroom. The kids were playing their perpetual game of soccer in the courtyard. Juan called to him. Still deep in thought, Simon did not respond. The kids laughed at him, and he carried the happy sound back upstairs.

He left the two pages from Vasquez on the guestroom's battered table and stepped to the window. Only the older kids were playing now, and they played well. Extremely well, in fact. Simon had played intramural soccer through his high school and college years. He knew talent when he saw it. The kids were playing some serious soccer. Their bare feet became a sunset dance, throwing up golden clouds of dust and laughter. He saw a happiness and simple joy, something he had thought lost to him forever.

He shut the window and returned to the table. But the lines of data didn't hold him. Simon rose from the stool and opened the professor's Bible. The book was well worn, the cover so supple he could fold it back upon itself. The onion-skin pages were heavily lined and annotated in the professor's illegible script. Simon had a sense of the professor standing behind him, watching in approval as Simon studied the pages for the first time in his adult life.

He set the Bible to one side and unfolded the photograph. The picture had been taken by a grad student on the day Vasquez had given Simon the key he still wore around his neck. Vasquez had his peculiarities. Most of the MIT professors and many of the students had some odd trait or another. The resulting jokes were a means by which the brilliant minds could be kept in human perspective. At the time that picture was taken, Simon and the professor were becoming very close. The professor had seen Simon as the student who would someday take his place and continue his research. The afternoon he had given Simon a copy of his key, Vasquez had revealed his secret research and his longing to provide free power to Mexico's poorest citizens. Vasquez had then bestowed the key like a king offering a loyal subject a crown.

And Simon had responded with a joke.

While the sounds of kids playing soccer filled his room with the music of heartfelt joy, Simon tried his best to tell the professor good-bye. But the professor's smile mocked his desire to turn away.

Simon unfolded the page he had taken down from Harold's board. The orphanage director's handwriting was almost as bad as Vasquez's. The two desires Harold had copied down were pitiful. They were certainly not funny. They mocked him as well.

Simon turned the sheet over. The blank page was an invitation. Not merely to write something down. Rather, Simon heard a faint call to move on. To start anew.

He was still staring at the blank sheet of paper when the kids went silent, and night drew a desert hush over his bare room. Simon rose from the stool and stretched. He cut off the light and lay down on the cot. He stared at the ceiling for a time. Finally he rose and turned the light back on and went over to the table. The empty page was there beside the professor's photograph. Waiting.

Simon knew if he didn't write, he would not sleep. He put down the number one and beside it wrote the words that had been bouncing around inside his head ever since leaving the professor's house.

To do something more.

He set the pen down and started to turn away. He wanted to, but he knew he was not done. The professor stared up at him. Waiting.

Simon picked up the pen and wrote the hardest four words of his entire life.

Beside the number two, he put: *To make things right.*

The words raked across his heart with talons of bitter regret. But after he cut off the light and lay back down, he discovered that the act granted him a sense of release. The burden he had been carrying for nearly a year was not entirely gone. But a tiny chip had been broken off. The weight was not so heavy. He breathed a little easier.

And for the first time since it had all gone down, Simon found himself able to say the word that had brought him two thousand miles. Too late to say to Vasquez, perhaps. But to say it at all offered him a sense of tragic conquest.

He whispered to the night and the man who was no more, "Sorry."

Then he rolled over and shut his eyes.

He slept and did not dream.

Chapter 16

Sofia's home was an apartment above a café and an art gallery. Her balcony overlooked the square and the orphanage gates beyond. The apartment belonged to Harold. He had bought it at the end of his first mission trip. Before returning to America he had wanted to anchor himself here. It was a move typical of Harold, planning for the future in concrete ways. By that point Harold knew this was where he had been called to spend his remaining days. The apartment was his way of not allowing the pressures of the outside world to change his mind.

Harold had offered her the place while she was still in university in El Paso. He had hoped it would be a way for her to maintain her connection, and he also wanted to heal the wounds caused by her departure and all the struggles that had preceded the move north.

Sofia carried her morning coffee and her Bible out to the balcony. Dawn spread out over the quiet plaza. Doves filled the trees that lined the square and filled the morning with their soft calls. She read a passage and prayed and reflected on her past. All while she was growing up, missionaries had visited from the U.S. Some came with church groups for a week, they worked around the orphanage, then they left. Others came with college mission groups or as couples on temporary assignment, stayed for a month or so, and then eventually they left as well. Sofia had gotten on well enough with most of them. But in her secret heart she had resented them. They had come and then they had left. They had abandoned her. Just like her parents.

The couple that had taken her north had been different. They had both retired from academic posts, and they knew and loved Harold and believed in his work. They returned every winter and taught for three months. They had recognized something more in Sofia, so they helped her apply for a stipend at their alma mater and helped her with the government forms for a student visa. Then one day she had simply packed her bag and walked across the Rio Grande and entered a new life.

For her, entering university had been like spreading her wings. When she returned the first time, full of trepidation and dread, Harold had welcomed her with open arms. For Sofia, his understanding and forgiveness had been the clearest answer to prayer she had ever known. Harold had never been one for quarrels. And he could see how happy and hopeful she had become. The arguments had been with Pedro. Her brother had felt bitterly disappointed. Her returns from university had been painful, for Pedro had silently accused her of abandoning him. Just like she had accused others.

She had no problem with Pedro's dream of running the

orphanage. People defined personal success in different ways, that was one of Harold's central precepts. Pedro had been born with a compassionate heart and a desire to serve. It was what made him so good at his job for the city. The people of Ojinaga trusted him. He was the kindly side of the local government, the human face of Enrique's push for change and growth. He would be ideal as the orphanage director once Harold stepped down.

What Pedro had not understood, what he had refused to accept, was that she had wanted *more*. But for her, having more did not mean giving up the orphanage.

Her attention was drawn back to the present by the orphanage bell. She sipped from her coffee, which had grown cold, and watched as Juan swung the gates open. The big doors caught the morning sun and turned the color of frozen honey. Juan grinned and waved at her. This was her favorite time of day.

Then Simon Orwell crossed the orphanage courtyard and entered the chapel.

Simon told himself he was only doing what his scientific training had taught him. Take whatever opportunity was available. Observe carefully and objectively. Analyze the results. Make necessary adjustments. Repeat or select an alternative. And above all else was the simple edict to *move forward*. Search for data. Analyze. Apply. But as Simon entered the chapel's shaded interior, he sensed he was doing the right thing. Faith had meant so much to Vasquez.

Simon slipped into the rear pew, as close to the exit as he could get and stay inside the sanctuary. Pedro came in soon after.

He started up the aisle. Then he stopped. And turned around. And smiled.

Pedro slipped into the pew beside him. "Is this seat taken?"

"Knock yourself out."

"You already did that, amigo. Seeing you here."

Simon was still searching for a comeback when he heard the swift footsteps across the stones outside the chapel. He knew it was Sofia before she stepped inside. He also knew she was going to glare at him.

What he didn't know, what he couldn't have suspected, was Pedro's reaction. He leaned forward from Simon's other side, and he glared at Sofia. Really shot her the stink eye. Sofia winced and faltered slightly. Then she gathered herself and continued up the aisle.

Simon stood and sat with the others. When the singing started, Pedro walked forward and was greeted with huge smiles from all the children. Simon listened to the singing and observed how Pedro managed to make the music both a joy and a game.

The song ended and Pedro started to dismiss the children. Then he shot Simon what could only be described as an impish grin. "Who wants to hear the angel sing this morning?"

The kids erupted in delight.

"It's been too long since the angel joined us, don't you agree?"

Even the villagers smiled and clapped this time. It took a while for a translation to be passed among the locals, as many of them clearly did not speak English. But the longer Pedro stood, hands on hips, waiting, the louder their applause grew. By this point the kids were jumping up and down in glee.

Finally Sofia called out crossly, "What if the angel doesn't want to sing?"

Pedro merely squatted by two of the youngest children and whispered. The kids raced over and took hold of Sofia's hands and pulled her up to the stage.

Sofia began to sing with the children's choir in harmony. Pedro exaggerated his movements, miming as though he wound a great wheel, trying to accelerate their tempo. He bounced on his toes to reach the highest notes. The children loved this. All the while, Sofia stood slightly apart, as though permanently separated. She sang with angelic purity.

The sound pierced Simon's heart. His entire being felt caught by her beauty and her voice. When it was over, Simon joined the congregation in applauding. He wished there were some way to tell her what it had meant, how much he wished he could sit here all day long. Separated from the world and his burdens by the slender silver thread of her voice.

It was during that moment, the brief respite before the beginning of Harold's message, that the idea came to him. He would never be able to apologize to Vasquez. So Simon should do something for him, here, in his adopted home. Make an act of contrition. Such words had never meant anything to him before this moment. Now they filled his entire being. They forged a legacy the professor would have approved of. They gave feet to his apology and made it *live*.

Simon was partly aware that Pedro returned to the seat next to him. He said something, but Simon couldn't focus on anything other than his new thought. Part of him watched as Harold walked down the aisle and hugged Sofia, and the woman scarcely responded. Harold approached the podium and called Juan forward. Simon saw all this. But at the same time, he remained captivated by the idea.

Harold put his arm around the grinning youth. "This is not Juan you see here. This is a baby elephant."

The children shouted their laughter. Harold waited until they quieted, then translated the words for those adults who spoke no English. Then he bent over and fastened a heavy chain around Juan's ankle. Harold slipped easily from one language to the other as he continued, "When the elephant is still very young, it has a chain attached to its hind leg. The chain is then bolted to a heavy concrete block. What do you think happens?"

A dozen young voices called back. Harold nodded vigorously. "That is absolutely right. The baby elephant is trapped. It can't move. It is imprisoned by this chain. Now watch."

On its face, Simon knew his idea was so simple, really. But the tendrils rose like a stop-motion photograph of a plant exploding from the earth and bursting into bloom. This was not just about an apology. This was not just in response to one wrong deed. This was an attempt to make up for all the mistakes that culminated in that one final night.

Up front, Harold bent over Juan's leg and replaced the chain with a length of twine. "I hope everyone is paying careful attention because this is very important. The elephant learns early on that it can't move, so when it grows up, it will be held in place with just this thin bit of string. The elephant believes that it can't break free if there is *anything* tied to its leg."

Simon nodded slowly, drawing Harold's attention. The words from the podium only hastened the growth of his internal idea.

Simon needed to do a penance. Not for Vasquez. The professor was gone. It was too late to say the words. But not too late to do the deeds. And heal the rift he had opened up. Within himself. And whatever future he might have.

Despite the heat, Simon shivered.

He turned to Pedro and whispered, "Can I borrow your pen?"

Pedro slipped it from his shirt pocket. Simon unfolded the sheet of paper and flattened it on the seat next to him. After the number three, he wrote: *Do something for the orphanage.*

He started to hand back the pen, then stopped and added: *Something big.*

Chapter 17

After chapel, Sofia followed the men across the courtyard. Sofia disliked how they were walking. The three of them—Harold, her brother, and Simon—moved as a unit. As though they shared something now. As though she had been excluded.

Pedro turned around when she passed through the outer doorway. The scalding look he had given her in the chapel was gone. She still felt ashamed by that look, in a way that banished her normal feistiness. Now, though, he simply glanced over and then turned back to Harold's office. She moved up beside them.

Simon took a paper from his pocket and unfolded it. He held it to the corkboard covering Harold's wall and smoothed out the creases with the flat of his hand. His motions were very deliberate. His face looked somber.

Harold stood beside him, his hand resting upon Simon's shoulder. He waited until Simon had pinned the page to the board, then leaned forward and read whatever was written there. He nodded slowly, then said softly, "Well done, son. Well done."

"It's the least I can do."

"It's more than that. A good goal is one worth investing that most precious of gifts—your life. And it needs to be *impossible*." Harold turned to Pedro. "Do you know where we stowed them?"

It seemed to Sofia that her brother had been expecting that very question, for he replied, "Ten boxes are in the cupboard under the stairs. The rest are in the back of the garage. I didn't have the heart to throw any of it away."

"Why don't you and Juan pull some of them out." To Simon he said, "Come give us a hand, will you?"

Through the open window, Juan protested, "Breakfast is almost over, Dr. Harold."

Harold had already turned to the closet behind his desk where all the orphanage records were kept. "Juan, Sofia, would you go ask them to make us up plates?"

She did not want to leave. But she did as she was told.

Sofia left the cafeteria with three metal plates. Juan scampered ahead of her and waved from the courtyard's other side. The three men had relocated to one of the empty classrooms. When she and Pedro had been growing up, there had been twice as many children. Now there was twice the need and less than half the funds. Harold had come to Mexico with an adequate pension and a sizeable nest egg. Now the savings were all gone, and his bank had refused to loan him any more with his pension as collateral.

Harold had invested everything into the orphanage. He begged what he could from U.S. churches. He received some funding from mission organizations. But the number of orphans was rising exponentially. The thought of losing young children to the Mexican orphanage system ate away at him. He was in his late seventies and his health was being affected by his worries. Sofia hated how helpless she felt in the face of such dire need.

Harold had chosen this particular classroom because it had three windows facing the courtyard. The front table was covered with large sheets of paper bearing electronic diagrams. Sofia had seen them before. The pages were kept from rolling up by dusty boxes. Sofia set the plates down by a black duffel bag she did not recognize. Then she retreated to the doorway.

Harold said, "What we need is a source of funds that we control. Something we can rely on. So we can start building again. We own another acre behind the admin building. We could build. We could triple the number of children."

Simon nodded and traced a finger over the schematics, his gaze flashing about the pages. Then he shifted one of the boxes and allowed the top page to roll back up. He bent over the next sheet. Intent. Focused.

Pedro said, "We invested in these solar lanterns hoping we could train some of the older children to assemble them. Then we could sell them directly or give them in return for donations."

"Financial stability." Harold rubbed the point over his heart. "We need this if we're going to guarantee the children a place to grow up."

"But the assembled lanterns don't work," Pedro said. "We showed the pages to the owner of the electronics shop here in Ojinaga. He could not help us."

Simon turned to the third page of diagrams. "My guess is, you have a problem in the connectors between the power supply and the battery."

"Can you fix it?"

"If I'm right, absolutely." Simon grinned. "And maybe even if I'm wrong."

Sofia saw the hope shine with the laughter on the men's faces. As she watched Simon study one component after another, she realized that the seed of hope had sprung within her as well. She hated the sense of rising conflict, of hope and fear in equal measure. She turned to the door. "I must go to work."

Sofia's business was located in the industrial zone by the border. She rented a portion of a newer building, a glass-fronted area with a warehouse and a loading dock. She made what should have been the reception area into her office. Neither the orphanage nor her apartment was air-conditioned. She hoped she never took the office's easy spill of coolness for granted. She loved watching the activity in the other buildings and the rush of traffic on the highway beyond the fence. She had two employees—a warehouse manager, who also served as her second driver, and a nighttime guard. It was enough.

She was busy with paperwork when her phone rang. The industrial zone was the one area of Ojinaga that almost always had both power and cell-phone connection. In most of the border zones, the local Mexicans paid for a cell phone from the other side of the border. Even the locals who had never crossed into America had their children or grandchildren bring back a phone, because the U.S. system was both cheaper and more reliable. This did not work in Ojinaga, because the U.S. town across the border was just as isolated. Presidio was surrounded by desert and mountains and the Big Bend preserve, a wildlife region larger than Rhode Island. But the maquiladora was a federally controlled region all to itself. The bribes and corruption that dominated so much of Mexican village life was severely constricted. So long as she was here, she could take and receive calls with ease. "Hello?"

"Darling, I love the sound of your voice. Tell me hello again."

"I'm working."

"You're always working. I am the mayor and I am running for governor and you run circles around me. Let me send you an aide."

"I don't want an aide. My business relies on personal contact. People trust me."

"Yes, I am aware how much everyone trusts you. I trust you. You are the most trustworthy person I know. Which is why I want you to join with me and let us show the world what two people who trust one another can achieve."

"You sound like you are practicing a speech."

"I might be. It sounded good, no?"

"Yes, Enrique. It sounded very good."

"Isn't that what Harold is always going on about, achieving all you can? Think of what we can achieve together. And say yes." He went silent for as long as he was able, which was not very long. "Well? I am waiting for you to accept my proposal."

"You told me to think. I am thinking."

He laughed. "How can I criticize you for doing what I asked? And yet you do exactly what you want, and you force me to do what I *don't* want, which is to be patient. You will make an excellent politician."

"Thank you, Enrique, for your patience."

"You are welcome."

"I know this is hard for you. It is hard for me too."

"Only because you make it so."

"Is that why you called, to make me impatient with myself?"

"Partly, yes, of course, if it will make you decide any quicker. But mostly no, it is not why I called. My mother is coming to Juárez. She is attending a gala event where I am speaking. She asks if you will join us."

Sofia had met Enrique's mother. Three times. "She asked for me? Really?"

"Well, no. Not exactly. She asked if you were coming. She *hoped* you would be there."

"Enrique, your mother wants you to marry that rich lady from Mexico City."

He was silent.

"I saw the photo of you two. Your mother had the society magazine open to the page the last time we met. She wanted to be sure I saw it. You two looked very nice together."

Enrique sighed. "My mother is very old school."

"She loathes the ground I walk on."

"She does not hate you. She . . ."

"She thinks you would be better with the society lady on your arm. What do the Americans call it? Eye candy."

"The event in Juárez is in four days. Say yes."

She did not need to check her calendar. "In four days I have appointments at the clinics in Potrero del Llano and El Mangle.

I am meeting with the doctors and bidding on the new clinic. I want to supply everything, and I think they might—"

"Oh, very well. I suppose I'll just have to call the eye candy in Mexico City."

"Don't you dare."

"She meant nothing, that one. She is the daughter of my father's oldest friend."

"You have told me all this before. Where are you today?"

"A fund-raiser Chihuahua City, then I dedicate a new dam. Then a city council meeting that will go very late. I will miss seeing you."

Sofia saw her brother's truck pull up in front of the shop. "Pedro has just arrived."

"Let me have a word with him, please. And Sofia, think hard about what I have said, please. Think very hard."

Pedro considered himself a keen observer. It was a talent, like his singing, something that held a special significance to very few. But it helped him immensely. Enrique claimed it made him indispensable. The mayor tended to exaggerate sometimes, which was a failure of most politicians Pedro had met. But in this instance, he had the impression that Enrique meant what he said.

Pedro knew the instant he stepped through the office doors that his sister was on the phone with Enrique. He saw the tight slant to her gaze, the way she studied the sunlight on the glass, as though drilling for faults that Pedro did not believe were there.

Enrique had proven his worth a hundred times over since coming to office in Ojinaga. He had stood up for the people of

Ojinaga when no one else had, not the police or the army or any former politician.

Pedro could not understand why his sister did not leap at the chance to marry Enrique. He worried that she might delay and fret until Enrique grew impatient and moved on. He had not felt more helpless since childhood. "I need a word with Enrique."

She handed him the phone. "He has just said the same thing."

Pedro exchanged greetings, then listened as Enrique sketched out several matters requiring urgent attention. Finally Pedro said, "*Padron*, there is a matter we need to discuss."

"I should be back in my office by six."

"This cannot wait. And you do not want to discuss this in your office." Pedro described the trip to the professor's house. And the attack with the same hunter that had been after Simon.

When he was done, Enrique's good humor had been replaced by a weary grimness. "It was a bad idea, taking the American to the home of Vasquez."

"With respect, I disagree."

"You put yourself at risk. You endangered Señor Simon, when we already knew the bad ones sought him. You might have brought them back to the orphanage. How could this possibly have been a good idea?"

"Señor Simon said he could possibly make the apparatus work. But to do so, he needed information that only Vasquez had."

"The police tell me the home has been thoroughly searched."

"Simon found something the hunters missed."

Enrique huffed in surprise. "How is this possible?"

Pedro described the globe Simon had recognized from Vasquez's MIT office. And the secret compartment that opened with the key Simon still carried around his neck. "Inside were the professor's Bible and two pages of data. Simon tells me the information could prove vital."

"Perhaps we should move the American somewhere else."

"Harold wants him to stay at the orphanage."

Enrique let out a loud sigh. "We must ensure the children's safety."

Pedro relaxed. This was what he had been after all along. For Enrique to take responsibility for the orphanage's protection.

Enrique asked, "You truly think the American can accomplish what the professor could not?"

"Vasquez was certain of this. Harold thinks the same."

"I will make the necessary arrangements. For five days. Once he obtains his new passport . . . one way or the other, our world will go back to the way it was before he arrived."

Pedro hung up the phone very softly. His sister's face had the pinched expression she wore before an explosion. "What were you thinking, taking Simon to Armando's home?"

Pedro remained silent. Any response was futile. As was any possible reason he might give.

But for once, the tirade did not begin. Instead Sofia closed her eyes. "Do you really think Simon is part of God's plan?"

He grinned. He could not help it. "Harold thinks so."

"I asked what you think."

His grin grew broader still. "I think the changes in this gringo have only just started. And when God has time to grow in him . . ."

A faint tremor touched his sister's voice. "Yes? What then?"

Pedro leaned across her desk and whispered, "Boom."

Chapter 18

That day Sofia had a long hard drive, and in two different directions. The two-lane desert highways were ribbed with constant repairs. In the mountains the steep inclines and sharp curves were rimmed by rusting guardrails or none at all. But there was little traffic, and Sofia knew the roads very well. Once she was through the mountains, she settled into a comfortable speed and cruised. Her thoughts made for noisy companions.

She did not reach any conclusion. But she had not expected to. So she prayed. Again. She had been praying about it daily since Enrique had asked her to get married. And as usual, there was no sense of guidance from above. All she knew was the same silence, as vast and nebulous as the desert that surrounded her.

It was dark when she finally parked in front of her apartment. She was too late for dinner at the orphanage, so she fixed a salad and ate it standing at the kitchen counter. She loved the counter. It was made of Mexican cedar, shaped and planed by hand and left unfinished. Every time she used it, she smelled a hint of the wood's fragrance, like a distillation of everything that was good and fine in her desert land.

After dinner, she walked across the square, greeting two of her neighbors who were minding their grandchildren and letting them run around a bit before putting them down for the night. She entered through the gates and stood there. She often did this at the end of a long day. She breathed the fragrances that had shaped her world as a child, the evening meal and the dust and the children and the same cleanser Harold had always used. She considered it as beautiful a bouquet as the cedar counter.

Her biggest goal in life was to be there for others. Just like Harold had been there for her. She wanted nothing more than to be that someone, at that point in time when they were most alone.

That was what drove her relationship with Enrique. He helped propel her to do greater things. He invited her to step forward and stand upon the national stage. Beside him. *With* him.

But she was troubled by the absence of love.

She told herself that many good marriages had begun on friendship and shared goals. And she was fond of Enrique. She really was. She often tried to tell herself that she loved him, at least a little.

But deep in her heart she yearned for more.

And yet . . . and yet, what right did she have, an orphan with no family and no name and no title, to ask for even this? Enrique was rich and powerful and destined for greatness. What was she doing dragging her feet and yearning like a child, seeking a love that might not even exist?

No matter how hard she prayed, no matter how many times she begged and pleaded for guidance, God remained silent.

Then she noticed something out of place.

She walked across the orphanage's courtyard. In front of the last classroom stood the front table. In the moonlight glinted bits and pieces of what looked like electronic devices. Just sitting there. Out in the open.

She realized none of the lights were working. Which was hardly unusual. They had been restricting power usage since the money became tight. But there was not even a lamp glowing in Harold's office. "The power company cut us off?"

"This afternoon." Simon bustled out of the classroom. "And you are exactly what we need, another set of hands. Juan, give her the flashlight."

"What are you doing?"

"Making solar lanterns."

"But they don't work."

"I'm pretty sure I solved the problem. Can you move over about three feet? No, the other way. Now bring the flashlight in, closer, okay, stop. Keep it steady. Juan, you got that piece?"

"Here, Señor Simon."

"Great. Grab that wire. Okay, hold it steady while I solder, that's it. Good job."

Juan's teeth flashed in the dim light. "You want the bulbs?"

"Where did I leave them?"

"The box is under the long table."

"My man." As Juan scampered into the classroom, Simon swept the hair from his forehead. The bandage glinted white in the light. "He's one amazing kid."

"Why can this not wait until tomorrow?"

"Because—"

His reply was cut off by a thin wail. It was a tragic sound, a faint warbling of childhood woe. A broken heart unable to even shape a word.

Juan hurried back out. "Gabriella, she is starting again."

"Yeah, I heard. Sofia, aim that light on my hands. Good. Okay, hold it steady, let's see if it fits." There was an audible snap. "Bingo. Where's the housing?"

"Here, Señor Simon."

There was a trio of further clicks, then, "Here goes."

A soft light pushed back the dark, illuminating two tired and sweaty faces. Simon and Juan shared a huge grin. Simon said, "High-five. No, no, raise your hand. That's it." They slapped palms.

Simon wiped the device with his shirttail and headed for the girl's dorm. "We've been charging the lantern batteries all afternoon while I worked on the circuitry. The lantern should glow now until daybreak."

Juan explained, "Gabriella is afraid of the dark."

Sofia followed Simon across the courtyard and up the stairs and across the veranda. Harold sat in a chair beside Gabriella's bed. A lone candle burned on the bedside table. He blew it out as Simon set down the lantern and asked the little girl, "Can you thank the gentleman?"

Gabriella looked so small, lying there. So beautiful. She was a fragile little bird with enormous dark eyes that darted from one adult to the next. Fearful. Alone even in the midst of all these people.

Harold said, "Simon and Juan have worked all day, just so you would not be afraid. You are surrounded by people who care very deeply for you. And who will do everything to keep you safe."

He rose from the chair and motioned them out. Simon looked both exhausted and immensely pleased with himself.

Sofia stopped in the doorway and turned back. Gabriella still lay there, watching. Sofia walked back over and bent down and kissed the girl's forehead. "Sleep and do not dream."

When she emerged from the dormitory, she found all three men waiting for her. Harold had one arm around Juan's shoulders, the other rested upon Simon's arm. As though he wanted her to see this act, and understand.

She needed to accept that Simon was becoming one of them.

Simon woke up to the pale wash of a new day. He carried a fragment of an idea with him as he rose and washed his face and dressed. He flipped the bathroom switch, and when the light did not come on, he slipped downstairs and across the courtyard and into the boy's dormitory. The beds were separated by chest-high wooden barriers, like stalls with their fronts open to the central aisle. He touched Juan's shoulder. The boy came instantly awake. Simon turned and walked back outside.

When the boy joined him, Simon asked, "Has the power come back on?"

"No, Señor Simon."

"This can't be good."

"Harold is worried about all the food stored in the freezers."

Which meant it was time to act first and ask later. Simon's favorite way of moving forward. "I need the thickest electrical cable this place has."

"There is some in the garage."

"Great. And a knife and a pair of pliers and some big alligator clips, you know the kind?"

"Like when the van does not start, yes?"

"Perfect."

Juan was a kid made to be excited. "Come with me, Señor Simon!"

According to Harold, the orphanage had once belonged to the wealthiest landowners in the village. They had shared the buildings lining the courtyard with household servants and trusted staff. The garage had originally held a blacksmith's shop and stables for a dozen horses. The forge and anvil were still there, in the far corner of the huge space, beneath a leaf-strewn skylight. The garages and work space were empty now, save for the dilapidated church van, an ancient Model T that Harold had acquired with the house, and several dozen boxes holding more components of the solar lanterns that did not work. Yet.

Five minutes later, Simon was unfurling a dusty cable, his hands protected by a pair of work gloves. The gloves' canvas was cracked and stiff, but they helped in laying out the cable. Simon slung the cable over his shoulders and scaled the rear wall, next to the orphanage's mains. With Juan feeding the cable, he transitioned to the telephone pole and climbed up to the transformer.

Simon had studied electrical engineering because it had come naturally to him. The logical step-by-step order was easy for him to memorize. He could do most of the schematics while half asleep. Or hungover. Which he had been, more often than not.

Vasquez, on the other hand, was a particle physicist. Vasquez and he had linked up Simon's second year. Vasquez had seen something in him. Twice he had even broached the subject of Simon staying on to do graduate research under his supervision.

And look how Simon had repaid the man.

Simon tested the leads and was rewarded with a sizeable spark. He made a note to thank the kid for the gloves and saving him from some nasty burns. He fitted on the clips. "Juan."

"Señor Simon!"

"Go try a switch."

The kid vanished and was soon back, dancing in place. "There is light everywhere!"

"Then we're good to go." He could come back later with some rope to hold it all in place. Simon slipped back onto the clay tiles lining the wall, then bounced down to the ground. "High-five."

As they slapped palms, Harold emerged from his rooms in the admin wing. He spotted them, studied the situation for a moment, then walked over. Juan instantly froze, his shoulders shrinking down and caving inward, the perfect picture of a guilty teen. Simon's grin faded, despite how he had a hundred arguments, all of them excellent.

But Harold did not say anything. He stood there with his arms crossed, studying the cable connected to the mains and snaking up the rear wall and connecting to the transformer. Then he gripped the cable and pulled hard. The clips popped off with a crack and a spark and fell to his feet. "We do not steal."

"You've got a kitchen full of rotting . . ." Simon stopped. There was something in Harold's gaze that faded his words to nothing. Simon could have handled anger and condemnation. But Harold was not angry. He was disappointed.

Harold said again, "We do not steal." He then squatted down beside Juan, bringing himself to eye level. "This is how it begins. The one small act, done for all the right reasons. The act that opens the floodgates. We do not lie. We do not steal. Do you understand?"

Juan hesitated, then nodded. "I am sorry, Dr. Harold."

Harold rose to full height. "Go ring the bell for chapel."

When the kid scampered away, Simon said, "I just wanted to help."

"My one goal in life is to give these kids a strong moral foundation and to help them realize they are valuable in God's eyes. I have to shout against the world to be heard." Harold pointed through the open gates. "Out there, they are seen as nothing. More throwaway kids, destined for the gangs and jail and an early grave. In here, I arm them with the gospel and with an awareness of their own potential."

There was no criticism in his words. No condemnation of what Simon had tried to do. Even so, he felt ashamed. More than that. Simon felt as though he stood before a mirror, one that revealed the person behind the deed. The dark corners, the cynical attitude, the easy swagger that led him from one quick high to the next.

"I don't hide it from the kids that we're facing a hard time. I try to shelter them and hold this place together, but what is most important is that they see how the fundamentals of a good life remain in place, no matter what happens. Even if the orphanage has to shut down, even if I go bankrupt, even if they get shipped off to . . ." Harold stopped and massaged the point over his heart. "I hope and pray they'll carry these lessons with them for the rest of their days. To identify their gifts and reach for the stars. To accept that the Scriptures lay out a path for them to follow, in realizing their full worth."

Harold stood there a moment, as though seeking to imbed the words more deeply through silence. Then he turned and walked away.

As he slipped into the last pew, Simon saw this was not the first time they had lost power. Not by a long shot. A number of the older kids, Juan included, moved around the front, lighting candles and placing them in little stone holders. Juan refused to meet his eye. Simon could understand that. He knew now that he had taken the kid in the wrong direction. It shamed him as well. When Pedro slipped into the pew beside him, Simon could not even bring himself to return the man's greeting.

Harold led the kids in song, then prayed, and spoke, and prayed again. Simon listened, but he really didn't absorb anything. He was too intently focused on the kids, and on Harold. The kids didn't merely obey him. They loved the old man. They trusted him. They listened with their entire being. They followed his direction. And he led them to God.

Harold had been a successful businessman. He had stamped his mark in the competitive world of international industry. He had been a NASA scientist. He had done so much, but Simon knew this was what the man considered his greatest triumph. This was where his entire life had been leading. To this moment. Standing in front of a group of castoff kids in an orphanage on the brink of closure. Teaching them the right way to live.

The difference between these orphans and Simon's early years could not be denied. His clearest memory of his own parents was how they had shouted at one another. And the way his mother smelled when she leaned over him at night, the gin and the cigarettes on her breath and her clothes. His dad had been perpetually angry and often drunk. Simon had lived with his grandmother for a while, but she wasn't well, and he'd become a ward of the state. He'd lived in foster homes, some good, others truly awful.

But school had been a breeze, and he looked old for his age, so at fifteen he used a fake ID to land a job waiting tables. He aced the SATs and got accepted to MIT, earning a scholarship that he almost lost a half-dozen times, going up before the disciplinary board so often he knew all of their names. Getting kicked out had been a foregone conclusion. It was amazing he'd lasted to his senior year.

Only Armando Vasquez had refused to give up on him.

Which was when the shame threatened to choke off his air. The burning in his lungs was matched by the coal-like fire behind his eyes. Simon bent over his knees and fought for control.

He felt a hand come to rest upon his shoulder and knew it was Pedro. Which only made control harder to come by.

When he straightened, he realized that the chapel was empty. It surprised him, how he hadn't even noticed their departure. The air was clogged with the smell of old wax and smoke rising from a dozen extinguished candles.

Pedro asked, "You are okay?"

Simon swallowed hard. "Sure."

"Do you wish to pray?"

"I don't . . . Thanks. But . . ."

Pedro gave a slow nod, as though Simon's battered words were completely clear. "The power has returned. Come. Breakfast is waiting."

Chapter 19

After breakfast Simon returned to the classroom and opened the duffel bag. He had been avoiding this because of what he assumed he would find. A sensitive apparatus designed for laboratory conditions was never intended to survive a car wreck, much less a race across desert terrain and being dumped in a drainage ditch. Almost none of the connectors had survived. Three of the motherboards were shattered. The tuning crystals appeared to be cracked.

Expecting to find this did not ease Simon's disappointment. He dumped the contents on the table and started sorting through the debris. It was unlikely he could get the thing to work until after his return to Cambridge. But he could at least assess the damage and try to figure out how to apply Vasquez's final research.

"Señor Simon?" Juan stood in the doorway, half in the room and half ready to bolt.

"Come on in. It's okay." Simon hated seeing him like that, his enthusiasm dampened, his gaze dull. "Look, Harold was right and I was wrong, okay? And you're a great kid."

The boy's grin was blinding. "Can I help?"

"Not with this. But hey, if you can grab a few others, we can set up an assembly for the lanterns."

"And make Dr. Harold proud, yes?"

"You betcha."

Which was how Sofia and Enrique found them, three hours later. Simon heard them long before he saw them. The kids banged open some door and came rushing out in a great torrential flood of noise and laughter and skinny brown limbs. They danced around Enrique as he lifted his hands, the conquering hero, the leader with the perfect smile and the beautiful woman who stood slightly apart.

To his eye, Sofia looked confused. Disturbed. Not by Enrique, maybe. Simon was not certain she saw the mayor at all. Her gaze drifted around and finally settled upon Simon standing in the classroom doorway. She lifted two fingers and gave him a little wave. Simon thought she looked sad.

Enrique was too busy doling out handfuls of candy to notice. Then Harold walked over and solemnly shook the mayor's hand, Simon assumed for getting the power back on. Enrique played at being modest, waving it away and bowing his head slightly, the practiced humility of a man who lived for such moments. Simon turned and went back inside.

From his place at the assembly table, Juan asked, "Señor Simon, can I go have candy too?"

"Knock yourself out." Simon returned to dissecting the

apparatus. It was not the happiest of jobs, but he did not mind. A lot of lab work involved breaking down equipment, replicating experiments, and rebuilding demolished hopes. Seeing if the results obtained were merely a random event or genuinely the product of good science. He had done such tasks many times before.

Which meant he was totally lost in his work when Enrique stepped in. "Señor Simon, I have some good news, some better news, and some ashes for you."

Simon stopped what he was doing and gave the mayor an audience. Which was what Enrique wanted, of course. Someone to watch and admire as he paraded in and deposited a pair of sacks on the table beside Simon's work. "This was recovered from evidence obtained at Professor Vasquez's home."

Simon watched him unload the professor's device, which appeared to be in worse shape than his own. "How did you get your hands on it?"

"I have my sources. Both here and in Juárez, which is where I obtained your passport application." He unfolded the document and set it on the table as well. "Fill that in and we will get the process started this afternoon."

Sofia leaned on the doorway opposite Juan's perch. "Harold keeps a camera in his office for the children's official documents."

"This is great, thanks."

"And we have managed to locate your passport. Unfortunately it will not do us any good." Enrique set the charred remnants of Simon's passport on the table. "The police found this in the remains of your burning car."

"No sign of the guy who attacked me?"

"Not yet. But the police, they have been notified that he is still on the prowl. Since yesterday the police have stationed officers outside the orphanage. We must be vigilant in protecting these children."

Enrique was a finely balanced man of perhaps five foot ten, with broad shoulders that tapered down to a slender waist. His dark eyes were liquid and expressive. He wore fawn-colored slacks, pale brown loafers, alligator belt, striped dress shirt with gold cuff links, and a slender watch with a band of woven gold.

Despite the power and the looks and the woman and the station, the man appeared nervous to Simon. He took a small step back, another to the side, then returned to his station by the front table. He tapped the table with one finger, combed the hair from his forehead, touched the knot of his tie, flashed a smile at Sofia, then winked at Juan.

Simon said, "Thank you for your help."

Enrique took in the two devices with a sweep of one arm. "Can you make it work?"

Simon took his time inspecting the professor's machine. To an outsider it was only so much junk. But Simon had worked on worse. In truth his attention was mostly on Enrique. The mayor gave Simon the same tight inspection, and his voice carried the same hidden edge, just like the last time he had asked about Vasquez and the device.

Simon shook his head, wondering what he was missing. "Doubtful."

The lines of tension around his eyes multiplied. "Explain."

"There are a number of highly sensitive components. If any of them are damaged, nothing will work."

"Can you replace them?"

"Sure. In time. First I have to test each separately and isolate the flaw. If there is one. Which I'm pretty sure there will be."

"There is an electronics shop in Ojinaga. A good one. They supply the high-tech companies in the maquiladora with spare parts."

"Great. I'll check them out." Simon pretended to focus on disassembling the professor's machine and made his question as casual as possible. "So why is this so important to you?"

"A device that may deliver free energy? Is that a joke?"

"No. No joke. Just wondering."

"Power in Mexico is controlled by CFE. They have a monopoly in Chihuahua state. You have heard of CFE?"

"Vasquez mentioned it, sure."

"The only company more corrupt in all Mexico is the oil company. CFE is the means by which corruption flows through much of our national government. They are one of the reasons why I intend to enter national politics. I want to wipe them from the map. I want to *erase* them."

Simon almost believed him. Enrique certainly did show a proper amount of outrage. And it explained the tension that emanated from him. Almost. But there was a rehearsed quality to his words and gestures. As though he had practiced them endlessly for just such a moment. Here with Simon, or in a nationally televised interview, or a speech before thousands. It was all the same.

Simon was certain that more was at work.

"I'll give it my best shot."

"Splendid!" Enrique flashed his number-one smile. "You are a great help to everyone, Señor Simon."

Juan piped up, "He made the solar lanterns work."

"Did you indeed? Fantastic! Harold is desperately in need of something he can make and sell and build a source of revenue for this place." Enrique clapped Simon on the back. "I will leave you to get on with this work, Señor Simon. It is vital, do you hear me? Vital! Juan, you must show me one of these excellent lanterns."

Sofia remained inside the classroom as they departed. For once, she did not reveal the predatory gleam, the desire to argue or condemn. She simply stood there, watching him work, looking pensive.

Looking like a woman waiting for him to ask a question.

If only he had the first hint of an idea what to say.

Sofia tried to tell herself she needed to go join Enrique. There was really no logical reason for her to be here with Simon. And yet she remained in the doorway, until Simon said quietly, "Penny for your thoughts."

"I was thinking about Vasquez."

His hands continued to sort through the components. "So was I."

She could tell he feared she would ask why he had betrayed his friend. His hands slowed, and his face pinched tightly, and his shoulders bowed. He became the portrait of a man waiting for a strike he could not avoid. It was a powerful moment for her. Sofia realized Simon was changing. The cynical edge had vanished. His armor was down. Her brother was right. God was working in this man's life.

She recalled how Vasquez had described the *other* Simon.

The person kept hidden away from a world that had wounded him when he had been young and most vulnerable. The brilliant orphan, cast off to foster care after his grandmother died, hurt and angry and scared and alone.

Sofia felt her heart go out to him. There was a great deal of herself in him. He was the face of who she herself might have become, had she not been brought here. To the orphanage in Ojinaga, where Harold could heal and nurture and introduce her to faith.

So she said, "When the professor returned last year from America, we became very close. Armando was educated. He knew the world beyond the mountains and the desert. He had been to Europe and he had lived in America. And yet he came back here because he loved it. Even with all the problems we face, even though he had many other places he could go, he wanted to be here."

Simon kept sorting, but his gaze flickered back and forth toward her, not lingering. "Like you."

"Yes. Like me. We both had island fever. We loved it here, and we did not ever want to leave, and yet we were desperate for someone else who knew about the world. The first day after his return, I'll never forget. Armando was seated there in Harold's office and we started talking, and two minutes later, it felt as though we had been friends for years."

The pain of loss bloomed inside her. She did not often indulge her sorrow, or the vacuum Armando's passage had left in her life. Sofia swallowed hard. "He loved you very much, Simon."

He stopped. He did not move or speak. He merely stood there. One look was enough to know he was burdened by the same weight. And more besides. He looked so sad.

She heard herself say, "Armando described you as a son. He accepted your flaws as only a father could. He talked about you every time we met. You and the device. He hoped it would help the poor of Mexico and help you as well, finally bring you around."

Simon dragged in a single breath. It was not quite a sob. He started to speak, though no sound emerged.

The words were there. Waiting.

"Look at me, Simon."

His gaze was filled with the shadows of a thousand wrong moves. He stood there, defenseless. Waiting for her to attack and destroy him utterly.

She knew now why she was there. She needed to help another orphan. Deliver the message Harold had instilled in her. Help them move in the right direction.

"We all carry burdens. We all make mistakes. We all sin and fall short of the people we should be. We leave things undone. We do what we shouldn't and we give in to bad actions and worse emotions. We hurt those closest to us."

His gaze gave Sofia the impression that he was too filled with pain to weep. Her eyes filled for him, as though one of them needed to shed tears over the state of their fallen world. "But there is an answer. An eternal truth. That the Savior died so we might be washed clean. So we can be forgiven for all we have done, and all we have left undone. So our lives can be made whole. So we can speak that impossible word, *hope,* and believe it is true for us. So that we can know joy. And love. And claim them for ourselves."

She stood there, waiting. "Would you like to pray with me, Simon?"

All he did was turn his head and look out the window. But it was as clear as an audible denial. He had broken the connection.

Sofia turned and walked out the door. She stood in the sunlight and saw the children run and heard their laughter. And she felt whole.

Chapter 20

The assembling of Vasquez's and his device into one unit went far easier than Simon expected. The machines were almost identical. Not quite, because the two men had been working at a distance and communicating mostly by e-mail. They mirrored one another's work, to a point. Until, that is, Vasquez had come up with his new idea.

The professor had clearly waited to discuss his alterations once he had evidence that they worked. This was not unusual. He and Simon both tried a number of different directions and up to now none had succeeded. So they developed a sort of scientific shorthand. As in, *I have a new maybe*. That's what they had called them. New maybes. The name worked as well as anything.

What had been different this final time was the excitement. Vasquez had sounded electric the last couple of times they spoke. And the pages in the professor's globe had offered substantial hints. By midday, Simon had combined the working components of two machines into one functioning device.

He organized a dozen kids into a solar-lantern assembly line and appointed Juan their manager. The kids worked and chattered and laughed through the process. Juan proved to be a born dictator.

By late afternoon, the lanterns were finished and tested and boxed. Pedro joined them in loading the assembled lanterns into the orphanage's dilapidated van. They completed their work just as the chapel bell rang.

Simon joined the kids by the outside faucet, loving the sound of their young laughter and easy delight at having this gringo wash his face and hands with them. Chapel revived him, and dinner with the children was a time of rare joy. He sat with Pedro and Harold and Juan and Sofia, speaking little, savoring the simple delight of belonging.

Afterward Harold insisted Juan join him in the office for another voice lesson. Pedro and Sofia and Simon ambled through the long shadows and entered the classroom. Brother and sister settled by the entrance as Simon gave the assembled device one last check.

Sofia recalled, "Vasquez talked about retrieving lost energy."

"Okay, first of all, energy is never lost." Simon did not look up from his work. "The amount of energy in the universe is unchanging. It is a constant. Vasquez's dream was to retrieve energy that was *wasted*."

"He said it was your dream too."

Perhaps someday he would hear these words and not feel the bloom of guilt. "Vasquez had an idea. I helped make it happen. But it was his vision."

"So how does your device work?"

"Scientists have struggled with retrieving wasted energy for over a century. A physicist named Tesla claimed to have actually done it. And maybe he did. But it's been hard to replicate his device because his notes were both illegible and incomplete. But the cost of Tesla's equipment was staggering. He spent millions of dollars to collect about a nickel's worth of usable power."

"What makes your device so different?" Sofia asked.

"Quantum field theory."

"What is this, exactly?"

"That's the problem. There is no *exactly* in the quantum universe." Simon snapped the exterior cover into place, polished off the dust with a bit of old rag, and took a step back. There were two long scratches in the fuselage, probably from where he had shoved it down the culvert pipe. And a big dent in the top, which had cracked the motherboard now replaced from Vasquez's unit. All in all, it looked like a vacuum cleaner that had seen a lot of hard use. But the excitement in his gut said otherwise.

Simon turned and realized the pair was still waiting for him to complete his thought. "At the subatomic level, energy reveals the attributes of being both a wave and a particle. But at the level of Newtonian physics, that's impossible. Either it's one or the other. In the quantum world, both can exist at the same time. Not only that, the attributes they show depend upon the observer. If I set up an experiment looking for waves of energy, I find waves. If I look for particles, I find particles. Vasquez and I focused on the wave attributes of energy."

"That was your idea," Sofia recalled softly. "Vasquez called it brilliant. A game changer."

He could not go there, not and focus on the night and the work ahead. "Most wave attributes can't be proven. Because we're dealing with subatomic particles that can't be seen or measured with standard instrumentation, a lot of quantum mechanics remains stuck at the level of field theories. A field theory signifies a concept that has not yet been physically measured. But this doesn't mean the wave attributes of energy can't be utilized. Storm patterns are all the result of unproven wave calculations." He patted the cover and felt the latent potential surge through him. "Vasquez's latest results indicate we may have finally found our way to stardom."

Sofia asked, "What happens now?"

"We need to check this gizmo out. To do that, I need a very particular kind of setting." Simon described what he had in mind.

When he was done, Pedro glanced at his sister, who snapped, "Don't even think about leaving me behind."

"This is exactly what you were against all along," Pedro said. "Recklessness, risk, possibly danger."

"And sitting here worrying about you out there will somehow make it better? I don't think so."

"Enrique won't like you being with us."

"Then we had better not tell him."

"Or Harold."

"Of course not Harold." She jangled her keys. "Let's take my van. The seat in your pickup hurts my back."

Simon felt the same surge of electric tension he always knew when working on the fringes of proven science. It captivated him. It *called* to him. And yet it terrified him. Sitting in the van's broad seat, riding along a dusty sunset road, the realization struck him with the force of a blow to his heart. A scientist could not be a cynic. And cynicism had been his shield against all the pain and loss he had known. To take up his role, to live up to the potential Vasquez had seen, Simon had to set down his shield. And that simple act terrified him. It stripped him bare. It laid his pain and suffering and past and all the wrong acts out in the open.

He couldn't do it.

It was that simple. He did not have the strength to change. As long as he insisted on doing so alone.

The thought pushed him back in his seat. The hot dusty wind through the open windows punched at him. He felt robbed of air. Because that was the other side of his cynical nature. He was always alone.

The only time he permitted others entry was when he worked in the lab. There he was surrounded by kindred spirits. People who discounted whatever personality traits he might have, shrugged them off, because they communicated at the level *beyond* the personality. They were bonded by the realm of the unseen.

Which was happening here. Now. With these people. Outside the lab.

The same, yet different.

Simon realized they were both watching him. "Sorry."

"Don't apologize," Sofia said.

"I was thinking . . ."

"We know," Pedro said. "It was like sitting next to a pressure cooker."

"A power generator." Sofia nodded from behind the wheel. "Just like Vasquez."

Simon thought of how they had both offered to pray with him. As though they were bound by invisible bonds to a source he could not even name, much less fathom. He knew if he said the words, they would do it with him. Now. This very instant.

He tried. He opened his mouth and tasted the dusty heat. But he could not fashion the words.

The transformer substation was situated on a grimy hilltop overlooking a pair of massive factories. The city of Ojinaga sprawled in the valley beyond. The factories to their right manufactured cement and paving materials. The air was clogged with the odors of hot asphalt and chemicals. Smokestacks threw out great plumes. Machines bellowed and ground and churned. Simon thought it was a perfect setting for his attempt to change the world.

They drove through the workers' lot and climbed the gravel track to the substation. Pedro assured them that as assistant town manager, his visits to such locations were perfectly acceptable. As they parked, Pedro had a quiet word with a lone guard, who offered a languid salute and strolled on.

Simon set the apparatus just outside the transformer's protective fencing and made his final adjustments. "There's this huge battle going on between Newtonian physicists and the quantum guys," he told them. The excitement made him garrulous, as though talking helped draw them closer together. "The struggle gets pretty ferocious at times. There may not be blood on the streets, but wrecked professional careers litter the halls of most universities. Vasquez called that a complete waste of time."

"Actually, what he said was, it's a complete squandering of human potential," Sofia said. "All burned to ashes on the pyre of ego."

Simon looked up from where he squatted on the ground. "Yeah. He did."

Pedro asked, "So what was his answer?"

"Basically, that both were right," Sofia recalled. "He said the arguments were a perfect example of man trying to fit creation into a comfortable box. The two directions are not exclusive. Both live in harmony. Or they would, if man let them."

Simon stared up at her. The sunset was directly behind her and cast her in glowing silhouette. "He never told me that."

Pedro walked in a circle, following Simon's direction, planting lightbulbs in the earth. "Remind me why I am doing this."

"Vasquez used unconnected bulbs to prove he could harness and channel wasted energy. I'm trying to replicate his results."

Sofia asked, "So what did Armando tell you was his answer?"

"He focused on the science." Simon bent back over his device, reflecting on how Vasquez had probably responded as he had because that was all Simon had been willing to hear. "Newtonian physics states that there are certain laws governing waves. One is called refraction, which means waves change direction when they meet a new medium, or substance, at an angle. And the amount of change is determined by the quality of the substance, which is called a boundary, and the angle of the wave."

Pedro straightened and looked at his sister. "Does that make sense to you?"

"Perhaps. Yes. I think so. Go on, Simon."

Simon pointed at the substation to their right. "For our experiment tonight, we're going to treat this place as a boundary. In order to transport electricity, substations raise the voltage and lower the amperage. But because they are so inefficient, a lot of power is wasted. It's what makes the air tingle, this energy passing through our bodies."

"And Vasquez . . . ?"

"He applied quantum principles to a Newtonian problem. If I'm right, he said, forget identifying a *specific* vibratory pattern. There isn't one. Instead, look for harmonics. Look for a probability of patterns coming together in a combination."

He tested the hookups one final time. "Maybe now is a good time to back up."

Chapter 21

The device made promising noises, but nothing more. There were a hundred different reasons why it did not work. A thousand. Fragile components and connectors might have been damaged beyond repair. But Simon did not think so. He had checked each module in turn and then linked them together and tested them again. In truth, he did not mind the delay, not even when he had to call Pedro and Sofia back over so they could hold flashlights to illuminate his hands. He figured if they really got bored, they would let him know, and he'd return to the orphanage, and sleep, and get up, and try again.

But they did not indicate any desire to leave. Instead they talked in quiet tones, an intimate conversation. Simon spoke no Spanish, and yet he had the distinct impression that their topic was very deep, very profound. Their voices carried the musical lilt of caring concern and love. There was none of the combative edge that marked most of the conversations he had heard between them.

Pedro asked another question. This time, Sofia turned and looked out over the city and did not respond. Pedro continued to wait with a patience that was distinctly Mexican. As though he could best express his love for this fine woman in respectful silence.

Simon fitted the cover back into place. His joints had stiffened in the night's rising chill. He rose in stages. "If this doesn't work, we'll call it a day." He ushered them back to where the pickup was parked. And hesitated.

Finally Pedro asked, "Why do we wait?"

Simon pointed down the hillside to the vast parking area that linked the two factories. A thin stream of weary workers filed from the plants. They were coated with dried sweat and a grayish powder fine as milled flour. "We've waited this long. Let's give it a few more minutes."

The workers drove away in ancient pickups or they climbed into ancient busses. Pedro opened the driver's door and fished behind his seat. He came up with a metal thermos. "In that case, I'll go get us some coffee."

When Pedro was out of hearing range, Simon said, "Your discussion with Pedro got pretty intense there for a while."

Sofia stared out over the city. "We were talking about Enrique."

"The mayor."

"And soon to be governor of Chihuahua. Pedro doesn't understand why I don't agree to marry him."

The last of the busses pulled away. As the parking area went silent, Simon could hear Pedro speaking with someone inside the stall. There was no reason he should be disappointed. Simon knew, under the current circumstances, he didn't have much to offer a woman like Sofia. "Enrique seems like a great guy."

She was silent for so long, he assumed she was not going to respond. Then, "Enrique has no interest in changing. Not anything. Not ever. He wants me to adapt to his vision of what a proper Mexican wife should be. He looks at what I do for the orphanage and my medical-supply business as hobbies."

This close he could sense her incredible energy, as potent in its own way as the force emanating from the substation. Even when she was motionless and her voice quiet, Sofia radiated a barely contained force.

"Enrique sees himself as a hero. He wants me to stop trying to figure him out. He wants me to take him at face value. Accept who he is, and where he is going. And sign on for the ride."

"You would be great at it," Simon said.

"Yes. I would."

"The wife of the governor of Chihuahua. The First Lady of Mexico."

"The face of modern Mexico," she added. "The lovely young orphan girl who defied the staid culture of Mexico and became a self-made professional woman."

"I can see that in headlines," Simon said.

"And on billboards. And television. Enrique's public relations team go berserk every time we meet."

The lights over the factory entrances were strong and harsh as arc-lamps. The illumination cast the surroundings in stark etchings of black and white. Simon saw the truth and could find no reason not to say it. "You see yourself as a hero too."

Her dark eyes tightened. "How do you do that? You don't even know me."

"A good scientist is a professional observer. It's not something I can control."

"Enrique has never . . ." She turned away and faced the transformers and the hilltop. "I have had to be strong all my life. I've never let anyone be strong for me. Enrique wants to be that person. He's the easiest man I've ever known at being strong."

"Just like you."

"But he shows no weakness. Not ever. And I feel so frail around him."

"Maybe he's just trained himself not to let it show."

"Yes. Perhaps you are right. But why does he not show this to me? Why does he only show me the face he wants the rest of the world to see?" She sighed and shook her head. "When I am with him, it is so easy to ignore all the questions I do not have answers for. When I am alone . . ."

Simon continued to study her openly. He had never seen a more beautiful face, even now, sliced by the harsh lights into one side dark and the other light. "Do you pray about this?"

She lowered her head, and the hair spilled across her shoulder and cascaded about her face. "All the time."

"What does God say?"

"Nothing. God says nothing."

Simon suddenly felt ashamed of his false motives. He wasn't asking to help her. He was asking because he was attracted to her. Her answers revealed a woman's heart, open and yearning.

Sofia went on, "I fear that God does not speak because He has already given me the answer. Enrique is the man He has chosen for me, a perfect partner to help me do God's will. And I do not act because . . ."

Simon murmured to the ground by his own feet, "Because you are afraid."

"Because I don't *know*. Because I cannot . . ." She twisted her hands together in a knot of limbs and tension. "Because I cannot hear my own heart. Because I have fought so long and so hard, I am afraid to let someone else fight for me."

Simon heard footsteps climbing the hillside and turned to see Pedro walking toward them. In one hand he carried a steaming length of spicy sausage wrapped in wax paper. In the other sloshed the full thermos.

Simon felt the words push out almost of their own accord, forced through his normal cynicism by a need that turned his throat raw. "You are a good person, Sofia. I see why you and Vasquez were friends. Why he trusted you. Because you have what he had. A kind heart and a will to do what's right."

She slowly lifted her gaze. Only this time Simon could not meet her eyes. "Thank you, Simon. So much."

Pedro halted in front of them and looked from one face to the other. "What did I miss?"

This time, as soon as he hit the switch, Simon knew the device was going to work.

There was a very soft resonance. He would have ignored it, put it down as part of the background hum from the generators, but he had heard it before. Once. On the laptop's video image in Harold's office. The machine had given off this precise sound after Vasquez hit the switch. Simon recognized the sound immediately. It held a peculiar timbre, which he now understood. The resonance came from different units vibrating in harmony. Very soft. Yet utterly clear.

Out of the corner of his eye, he saw Pedro starting forward. Simon called out, "Stay where you are!"

"But nothing is happening!"

"Keep back." He could feel the resonance strengthening. Most of the vibrations were very low, almost out of audible range. But Simon could sense the power gathering. He felt it in his bones. His entire body resonated to the gathering force.

The lightbulbs began to flicker.

Sofia cried aloud, a soft intake of breath, echoed by her brother who whuffed in surprise. She said, "You've done it!"

Simon held up his hand. He dared not turn around. His observations of the next few instances were crucial. He had to determine a means to keep the device working. How to stabilize the effect. How to maintain the current. How to—

The lights stopped flickering. The illumination grew slowly, like the bulbs were sulkily waking up.

The light continued to strengthen, intensifying until Simon had to squint, until he raised both hands to shield out the light, until he could no longer see the apparatus. Until the bulbs buried in the ground were brighter than the overhead lights. Until he was forced back by their blinding power.

"It *hurts*," Sofia said. "Turn it *down*."

"I can't."

"But this isn't—"

Then the first bulb popped. The crack was like gunfire. It was followed by another. Then they were going off with the speed of machine guns. Simon backed up farther but he didn't turn away. He didn't dare. Because at the same time he saw the *other* consequence.

The power became visible.

Just for an instant. There and gone so fast, it would have been possible to claim it had never happened at all. But it did. And he saw it happen.

A ribbon of current began sweeping in from the substation. The energy held the same shimmering force as heat rising off the desert floor.

The device quivered slightly. A tiny little vibration, almost like it was shivering with delight. Like it was ravenous and feasting upon the ribbon of energy.

The air on the hilltop hummed. The harmonics were impossibly beautiful, as though electricity had been given a voice. It rose and rose and rose.

And then the lights started going out. Not those buried around the apparatus. Everywhere.

In the valley below them, Ojinaga vanished. It happened in stages, the farthest reaches going first. Blocks of darkness spread toward them, like a beast was taking massive bites from the city.

A bell inside the substation started clanging. A spark flared off one of the massive transformers. Another.

Simon stepped forward. The closer he came to the machine, the more powerful the sound and the force grew. His hair was standing on end, his muscles twitched, and he felt his motions grow jerky. He used the toe of his shoe to hit the switch.

The harmonics stopped with a massive *snap*. A spark fired from the machine to his foot, like the device was angry with him. Furious.

Simon was catapulted all the way back to the truck. He struck the front fender with a resounding thud.

Sofia might have screamed. He wasn't sure. All he knew was, just as the lights started returning, his own went out.

Chapter 22

The next morning, Simon's joints ached and there was a second bump on his head that throbbed in time with the first. He showered and dressed and joined in the orphanage's morning routine. He attended early chapel and then shared the kids' simple breakfast. Harold greeted him with the same friendly reserve, the same knowing gaze. Simon figured it was only a matter of time before the guy erupted over what had gone down the night before. Only it never came.

Simon spent the day going through his calculations and checking the apparatus for damage. Some of the components had been toasted, which was hardly a surprise. He disassembled the device. He taped the pages of frequencies to the blackboard and filled the surrounding space with calculations. When the board was filled up, he took sheets of large-lined paper from another classroom and filled them as well.

The kids were busy with their afternoon game of soccer when he finally left the classroom. Harold sat in a high-backed chair by his doorway, reading from his Bible and watching the kids play. When he glanced over, Simon tensed, waiting for the condemnation over his actions the previous night. Instead Harold said, "I can't thank you enough for assembling the lanterns, son. They could make a huge difference in our fund-raising efforts."

Simon started to respond in his normal offhand manner. But for once he checked himself and left the words unspoken. Perhaps it was Harold's look, a solemn gleam that revealed hidden depths. Simon could almost see the force that bound this man to the place and these kids. "You're welcome."

Harold shut his Bible, using his finger to hold the place. "Pedro tells me you managed some success last night."

"For about ten seconds. Before it shorted out a power station."

"Yes, it's the talk of the town." He surveyed the disassembled machine. "Can you resolve the problem?"

Simon studied the orphanage director. Harold's demeanor surprised him. "Hard to say. There are a lot of sensitive diodes that could be totally wrecked. And I don't have the money to buy new ones."

"But in principle you could rebuild it?" When he hesitated, Harold pressed, "Simon, there is a world out there waiting for this thing. Vasquez and I shared the same dream. Helping the millions out there who suffer and perish because of one simple reason: no access to power. With your device we could provide free energy to the poorest of regions. I shared his concept with an old NASA colleague of mine who now runs a major venture capital group. He told me that if we can demonstrate a consistent flow of energy, even for a short period of time, he's willing to fund the development of a full-scale project. That would replace the research grant the city council reneged on."

"You didn't tell him that Vasquez died?"

"Of course I did. But I also told him about you."

Simon saw the spark in Harold's gaze. The fire that defied everything the man faced. "How do you do it?"

"Do what?"

"You're facing ruin. Everything you worked for could collapse tomorrow. But you're talking about changing the world."

"Son, that's the power of dreams. If they're not big, if they're not impossible, they're not worth investing your life."

Simon backed up a step. "I've forgotten how to dream."

"Your problem is, you never learned." Harold rose from his chair and stepped into his office. He returned holding a book. "I want you to have this. Pedro and Sofia kept after me to write down the lessons I developed from my seminars and what I teach the children. They are keys to help you unleash your potential. Help you make sense of your impossible dreams."

Simon was still searching for a response when the soccer ball skipped over the dusty earth and landed by Simon's feet. Juan ran over. "Do you want to play football, Mr. Simon?"

"You mean soccer?"

Juan grinned. "This game is played only with your feet, no? So why do you call it soccer?"

Simon set his cup on the wooden planks. "Guy who scores first gets to name the game."

His entry into the courtyard was greeted with shrieks of delight. The game soon became a contest between Simon and the orphanage. When Simon stole the ball, they stopped him with a mass tackle. It was Simon against the horde. He shouted a protest, but it was lost to the laughter and he did not care.

Then Pedro stepped through the front gates, and Simon shouted, "Help!"

Pedro moved amazingly fast, a flitting shape that was one moment by the orphanage entrance and the next dancing between Juan and the goalposts. Simon stopped fighting against the shrieking army and watched the two of them, shouting at each other and throwing up so much dust he could scarcely see their legs. Then Pedro looked at Simon and grinned. The message was clear enough. He stopped and let Juan sweep around him and kick the ball through the posts.

The kids erupted in one unified cheer. Pedro and Harold stood on the sidelines and laughed while Juan did a victory dance and shouted to Simon, "Football!"

Sofia pulled up in front of her apartment just as the descending sun painted the western ridgeline. The palette was gold and russet and rose. The light played through the trees lining her little plaza. She climbed the stairs and stepped onto her balcony as several neighbors emerged to watch the silent symphony. She wondered if they were as tired and worried as she felt. But the faces she could observe were carefully composed. It was the Mexican way, to hide deep emotions behind politeness and gentle voices and the mask of indifference.

Her ability to enjoy the sunset was tainted by a day filled with unanswered questions. Such as, why did she feel so reluctant to marry Enrique? She had passed a dozen election billboards today. All of them smiled down at her. Reminding her that the clock was ticking. Telling her that she should be standing there beside him. Offering her people a better tomorrow.

She entered her apartment and prepared a salad with sliced avocado. She ate standing at the balcony. Dusk faded with desert swiftness. The chapel bell rang, and she decided that she did not want to go this evening. Instead she put away her dishes and brought her Bible out onto the balcony. She read a passage and she prayed, then she stopped when the children exited the chapel. She waited and she watched, and she realized she was hoping to catch a glimpse of Simon.

She sighed her way off the balcony and through her apartment and down the stairs and across the plaza and through the orphanage gates. Juan broke off from his soccer match to race over and say, "Simon played football with us. I won. He went back into his classroom. He has not come out."

"Not even to eat?"

"I went over and told him it was time for dinner. I do not know if he even saw me."

"Well, he'll certainly see me now." When Juan started to follow, she said, "No, you stay here."

"But I want to watch you argue."

"We're not going to argue, and you are an imp. Now go play."

She entered the mess hall and greeted the cook, who responded to her request for a plate of food with a knowing smile. "He is so very handsome, this Yanqui, no?"

"Not you too. I get enough of this from Juan."

The cook was a kindly woman who had six children of her own and played grandmother to the entire orphanage. "You do not have enough on your plate, flirting with Enrique? Why must you claim two of them?"

"I am claiming nothing. I am going to make him eat. And you are worse than the children."

"And you are not fooling anyone." She piled food onto the tin plate and crooned, "Simon, my darling boy, you must keep up your strength for the love."

"I am never speaking to you again. Now give me the plate." The cook's laughter was far too high pitched for her huge size, and it chased Sofia across the courtyard.

But what she saw as she entered the classroom erased all her exasperation. Simon leaned over the front table. His hands were balled into fists. His shoulders were hunched, and his hair draped down over his forehead. His work was spread out everywhere. The blackboard was one massive scrawl of calculations. Pages were taped to the walls. The apparatus was dismantled and covered most of the table. But he was not looking at any of that. He was studying Harold's book.

"I've brought you food." She turned on the lights by the doorway. "Juan says you've been working all day."

"Except for a *football* match this afternoon. Me against all the kids." He eased his shoulders and his neck, then seated himself behind the teacher's desk. "I'm starving."

"I imagine so. You remind me so much of Vasquez. He wouldn't eat unless I ordered him to take a break."

"Pedro said you never went to his house."

"He came here. At least every other day. He visited with Harold and he went to chapel and he helped out. We became his family." She hesitated, then asked, "Do you have family waiting for you back home?"

"My parents are gone. I have an aunt somewhere. But I haven't seen her since I was a kid."

The toneless way he spoke reminded her of children she had known in the state orphanages, who had learned the safest way to live was by stamping down hard on all emotions. He ate with a remarkable delicacy, his attention drifting back to Harold's book. Was he truly changing as Pedro predicted, or was it just her own growing affection for him? An affection she could no longer deny. "Have Harold's teachings helped you?"

"Helped and challenged both." He turned a page. "I'm still trying to make sense of this goal business."

"He makes everyone do it. Even Enrique."

Simon laughed. "No way."

"Enrique had his secretary write the goals out for him." She heard him laugh again and wished she could share the humor. Instead of thinking that it was just like the mayor. She knew he found such probings to be extremely unwelcome, even when they came from a trusted friend, even when the questions were meant to help, even when—

She pushed it away. "Why did you go to MIT?"

"Because I could. They offered to pay. I went."

"Why electrical engineering?"

"It came naturally. That and an old fear. As a kid I was afraid of the dark." He looked at her. "What tops your list of goals?"

The intensity of his gaze caught her unaware. "I want to help orphans throughout all Mexico." She had not shared that with anyone, not even Pedro.

Simon gave a slow nod. "That's a beautiful purpose for your life."

"Thank you, Simon."

"Marrying Enrique would probably help make that possible."

"It would." She wet her lips, tasting the dust and the chalk and the night. "But I wonder . . ."

"What?"

She rose from the table, amazed at herself. She had been about to confess the impossible to this man. How she wondered if this goal was worth giving up on the secret yearning for true love. "Good night, Simon. It's late, and we both need our rest."

Pedro was waiting for her as she approached the front gates. He often hung around at the end of a long day, checking on things, talking with Harold, helping to bed down the children. He had always taken his strength from this place. It was his character to support others. He would make a perfect orphanage director. The children already loved him.

She tensed as Pedro fell into step beside her. She could hear all his unspoken questions. Why was she so interested in Simon? Did he represent a threat to Enrique in her heart? Was she ever going to accept Enrique's offer of marriage? What was she waiting for? What did she want? She knew all the questions. And had answers for none of them.

But she was wrong. Pedro surprised her by asking, "What happened between Simon and Vasquez?"

She stopped. "Why are you asking me that?"

Pedro turned and looked back at the classroom where the lone light cast the empty courtyard in a dusky glow. "I like him."

The simple words made her eyes burn. "I like him too."

"He carries burdens. That much is clear. And I think he has known his share of hard days. But he listens to Harold. He thinks." Pedro shrugged. "I asked him to pray with me."

"I did also. What did he say to you?"

"He thanked me." Pedro's teeth flashed in the gloom. "It was the nicest turndown I have ever received."

"He was reading Harold's book when I brought him dinner."

"Then he is still asking questions, no?" Pedro's smile flashed in the night. "Harold believes Simon is moving in the right direction, and all he needs is a little more time."

"Harold can predict when a man will give his life to Jesus?"

"I am thinking, with this one, maybe yes."

The burning behind her eyes only grew worse. "What happened between Simon and Armando was very bad."

He replied easily, "Who has not fallen short in the eyes of God and man?"

Sofia studied her brother. "You have been thinking about this."

"What I have been thinking, sister, is that Harold is right. And for this I am happy that Simon will be staying here for a few more days."

Chapter 23

When Simon woke the next morning, the eastern horizon held the first faint wash of dawn. He lay and recalled the previous day and felt anew the strength of their invitation. Beckoning to him, enticing him. To join with them in renewing his life through the eternal.

When the morning bell rang, he left the classroom and joined the flow into the chapel. He did not see Sofia, which saddened him. It was silly to hope for anything between them, really. Her engagement to Enrique was only a matter of time. The two of them would make a beautiful couple and accomplish great things. Mexico needed them. Which only made his longing worse. As though he looked beyond Sofia to the man he was, and the changes he needed to make to deserve the love of someone like her.

Pedro and Harold joined him for a silent breakfast, then followed him back across the courtyard. As they entered the classroom, Simon said, "I have a problem. Actually, two. The first is with the components. Like I told you yesterday, some got fried in our little outing, and I can't afford to replace them."

"We're looking at money coming in from the lanterns you helped us with." Pedro pushed himself up onto the window ledge. "A church group in Texas has offered to buy the entire load. I'll drive the van up tomorrow."

Harold settled into the chair behind the desk. "Let's see if the Ojinaga shop can meet your requirements and how much they cost. If we can handle it, we'll put it down as an investment."

Beyond the easy camaraderie, Simon heard the message that he was accepted. One of them. He swallowed hard. "The second problem is with the science."

Harold nodded. "With the control of power through the apparatus."

"Right. I assumed the answer would be found in the connection of frequencies that Vasquez listed on his sheets. I mean, we all heard the harmonics before the power surge."

"Like heaven sang for us." Pedro nodded.

"But something tells me I'm looking at it all wrong. Like I need to rethink the whole frequency equation."

"As though your question is right, but the perspective is wrong," Harold suggested.

"Exactly."

"Sometimes the direct approach is the wrong approach. Back at the beginning of the Apollo program, the number-one problem we faced was heat control. Most scientists assumed astronauts would either freeze in space and cook on reentry. Hull temperatures during the capsule's descent would exceed a thousand degrees. Hot enough to melt iron. Which meant we had to wait until some new technology was invented or a new material could be found, one that absorbed heat and would not melt."

Harold stretched out his long legs. Holding no airs. Needing no spotlight. "I wasn't the smartest guy on the block. And I won't say God reached down and handed me the answer. But what I will say is this. My faith gave me the ability to take a step back. I was able to detach myself from the stresses and the problems and look at the situation from a different perspective."

Pedro's smile resurfaced. "Now you sound like the professor."

Simon had been thinking the same thing. It seemed as though Vasquez was standing in the corner, smiling in approval. For Vasquez, faith had been a significant part of everything.

Harold went on, "One day I was turning a chicken on a barbecue spit, when it hit me. If turning the bird on a spit can evenly distribute the heat, why can't we do the same thing with a spaceship? And that's exactly what we did."

Pedro said, "They even named it after Harold."

The two men shared a smile. "Not exactly."

"They called it the barbecue roll," Pedro said.

"What I'm saying is this. Sometimes the riddle is bigger than our limited knowledge. You've got to tune into the right frequency. And by that I mean prayer."

Simon was still mulling that over when Juan bounced through the doorway. "The mayor is on Harold's phone for Pedro. He says it is urgent."

Pedro was gone less than five minutes. When he returned, it was to inform Simon, "We must go. Enrique wishes to speak with us both. Immediately."

As they were leaving, Harold said, "Just one thing. I heard from my friend at NASA, the hedge fund investor. He'll be down this way in three days and wants to see the device for himself."

Simon stifled a groan. "The machine doesn't work."

It was Pedro who replied, "Tell him yes."

"You were there," Simon protested. "You saw the disaster."

"What I saw was an unfinished miracle. And so should he."

"I don't know . . ."

"I do." Pedro turned to the sunlight and the waiting day. "Now we must hurry."

Simon remained silent through the drive, his mind flitting from one unresolved issue to another. Pedro left Ojinaga and headed south along the desert highway, then turned through wooden gates and drove along a washboard road. The restaurant was built within an old ranch, bordered by a dilapidated barn and feeding troughs and a wind-driven well with squeaky fan blades. Longhorn cattle grazed the surrounding scrubland, drifting through the midday heat. A massive helicopter stood gleaming in the rear corral, utterly at odds with its environment.

The restaurant's interior was polished and rustic at the same time. The lighting was muted and the windows heavily draped. The walls and floors were varnished the color of frozen honey. A surprising number of people were dining and talking and having a good time. The air was rich with the fragrances of wood smoke and steaks.

Enrique was seated at the back of the restaurant. The walls between what had probably once been the living and dining areas had been torn out. The two rooms were divided by struts the thickness of tree trunks. Enrique's table could have held six. He sat there, alone, while three people stood in front of him talking softly. He ate with gusto, his knife and fork clattering as he listened to the trio. Simon stopped at the entry to the second room because that was where Pedro halted. Waiting to be recognized.

Enrique spoke a few words, and the trio bowed from the waist and turned and walked past Simon, their eyes downcast, their faces blank. Enrique called to Pedro, who motioned for Simon to remain where he was. The assistant town manager approached the table and stood where the trio had been, his hands clasped before him, the patient supplicant. Enrique spoke for a time, then dismissed Pedro with the hand holding the knife. Pedro walked past Simon without meeting his gaze and slipped from the room.

"Simon! How good to see you. Please, join me." Enrique used a foot to push out a chair. "Are you hungry, my friend? This place has the best cuts of beef in all Chihuahua state. My favorite is aged Kobe beef. Imported from Japan."

The smell left him famished. But the way Enrique had dismissed Pedro galled him. "Thanks. I'm good."

A man stood in the corner between the window and the support beams, as though he intended to disappear in plain sight. Simon recognized him as the driver who had brought Enrique to the orphanage. He wore dark pants and white shirt and steel-toed boots. Aviator glasses dangled from his shirt pocket. He watched Simon with unblinking intensity.

Enrique gestured at his plate with his knife. "Are you certain you will not join me? The orphanage food cannot be a culinary delight. No? Well, then, why I asked to speak with you. Am I correct in understanding that you took Sofia with you to the power station?"

"She wanted to come."

"This, my friend, cannot be permitted. She is, after all, the fiancée of a candidate running for office. The press would have a field day with such an item."

Simon had the feeling that Enrique was waiting for him to correct that statement, and point out that Sofia had not yet agreed to marry. "It won't happen again."

"Splendid!" Enrique beamed. "I knew I could count on you. After all, you will be leaving us soon, no? Returning to your life north of the border? And we will be left here in Mexico."

Simon took that as his dismissal and rose to his feet. "I guess I'll be getting back to Pedro."

"There is just one more thing." Enrique made a production of lining up his fork and knife, dabbing his lips with the napkin, then folding it and settling it beside his plate. "I understand the blackout that struck most of Ojinaga was your fault?"

"Far as I can tell. I'm really sorry about that."

"So this device of yours, it is dangerous, no?"

"Control of the power is the next problem to address," Simon replied. "It's supposed to create light, not darkness."

"And yet the city experienced a similar blackout the night that your professor died." Enrique waved that aside. "I have been approached by an investor who is interested in purchasing your device. He agrees with you that the problem could be corrected. And it could make you some fast money."

"Vasquez left his share of the discovery to the orphanage," Simon pointed out. "Harold has to be involved in these decisions."

"Harold is a charming old man, no?" Enrique seemed to find that amusing. "Then I will bring up the issue when we next meet. After all, we both want the same thing. In the meantime, I must have it back."

"Excuse me?"

"You will cease work on the device and return it to the city. I have been contacted by the state prosecutor. The professor's death is still under investigation. His device is evidence."

Simon noticed how the driver pushed himself off the wall, as though readying himself for combat. The man was small and slender, yet he carried himself with an air of tightly controlled menace.

Simon turned back to Enrique. "You're the boss."

"Excellent! My driver will stop by this afternoon." Enrique's smile was brilliant. "We must not keep the city waiting, no?"

When Simon emerged from the restaurant, Pedro stood beneath the front awning's shade, watching a steer sharpen his horns on a fence railing. The horns were three feet across. The bull stopped scoring the fence long enough to look at Simon. Then he snorted and went back to digging another furrow in the scarred fence.

Pedro asked, "What did Enrique want?"

"He said the professor's device is evidence and the city wants it back. I had the impression the man's got a totally different goal in mind." Pedro winced and Simon regretted having spoken. The mayor was, after all, this man's ally. "Maybe I'm just blowing smoke."

"This is Mexico," Pedro slowly replied. "You mess with the bull, you risk meeting the horns."

Before Simon could ask what he meant, Pedro turned and walked back to the pickup. When they were back in the pickup and heading for the orphanage, Pedro asked Simon, "Will you tell me what else Enrique said to you?"

"Basically, back off your sister. Which is kind of weird, you know? I mean, what's the deal? It looks to me like he's got that all sewed up."

"Weird, yes, I agree." Pedro drummed his fingers on the wheel, squinting at the sunlight on the windscreen. "Enrique told me to pass on two messages to Harold. First, your passport should be ready in a few days. Second, you had trouble with the police. You were arrested at the bar where you worked, and this arrest led to Vasquez being deported. Is this true?"

The pain was so fierce, it felt like a blade of shame was jammed between his ribs. "The charges were dropped. But yeah. It's all true."

Pedro drummed on the wheel and did not speak.

Simon struggled to fashion a genuine apology. Over how he had let down so many people. How he had felt a change taking shape inside himself. How he didn't want to let anyone else down. Especially the orphanage.

But Pedro surprised him by saying, "I share your impression that what Enrique said was not what Enrique meant. We need to discuss this with Harold."

The pain stabbed Simon anew as Pedro passed on Enrique's message. But Harold did not condemn him as Simon expected or expel him as he feared. Harold said simply, "Vasquez told me about the incident. He also told me he had forgiven you. How could I possibly do anything else."

Simon fought against himself, and managed, "I didn't come down for the machine."

"I never thought you did."

"I wanted to apologize."

"Son, you still can, and you know this." He gave Simon a chance to argue, then pressed on, "There is one act above all else that would validate the confidence Vasquez has shown in you. Reach beyond where you are. Acknowledge that you can't make a success of your life alone, that you need help, and that it is there in front of you. Waiting for you to ask. Ready to give you wings."

For the second time in as many days, Simon found himself willing to push away the cynical response that came bubbling up. "I hear what you're saying."

Harold studied him a long moment. The light in his eyes belonged to a man half his age. "Let me show you something." The orphanage director unfolded the professor's pages. "Four of the frequencies are circled."

"Right. Those are the ones I used when I powered down the entire city."

"Good. Now look here." Harold ran his finger along the letters written down the page's left border. "Three are underlined."

"I've been over them and over them," Simon said. "They don't correspond to any standardized calculation or frequency pattern."

"Then it obviously means something else. You know Tesla used a cryptogram to hide his most-sensitive data. Letters for numbers and vice versa."

"Vasquez was fascinated with the guy," Simon recalled.

"I applied Tesla's system and came up with this." Harold handed him a sheet.

Simon read, "Juan, eight one two."

Pedro exclaimed, "It's a clue!"

"Eight hundred and twelve is not a viable frequency," Simon replied.

"I've told you before, look beyond the obvious." Harold stared out to where the children played their afternoon game of soccer. "Armando was both very excited and very afraid. He sensed that someone was after his device. So he demonstrated to you the obvious. He revealed how far he had gotten, what he knew would work."

Simon nodded. "Which was what anybody else who was observing Vasquez knew as well. The device worked, but turning on the power resulted in a catastrophic blackout."

Pedro said, "Last night was not the second time the city has recently lost power. It was the third."

Simon felt a new energy course through him. "Which means Vasquez tested the device once. He saw the problem. He realized someone was tracking him. He tested it a second time and recorded the results. He was killed."

"The police say otherwise," Pedro said.

"Forget the police," Harold said. "We have needed to discount everything they've said."

Simon went on. "Between the first and the second blackouts, Vasquez realized what the answer was."

"But because he was being watched, he hid his discovery," Harold confirmed. "Why don't we go see if the shop in town has the components. We can talk to Juan when we get back."

"What about Enrique?"

Harold said to Pedro, "For a start, can you give him enough to satisfy the city attorney?"

Simon swept up the fried components and dumped them in Armando's case. "Done."

"Leave it with the officer standing guard by our gates."

Pedro's concerns resurfaced. "I'm still not certain Enrique told us the truth."

"About anything." Simon agreed.

"Neither am I," Harold said. "But we can't react to what we don't know. Let's focus on getting the professor's device ready for the visit of my investor."

Chapter 24

For a time, Sofia had considered making Juárez her home. Her first year at the University of Texas at El Paso, she had crossed the border several times a month. The culture in an American university had been jarring. She had thought she would never settle in comfortably. She had traveled back with other freshmen from Mexico who had felt the same way. They had walked along the market streets and dined in family-style restaurants. Gradually she had come to think of Juárez as a home away from home.

During her first two years at university, Juárez had been vibrant and filled with a growing prosperity. The border factories had employed almost two hundred thousand people. The smaller local companies who supplied them had created another quarter of a million jobs. The entire city vibrated with new energy and promise.

Then the year before she graduated, the nightmare came to Juárez.

Sofia had adapted to the American university and culture. She had made friends. She had become active in two of the campus ministries. She was involved in her studies. She had entered the honors program. Her junior year, she had not entered Juárez at all. Of course she heard about the change. She saw the worried expressions of those who returned. She heard the stories whispered around the halls. But there was a very real difference between reading the stories in a newspaper and witnessing the change.

She went in late October of her senior year. The border crossing took twice as long as before. The patrol officers were different, very grim and cautious. It was the first time she had ever seen body armor. The streets of Juárez were drenched in unseen shadows. Every face she saw was creased and stained with fear.

Today as they approached the city's outskirts, a ghost town rose up around them. People flitted into sight, then vanished just as quickly. Cars raced down the side streets, the engines sounding a shrill note, as though echoing their passengers' fears. Stoplights were meaningless things. They might as well have spelled out the word *flee.*

Then the army came into view.

Armored-personnel carriers appeared on the corners. Soldiers loitered in the plazas fronting the churches and municipal buildings. Their guns were stacked like cordwood. They hung their thumbs from body armor and eyed the passing cars from behind mirrored shades. Juan gaped at them, then turned round eyes toward her.

Sofia said, "You must stay close. You do not point at anyone.

If a man glares at you, look down. You remain silent while we are in public."

"Yes, Sofia."

She pulled into a multistory parking garage and waited while three guards inspected the car's interior and trunk, then passed mirrors underneath. They entered one of the safer shopping areas, which meant enduring bag searches and X-ray machines like were found in the American airports.

She first took Juan for a haircut, then to a men's store where she bought him his very first jacket and dress slacks and shoes and white cotton shirt. The sight of him emerging from the dressing room caused her eyes to burn with tears she was determined not to shed.

She took him to a restaurant on the top floor of a high-rise building connected to the shopping area. She selected a table where they could sit and look out over the Rio Grande to El Paso beyond. She pointed out the spires of her university. She described the people and the life. For a few minutes, the grim nature of the city below was forgotten, and they were simply two people enjoying a midday meal.

Juan surprised her by announcing, "I like Simon."

"So do I. Very much."

"He did a bad thing to the professor."

"How do you know about this?"

"I heard you two talking about it one night."

"You young imp. What have I told you about listening at windows?"

Juan paid her scolding no mind. "The professor loved him. I heard Vasquez say it himself. Why would Simon do this?"

Dressed in his new outfit, Juan looked as though he was perched on the border of manhood. That and the distance between them and the orphanage made it easy for her to say, "Sometimes when I look at Simon, I see what might have happened to me."

Juan nodded. "If Harold had not found us. If we had not learned how to trust. And how to hope. And how to pray."

The burning sensation returned to her eyes. "You are a truly remarkable young man."

"Do you love Simon?"

She started to deflect the question, then decided otherwise. "Can I trust you to keep this completely between us?"

"Always and forever."

"The answer is, I don't know if I feel what the professor felt, or if it is really what I have come to feel myself for Simon."

Juan looked out over the cityscape, his expression thoughtful. "Or perhaps it is God placing this in your heart, so the professor's love can live on."

Sofia found it difficult to shape the response. "Perhaps."

Juan looked at her with a gaze far older than his years. "God is right to trust you with His love."

She used both hands to wipe her face. "What makes you say this remarkable thing?"

"Because who could be better at showing Simon what love really means?"

As they approached the tallest building in Juárez's business district, Sofia saw the helicopter descend onto the rooftop landing zone and knew Enrique had arrived.

The soldiers surrounding the central plaza were backed up by agents wearing suits and carrying walkie-talkies. The absence of uniforms made them more dangerous, not less. These people did not follow the normal rule of law. In today's Mexico, such agents *were* the law.

Juan was cowed by the military and the guns and the tension. He shrank back as an agent recognized Sofia and saluted her and ordered the military to pull up the barrier so she could park in the VIP section. She cut off the motor and said, "Everything is all right, Juan."

He nodded but did not speak.

Halfway across the sunlit square, she squatted down in front of Juan and waited until he met her gaze. "You know I am dating the mayor of Ojinaga, yes?"

"Yes, Sofia, of course."

"You also know that he is running for the governor of Chihuahua state?"

"Everyone knows this."

"This is the other side of Mexican politics. The threat can only be met by real force. We are going to observe Enrique as he is interviewed by the national television. And then we are attending a rally. Do you know what a rally is?"

"Of course, Sofia. I am not a child."

"No, that is certainly true." She straightened his jacket and smoothed his hair. "You look very handsome, Juan."

He beamed. "I am dressed like a prince."

"Indeed you are." She rose to full height and said to the hovering agent, "We are ready."

Chapter 25

"Jefe, with respect, I can take them all here on the road into Ojinaga. No one will—"

"I know what you are capable of." The boss's voice was distorted by the whine of a massive engine. Carlos knew the jefe had waited for this call until the helicopter had landed and the people with whom he traveled had exited the metal bird. The decelerating rotor made a huge noise through the chopper's open rear door, which meant the jefe's words were inaudible to anyone but Carlos. He had used this technique many times before.

"You do not see the big picture, Carlos. That is my job. Your job is to follow orders."

Carlos kept three cars between Pedro's pickup and his SUV. Simon sat between Pedro and Harold. Carlos watched the orphanage director throw his head back and laugh. What could possibly be of such hilarity to people like this? Trapped inside a run-down orphanage, full of castoff kids. "You want me to be arrested."

"Listen to what I am saying. The assistant town manager saw you enter the house where the professor was killed. He has seen the bloody evidence. He knows the police lied about Vasquez suffering a heart attack."

The solution seemed as clear as the sun through his windscreen. "Then the town manager must die."

"Again you do not see the big picture." Even when almost shouting, the boss showed a practiced patience. "Another death at this time would disrupt the entire process I am trying to put into place. Plus I have told you that the orphanage must remain safe."

"Jefe, I have been to prison. I do not wish to return."

"It is only for a few hours. A day or two at most. Long enough for the police to appear to be doing their job. Then I will personally see to your release." When Carlos did not instantly agree, the tone sharpened. "I expect you to obey me, as usual."

The worms of fear gnawed at his gut. The boss was correct. Carlos had no choice. "I will do as you say, jefe."

"Of course you will. Now pay attention. This is how I want it to happen."

As Carlos listened, his gaze fastened upon the middle figure riding in the pickup. The American might think he was safe. He might assume his strength was enough. But it was only a matter of time. When the boss finished speaking, Carlos replied, "Tell me the Yanqui is mine."

"Did you not hear a word I have said? His end is precisely why you must be arrested. The American handed over the professor's device to the guard at the front gates. He still has his own.

The guard has inspected the classroom this American has been using as a lab. The device is not there, which means it is with them now. You are following him into town, yes? Most likely he is going to the electronics shop. You will go there, you will rob him, you will deliver the second device to my driver, and you will be arrested."

"Jefe, it would be so much simpler—"

"We are not after *simple.* We are after *clean.*"

Carlos thought again of what he had endured as a child in the adult prison. But he could not refuse this man anything. "*Sí,* jefe. I will obey."

"The American has finished dancing to my tune. It is time for him to take his last breath."

Sofia and Juan crossed a massive foyer with four floors of balconies rising to a glass roof. The rich and powerful of Juárez milled about. Waiters circulated with drinks and trays of food. A string quartet played in the far corner. The noise bounced off the polished stone floor and high ceiling, forming a chaotic din. A number of people recognized her and pointed her out to others. Sofia pretended not to notice. Would she ever grow accustomed to such moments?

Sofia wore a Chanel suit, the only designer fashion she owned. She had found it at the discount mall outside Dallas when she had gone up to speak at a church. She did most of her shopping in such places. It made her infrequent journeys to America all the more special.

The suit was a woven blend of silk and cotton and light as a feather. The color was somewhere between blue and gray and highlighted her hair and eyes. She knew she was beautiful in it. To say otherwise would be false modesty. Even so, as the eyes raked her and Juan, she felt as though all the secrets of her past lay exposed. As though she would never fully belong among these people, their easy wealth, and their sense of entitlement. As though they had already dismissed her as unworthy.

The agent led them through guarded doors. They entered a second chamber only slightly smaller than the first. More people were gathered here, many of them recognizable from newspapers and magazines. One corner had been sectioned off and was rimmed now by television equipment and lights.

Sofia had attended a number of such events since she started dating Enrique.

At first she had assumed he was trying to show off for her, demonstrate how powerful he was becoming, how far she could go with him. And there was certainly a hint of this. Enrique liked to preen and show off for a beautiful woman. But Sofia soon realized he was also testing her. To see how she reacted to this dimension of his life and his world. And the answer was, she really didn't care. She knew who she was. She had no desire for public acclaim. She knew it was a part of his life, so she accepted it. That was all.

One night, after a reception where Enrique had been feted by the president himself, he had asked her, "How do you feel about this?"

"I don't know enough to have an opinion."

Clearly the handsome and wealthy gentleman was expecting a different response. "But . . . don't you have feelings for me?"

"Of course, Enrique. But there is a difference between

feelings for you and all this . . ." She waved a hand back at everything they just left behind. "The responsibility. The attention. The public nature of your life."

He smiled then. And perhaps it was the first time he had actually revealed the man beneath the mask. "It is precisely because of how you speak that I am falling for you, Sofia. Shall I tell you why?"

"Yes, please."

"You do not act thrilled by the power or the money or the public eye. You speak of *responsibility.* Do you have *any* idea how rare that is?"

"It is natural for me."

"Yes. I see that is true." And he kissed her then.

Juan brought her back to the present by asking, "Are there always so many soldiers and police and other men with guns?"

A voice behind Sofia said, "No. Not always. Today is special."

Sofia turned and discovered Agent Consuela Martinez, the woman serving with the antidrug force who had delivered Gabriella to the orphanage. Sofia shook her hand. "Forgive me for not saying hello. I didn't see you."

"I have been in a meeting. We used this gathering to hold a conference." She smiled at the young man standing beside Sofia. "Juan, do I remember that correctly? You certainly look grown up today."

He returned her smile, then went back to staring out the window. The view overlooked downtown Juárez, to the sparkling waters of the Rio Grande and the border fence. Martinez looked out with him and said, "I heard on the radio the wait to cross through the border today is almost six hours."

"Because of Enrique?"

"Because of everything going on today, yes. How is the little one I brought you settling in?"

"Gabriella still has nightmares," Juan said.

"Don't we all," Martinez replied.

Sofia asked, "Why are there so many officials?"

"Enrique has declared war against El Noche. You have heard of him?"

"The name, of course. He runs a cartel, yes?"

"His gang has been moving on Juárez. Enrique has promised to make a restoration of order to this city his first priority as governor." Martinez hesitated.

"You might as well tell us the rest," Sofia said. "We will hear about it soon enough."

"An hour ago, El Noche responded that Enrique would not survive to take office. Frankly I am surprised he has not warned you of this."

"I turned my phone off before we left Ojinaga. I did not want to be bothered with work." She fumbled in her purse, found her phone, and turned it on. "I have six messages from Enrique."

But before she could key her voice mail, Enrique emerged from a side room, his arm draped around an older gentleman. As soon as he spotted Sofia, he broke off the conversation and hurried over. "I have been trying to reach you for hours." He frowned at the sight of the young man standing beside her. "Juan?"

"Hello, sir."

He lowered his voice. "You have heard about El Noche?"

"Agent Martinez just told us. We can leave immediately if you wish."

The federal agent offered, "I can arrange an escort."

"Thank you, but Sofia, you are now here, so stay."

"Perhaps it would be best—"

"No, no, an hour one way or the other makes no difference." He struggled to shape a smile. "And besides, there is someone who asked for you especially. Come."

Sofia accepted his outstretched hand and allowed herself to be swept into his world. All the eyes on the room were upon her now. The young orphan woman whom Enrique wished to marry. She saw the speculative looks and the calculating gazes. And she tried to tell herself their opinions did not matter.

Her unease only strengthened when Sofia realized who awaited them.

Enrique's mother, Magda, was a woman born to rule. She had the polished exterior of an ancient marble statue. And she was just as cold. Her dark eyes held a brutal intelligence, a cold willingness to do whatever was required without an instant's regret. She was a woman who could kill with a smile.

"Sofia. How nice."

"Mrs. Morales. Enrique told me you were hoping to join him today."

"I try to attend as many of my son's events as I can. It is part of the process, no? Supporting Enrique's campaign however possible. No matter how difficult it may prove. That is part of what it means to be family. Don't you agree?"

Sofia knew she should not allow the woman to bait her. But she had never been one to silently accept the slights of others. "So difficult, yes. Wherever did your helicopter manage to land?"

The eyes tightened, but the woman did not respond. Sofia duplicated the older woman's tight slit of a smile. Enrique held his arms out wide, seeking to draw the two women together. "Turn this way, ladies. The photographers wish to take your picture."

"Should this not be limited to family, my son?"

"Nonsense. Step closer, please, Sofia. And smile."

While the lights flashed in blinding sequence, Magda asked around her son, "Who's the waif who accompanied you, my dear? Another of the sweet little lost ones?"

"His name is Juan." Sofia waited until Enrique waved the photographers away to bare her own knife. "What a charming frock you are wearing, Mrs. Morales. Did you sew it yourself?"

Enrique clapped his hands. "Enough, the both of you. How can I hope to build peace on the streets of Juárez when I can't do this in my own home?"

Sofia felt instantly contrite. "You are right. I am sorry for my words, Mrs. Morales."

The woman's gaze tightened further, as though she had never actually heard a heartfelt apology before. Enrique, however, gave her a one-armed embrace. "Thank you, my dear one. And now I am being directed to the eye of the hurricane."

Enrique allowed a nervous aide to lead him through the cameras and the lights onto the carpeted dais and into one of the swivel chairs. The newscaster, whose face was one of the most famous in Mexico, reached over and shook Enrique's hand while the makeup lady worked on him. A producer called out the countdown seconds. "We are live in five, four, three . . ."

Sofia tried to pay attention, but she sensed Enrique's mother moving up beside her and tensed for the next incoming barb.

Enrique was by nature a lonely man. It was a trait Sofia felt most drawn to. He needed a woman who would truly care for him. No doubt Magda did in her own way. But Magda also used her son. She was *invested* in him. She was intensely shrewd and very focused upon building the family empire.

Magda said softly, "At first I thought you were just another of my son's little rebellions. I was wrong, of course. Much to my dismay."

Sofia gave no sign she even heard the woman. But she found it increasingly difficult to focus upon the two men under the lights.

Magda went on. "He is right about many of your traits. You are intelligent. You are fierce. You are independent. You have managed to rise from nothing. But there is one thing my son fails to recognize. It is the attribute that makes you utterly wrong for him, and for us. Shall I tell you what that is?"

Sofia kept her face turned toward the lights, though she no longer saw the men at all. *Here it comes.*

"It is that Protestant song and dance of yours. What an utter waste of time." The woman's quiet words dripped with scorn. "You have fallen for the lure of unseen hope."

Sofia faced the woman. "That is the finest compliment anyone has ever given me."

"My son needs someone who understands that what you see is all that matters."

"I have nothing more to say to you. Except this." Sofia stepped in close enough to feel the woman's sharp intake of breath. "I will pray for you."

Sofia turned from the lights and the power and the wealth. She walked to where Juan and Martinez stood by the rear windows and announced, "We are leaving."

Chapter 26

Ojinaga's market area was located half a mile from the central square. The main streets contained offices for national utilities like the power company and the banks and the city's more expensive shops. The narrow side streets held a variety of smaller shops and open stalls. The market sparkled like a desert rainbow. The boisterous, good-natured crowds defied the heat. At every intersection, street performers competed with beggars for attention.

Pedro led Simon into the city's main electronics store. The shop was a throwback to another era. Dishwashers and flat-screen televisions and computers and toys all competed for space. The wall separating the shop from what appeared to be a repair station was lined with shelves and drawers. As Pedro greeted the shopkeeper, Simon set out the seven components from his own device that were fried beyond repair. Pedro swept a hand over them and asked a question.

The shopkeeper picked up one of the circuits and fitted a jeweler's loupe into his eye. He spoke and Pedro translated, "He wishes to know what happened."

Simon kept his response to the bare minimum. "I overloaded the device."

The shopkeeper went through the components carefully, then confirmed he had all but one in stock. As he laid the fifth component on the counter, he asked another question that Pedro translated as, "What kind of device are you working on?"

But while Pedro was still translating, the shopkeeper's eyes widened, and fear rippled across his face. He jerked his hands into the air.

Pedro and Simon turned together to find the bearded hunter standing in the doorway. He was smaller than Simon remembered. But the feral expression was the same. As were the glittering eyes. And the shapeless leather coat.

The gun, however, was new.

The hunter barked at Simon. Pedro translated, "He wants your case."

"Tell him the machine doesn't work."

"Then you can give it to him, no?"

Simon spotted Harold rushing up behind the attacker. The orphanage director dropped his briefcase and hefted a ceramic vase from the shop next door.

The hunter screamed something, his voice rising to impossible heights. Pedro said, "Give him the bag."

"Sure thing." Simon held it out.

Harold dropped the vase on the attacker's head. The man shouted and wheeled about. As he did so, the gun went off.

The shot was impossibly loud. The narrow shop compounded the noise, turning it into an assault on Simon's brain. Pedro, however, seemed unaffected. He grabbed the shopkeeper's laptop and slammed it down on the attacker's head.

The bearded man went down hard.

Simon's relief at having survived was short lived. He saw Harold holding his shoulder, with blood seeping from between his fingers.

The shopkeeper pressed an alarm, and a siren blared from above the entrance. The three of them stumbled out, Pedro and Simon supporting Harold between them.

The entire plaza emptied in a flash of screaming panic. The streets became silent as the grave. Even the stallholders had vanished. The only motion he could see came from a lone car. It zoomed toward them and slammed on the brakes. As soon as Pedro saw who was behind the wheel, he groaned.

Simon recognized the driver and a chill struck his bones. The car was driven by the woman who had led the council meeting. The one who had offered him a thousand dollars for the device. The woman in the photograph in the professor's office. The one supposedly engaged to Vasquez. The one Pedro called a *bruja*. A witch.

Dr. Clara pushed open the driver's door and screamed across the car, "Get in!"

Pedro did not move.

She pointed behind them. "Your attacker is coming!"

Simon glanced back and saw it was so. The bearded man was up on his knees, one hand clamped to the back of his head, the other scrabbling for the gun.

As a police siren rose in the distance, the woman's voice lashed at them. "You wish to risk your friend's life? The police will come and lock him in a cell. He needs a doctor! *Move*!"

Simon sat in the front passenger seat, turned so he could watch the two men in the backseat. Pedro's face was washed of all color. Harold's features were etched with pain, and the hand holding his shoulder was soaked through.

Dr. Clara glanced in the rearview mirror and snapped, "Don't sit there doing nothing!"

Pedro asked dully, "Why are you here?"

"Never mind that. You need to apply pressure!" She swerved around a corner, taking it fast enough to pop the car up on two wheels. When the vehicle righted, she snapped at Simon, "Give him your shirt!"

Simon pulled the shirt over his head and passed it back.

"Bind it to him tightly and press down on the wound."

"It hurts," Harold complained.

"Of course it hurts. You've been shot."

Pedro said, "Why are you going this way? The hospital is behind us."

"So too are the police behind us. You want Dr. Harold to die in custody?"

"I will call Enrique."

"You will keep pressure on that wound. The mayor is in Juárez."

"Where are you taking us?"

"Is the police officer still on guard at the orphanage gates?"

"Yes."

"We will go there."

Simon shared a worried glance with Pedro. "How do you know about the police guard?"

"So many questions," she replied. "You sound like Vasquez."

"Here's another one. Why are we running from the police behind us when there's another one up ahead?"

Pedro replied, "The guard at the orphanage is Enrique's trusted man. The police who come to the square, who knows?"

"But you're the town manager."

"Assistant manager. And that means something only to Enrique's allies. To the others . . . Perhaps she is right."

"Of course I am right." She held up a finger in Simon's face. "No more questions. I drive. You sit and you breathe and you be glad you are alive one day more. Questions can wait for a safer hour."

Chapter 27

Agent Martinez insisted on driving Sofia and Juan back to Ojinaga in her car, while her partner followed them in Sofia's van. Martinez expressed the invitation as politely as she could, but the steel was there in the policewoman's voice. Sofia assumed it always was present to a certain extent. As they passed through the cordon of soldiers ringing Juárez, Sofia wondered at the things this woman must have seen.

The agent drove a late-model Ford SUV with an oversized engine and dark tinted windows. The seats were woven leather and the steering wheel was burl. The dash and the central console and the doors were rimmed in chrome. Sofia ran a hand over the soft leather door handle. "Very nice."

"It was confiscated in a raid on the cartels. Many of the best police equipment comes to us care of our enemies."

Juan asked from the rear seat, "Have you always wanted to be a policewoman?"

"Not always. When I was your age, all I wanted to do was run track."

"What happened?"

"I come from Sonora. My father is a pastor. I see I have surprised you. Yes. We are trained not to speak of our past. It is a way of protecting our families. When I was in high school, I won the state championships. I was a sprinter. I went to the junior nationals and placed in the hundred meter, the four hundred, and the relay." She smiled tightly at the memory. "In those days, if I was going anywhere, I *ran*."

"And then?"

Her smile slipped away. "I was in a car accident. I damaged my knee. It was repaired well enough. But my running days were over."

"And the police?"

"My father let me wail and weep over my fate for a time. Then he asked me what I wanted to do with my life. What would give me a purpose worth living for. Because whether I saw it or not, surviving that wreck was a gift from above. In time I realized that my father was right. And the simple fact was, I was a fighter. Sprints are all about power, about transforming the body into a bullet. And my father and my upbringing had taught me a strong sense of right and wrong. I hated seeing the changes that were happening to my country. So I decided I was going to do something about it."

"What . . . ?" Sofia's phone rang. She checked the readout and saw it was Enrique. "Excuse me, I must take this."

He demanded, "Where are you?"

"Twenty miles east of Juárez."

"Why did you leave?"

Sofia did not try to hide the acid she felt rising with her answer. "Ask your mother."

He sighed. "My love, did it ever occur to you that your response was precisely what my mother was after?"

Sofia mulled that over. "It did not. No."

"She is finally accepting that my affection for you is genuine. She does not approve. She will not say this, because she knows that for once I am not bending to her will. So her only hope is to push you away."

"She succeeded."

"Sofia, I hope you are listening, because I will only say this once. This indecision of yours only makes it worse for everyone. It is important—"

Sofia broke in to ask, "Do you truly believe in God?"

Enrique went silent. Martinez glanced over but did not speak.

"This is not a difficult question, Enrique. Do you accept Jesus Christ as your Lord and Savior?"

"Sofia, my dear, we have spoken of this so often."

"And we will continue to speak of it for as long as we are together. For as long as I have breath."

"But why now? Why over a phone in the middle of a frantic day?"

"Because of something your mother said."

"My mother the troublemaker. Can we please have this discussion another time? I have a building full of people waiting for me and an empty chair beside my own."

"Yes, Enrique, we can discuss this any time you like." Sofia cut the connection and clenched the phone with both of her hands. It all came down to that.

Juan asked, "The mayor does not follow Jesus?"

"He has said . . ." Sofia shook her head and stared at the road ahead. "He has said many things. And I have been willing to hear what I needed to, instead of what he has *not* said."

Martinez spoke quietly, "He is a politician."

Sofia studied the woman seated beside her. The strong hands, the tensile strength to her slender frame, the dark hair cropped short as a man's. "Juan and I thank you for this gift of safety."

The policewoman smiled into the rearview mirror. "You and our handsome escort are both welcome." She hesitated, then said, "I would like to ask you something. It may not be proper."

"Please. Ask."

"The orphanage, Enrique mentioned that it has financial difficulties."

"Very serious ones. Harold's money is almost gone, and the American churches are giving less because of the recession."

"And yet, the mayor, he is rich."

"His *family* is rich. All the assets are parked in trusts." Enrique had explained this often enough, the frustration he knew over his inability to do more for Harold. "He hopes that his family would offer a larger payment as a gift for our marriage."

"A dowry."

Juan asked, "Enrique will save our orphanage if you marry him?"

"Perhaps. If his family agrees. He hopes they would see the orphanage as something to hold up to the press. A symbol of where I came from. They could not do this if the orphanage were to close."

"Then why . . . ?"

Sofia admired Juan for not fully shaping the question. She reached back between the seats and took hold of his hand. "I do not know why I haven't accepted his marriage proposal. I have prayed and prayed for guidance. I have asked the Lord to take away my fears and my reluctance. But God has been silent. I have never felt farther from Him than over these past weeks. And so I wait. And I pray."

Juan declared, "I will pray with you. Every day."

She turned to offer him a from-the-heart smile. "You are more than my family. You are my friend."

They broke midway through the return journey for an early dinner in the last village before the mountains. The sunset turned the vista into a field of gold beneath an azure sky. They sat on the covered veranda and watched children play hide-and-seek around a dusty plaza. Three times Martinez rose from her chair to field phone calls, each time returning more somber. When they had finished, Consuela signaled to her partner, a taciturn man with a powerful build and fathomless eyes. He rose to his feet and spoke for the first time that day, asking Juan if he would like to inspect his guns.

When they had strolled back to the police vehicle, Consuela asked, "Do you object to my partner showing Juan his weapons?"

"Did you see his response? Juan was as delighted as any other fourteen-year-old boy."

"I need to ask you something. But I don't know how to shape my question."

"Is there a problem?" Sofia frowned.

"There is. Perhaps. Yes."

"With the orphanage?"

"Not that I am aware. Well, that is not entirely true."

"Your hesitation is scaring me."

"I spend much of my days being afraid." Consuela cast her a long look. "I would like to ask that you trust me."

"I do."

"Just like that?"

"We have known each other for how long, two years? In that time you have delivered almost twenty children to the orphanage. I see your care and concern for the little ones. I wonder at how you can remain a good person and see the things you must. Of course I trust you." Sofia fought against the constriction in her chest. "Now tell me what is so bad you are afraid to share the news. Please."

"It is not the news that is the concern. It is the need to ask related questions. Possibly."

"You need to ask me something difficult."

"I do. Yes."

"It doesn't have to do with the orphanage, your questions."

"No."

She saw the formal way Consuela sat, the cautious blankness to her gaze. It could only mean one thing. "You want to ask me about Enrique."

Consuela responded with a fraction of a nod. "Before I do this thing, I wish to share with you a confidence. By telling you this, I place two lives in your hands. My own and another."

"Are you certain you must?"

"No. But I think I should."

Sofia braced herself. "Very well. I am ready."

"I am escorting you and Juan back to Ojinaga because it offers me a cover, an excuse that I can display publicly. I have a confidential source in Ojinaga. A highly placed secret informant. It is why I was transferred from Mexico City to the state police. So that I could handle this source. She sought me out, you see. Apparently she knew my father."

"What does all this have to do with me?"

"She has been feeding me information for some time, this source. Occasionally there have been items that have made no sense. Until today, I have discounted the evidence. But it does not mean she is untrustworthy, this source. She could have been intentionally misled. It happens."

"This information, it has to do with Enrique?"

"Perhaps." Consuela's words grew very slow, as though each required great effort. "I have been very reluctant to even consider such a thing. But lately . . ."

Sofia straightened in her chair. "Ask your questions."

Instead Martinez glanced over her shoulder and shook her head. Sofia heard her partner offer Juan an ice from the sweet shop across the plaza. Martinez waited until they moved away. "Harold has been shot."

"What?"

"There was an attempt to rob Simon in the central square. Or so the police have claimed. And the report could of course be true. But Ojinaga does not normally attract the sort of violent person who would hold up a tourist in the middle of the day in the town's central market."

Her head was spinning. "Harold was shot? Or Simon?"

"Harold. Simon was with your brother in the electronics shop. A man came in demanding Simon's carryall. Harold hit him with a vase. A gun went off. Harold was grazed. He is fine."

"I must go to him. He is in the hospital?"

"No. My . . . source felt it was not safe. She took him back to the orphanage."

"I don't understand. Your source happened to be there?"

"This was no coincidence. She has been following them ever since she received word that certain people in power were showing a keen interest in Simon Orwell."

"Wait, please. If Harold is not in the hospital, how can your source be certain he is all right?"

Martinez leaned across the table. "My source is Dr. Clara."

"*No.* The bruja? Impossible."

"I assure you, it is so. And she is no witch. She is a doctor who became sickened by seeing so many young men die a senseless death. So she came to me and asked how she could help stop the violence. We trained her. Then slowly, slowly, she let it be known to the dark forces in our society that her loyalty was for sale. For six years now she has been the cartel's trusted ally in the Ojinaga city council."

Sofia felt her head swirling from multiple shocks. "What does this have to do with Enrique?"

"Most of the border regions have been placed under the watch of the military and my own task force. It is becoming hard for the cartels to operate profitably. We have heard they want to move into Ojinaga. But do so in total secrecy. Which means they must have a hidden protector."

"No," Sofia protested weakly.

"When Dr. Clara first suggested it was your fiancé, we of course discounted the possibility. But there have been hints recently. Fragments of evidence. Nothing definite, but taken all together they suggest that this may indeed be true."

She felt all her own doubts, all her hesitations, all her unanswered yearnings coalesce into one great lump at the core of her being. Sofia forced herself to say, "Ask your questions."

Martinez's face appeared carved from golden stone. "I would be grateful if you would tell me everything you possibly can about Enrique Morales."

Chapter 28

Dr. Clara pulled up tight to the orphanage gates. "Get him inside."

As Simon and Pedro helped Harold from the car, the police officer on guard duty started toward them. Dr. Clara crossed the road and spoke with him. Pedro held Harold by his good side. Simon walked on his other side, maintaining pressure on the compress bandage. Dr. Clara caught up with them as they passed the chapel. They hurried across the courtyard and into Harold's office. Simon heard the kids talking in the classrooms and hoped no one saw them.

Dr. Clara helped ease Harold into the office's one chair. "I don't have my equipment. Does the orphanage have a clinic?"

"First aid only," Pedro replied. "My sister carries a medical kit. But she is away."

"In Juárez. I know." Dr. Clara eased away the blood-soaked shirt. "Two bits of good news. First, the bleeding has almost stopped. Second, the bullet only creased the top of your shoulder. There should be no permanent damage. How do you feel?"

"Like I've been shot." Harold's tongue sounded overly thick for his mouth.

"Don't pass out on me."

Pedro demanded, "Who are you to be giving orders around here?"

She narrowed her gaze. "The one person who might save Simon's life."

Even Harold focused on that news. "What do you mean by that?"

"Later. First we need to cauterize this wound. Pedro, go to the kitchen and bring me a container of cayenne pepper."

But Pedro did not budge. "How do you know my sister is away?"

"That, too, must wait. Also I need a needle and thread. Surely your clinic has that, yes?" When Pedro still did not move, she snapped, "Go!"

Pedro rolled his eyes. "Make sure she doesn't poison him."

Simon asked, "Save me from what?"

Dr. Clara looked at him then. Really looked. Her face was flat, her features very squared off and tight. She reminded Simon of photographs he had seen of Incan Indians, an ancient race with very distinct features, very unreadable. She said, "You need to listen very carefully."

"This is coming from the woman who cheated me and lied with every breath, am I getting this right?"

Harold turned toward him then. "Simon."

"What?"

"You must finish the device."

Simon was reluctant to break away from the woman's flat gaze. "Shouldn't we talk about that later?"

"You need to listen to him," Dr. Clara said. "It all comes down to the apparatus."

"Which you tried to steal for a thousand bucks!"

Pedro rushed back into the room. "I have the pepper. And there was a surgical sewing kit in the clinic."

"Any antibiotics? Pain medication?"

"Just this bottle of Tylenol. Everything else is with Sofia."

"Then this will have to do." She lifted the pepper tin. "Hold still."

She dumped a liberal portion into the wound. Harold's roar shook the wall behind Simon. Dr. Clara chided, "The children."

Pedro hissed, "You are a witch doctor!"

"I am a specialist of modern medicine. But I have also studied ancient Mexican techniques. Cayenne pepper will clot a wound in ten seconds. It possesses antibacterial and antifungal properties. It also numbs the surrounding tissue. Watch." She threaded the curved needle and inserted it into Harold's shoulder. "Do you feel anything?"

"Everything hurts."

"But you cannot feel this needle, am I correct?" She swiftly inserted five stitches, then tied and snipped off the thread. "You'll be fine. Just drink lots of water. And rest."

"My head is pounding."

She shook out two Tylenol, poured a glass of water, then helped Harold drink. She said to Simon, "I need to give you something. Armando left you a letter."

Pedro was shocked. "Why would he leave such a message with you?"

"Armando and I were engaged to be married. He knew about other work I have been involved in. But that discussion will also have to wait." She reached into her purse. "Armando was very hurt by what you did. But he never stopped loving you. The closer he came to solving the problems with his machine, the more certain he became that he was being tracked. He feared for his life, but he refused to give up on his dream. So he reached out to you one final time."

"Praying you would finish his work." Harold's voice sounded weak but solid. "He told me this the last time we met. He prayed you would make his goals your own."

Clara handed Simon a wrinkled envelope. "He asked me to give you this."

Pedro started to ask something when the phone in Harold's office rang. The sound startled them all. He crossed to the desk in the adjoining room, spoke briefly, then returned to say, "The church in America wants to make sure I am bringing the solar lanterns. They have an event planned for tonight."

Harold said, "Of course you're going."

"I can't go while you are like this."

"We need the money. Go."

"But . . ." Pedro was halted by the sound of several vehicles pulling up in front of the gates. He ducked out, then returned to say, "More police have arrived."

Harold struggled to rise. "I'll go talk to them."

"You will stay exactly where you are. I'll speak with them myself. But it won't do any good."

Pedro demanded, "What is happening?"

"I am not yet fully certain. One thing I do know. Simon, you can trust no one outside these gates. Do you hear me? A smile can conceal great menace. Say nothing to anyone except me or Agent Martinez. And say nothing to anyone about this conversation. To the outside world, I must remain your enemy. Both our lives depend upon this."

"Your words are nonsense," Pedro complained. "Why were you after us in the city? How did you know about Sofia? Why are the police following you?"

"Your questions are valid, but you must hold them until later. Simon, are you ready?"

"For what?"

Dr. Clara's face shone with grim foreboding. "For a Mexican prison."

Pedro went out and spoke with the police who had gathered around the orphanage gates. He returned to Harold's office. He and Clara spoke in Spanish. She gave off terse replies, saying little in response to his questions. Twice she spoke his sister's name. Pedro returned to Harold's office, dialed, and cut the connection. He spoke two words in English, "Voice mail."

"Go speak to the children while they're still in class," Clara urged.

"What should I say?"

"Harold is unwell. But he will soon be fine. That is enough."

Pedro glanced at Simon. "And about the police?"

"They will be leaving soon."

When Pedro departed, Simon said, "A few answers would be nice."

"A little information will do you no good, and there is not time for more." She indicated the unopened letter. "Armando is waiting."

But Simon put the letter in his pocket. "I'm having trouble accepting you're not the enemy."

"Much in Mexico these days is not as it first appears."

"That's not much of an answer."

"Simon, I will tell you everything. But not now." She showed him an ancient's gaze. "I can't ask you to trust me. But I must ask you to be patient."

Pedro entered the office. "If I am to arrive at the Presidio church in time, I must be leaving."

"Go," Clara ordered. "You can do nothing here."

Pedro eyed the doctor with suspicion. "And Harold?"

She glanced through the bedroom's open doorway. "He is resting. Go."

Pedro crossed the courtyard and climbed into the van and drove out. The police halted him, had a long conversation, then inspected the boxes in the rear. Simon watched through the office window. He was fairly certain they had been making sure he was not hiding in the van's rear hold.

The second police car was joined by a third. They pulled in nose to nose, blocking off the entrance. But otherwise they did not disturb anyone. Clara announced she had to go to the clinic. When Simon started to demand some answers, she halted him with an upraised hand. "As soon as it is safe to talk, you will know. Until then, go with God."

Simon was still trying to find a response as she crossed the courtyard, spoke with the police, climbed into her car, and drove away.

Simon fought against a sudden urge to scale the rear wall and flee. He returned to the classroom and tried to work but found it impossible. The heat congealed into a lump at the core of his being, so vast and heavy he had difficulty breathing around it. Finally he picked up Harold's book and returned to the director's office.

He heard Harold's breathing from the back bedroom, slow and steady. Simon settled into the chair by the piano and found his place. The words on the page flitted in and out of his brain. Even so, it was comforting, as though he could hear Harold talking to him. Of a moment beyond this one. Of a future with meaning. Of hope.

Simon did not find peace in the pages, or even answers. But he did find patience. And just then, it was enough.

He was still there an hour later. More cars pulled up before the gates. Harold woke to the sound of car doors slamming shut, two, three, four, five.

Harold called through the open bedroom door, "What is it?"

Simon's chair was positioned so he could look through the office window and see the front gates. "Two more cops. Sofia. Juan. Enrique. The woman agent, what's her name, Martinez. And Pedro's back. He looks angry."

"Come help me up."

Simon entered the bedroom. "Clara said you needed to rest."

"I don't have strength to argue, son."

Simon gripped Harold's good arm and took most of the old man's weight. At Harold's direction, Simon slipped a shirt through the free arm and draped it around his shoulder. Then he supported Harold through the office and out to the veranda. As soon as they came into view, Pedro shouted, "How *could* you?"

Simon realized the assistant town manager was addressing him. Enrique demanded, "Who assembled these lanterns?"

"Me and the kids."

Harold demanded weakly, "What is going on here?"

Enrique reached behind him, and an officer handed over a solar lantern. He popped off the lid and turned it upside down. A plastic bag filled with white powder fell to the ground. A rustle of shock and indrawn breath flitted through the courtyard. Every kid knew what that plastic bag contained.

Enrique said, "Pedro is fortunate our friends on the police were tipped off about this shipment before he arrived at the border."

Pedro covered his face and bent over at the waist. His sister rushed to comfort him. Sofia gripped her brother by the shoulders and turned an angry face toward Simon. "Is this your deep, dark secret? That you used us to smuggle drugs?"

"I didn't do this." The protest was feeble, weak even before it was formed. "Pedro, listen to me. Harold, you have to believe me, I didn't—"

"Why don't you tell everyone why you really came to Mexico?" Enrique's voice rang in the silence. "Could it be for the same reason you went to prison in America?"

Simon watched from a great distance as two of the uniformed police moved toward him. The manacles glittered in the afternoon light. He opened his mouth, but the power of speech was gone.

"Should you tell our friends what you did to the professor? How you repaid his trust?" Even Enrique's outrage carried a polished quality. "Harold, do you know why Professor Vasquez left MIT? Shall I tell them, Simon? Because Simon *betrayed* him."

Simon wanted to speak, to explain, to object. But his throat was clogged by too much shame. Not even when the police swung him around and snicked the cuffs in too tightly could he speak. The officers gripped his arms and pressed him forward. Across the courtyard and through the gates and into the waiting car.

The officer slipped into the front seat and started the motor. Simon took a shaky breath and did not look up as they drove away. His one coherent thought was that cop cars all smelled the same.

Chapter 29

Sofia and Pedro helped Harold back into bed and propped him up with pillows. Sofia felt as though she observed everything from a great distance. She saw Juan move to his customary position, though his face was streaked with anxious tears. Pedro's features were creased by the very same concerns. The three most important men in her life, all wracked with pain and helpless worry.

Enrique planted himself in Harold's office. He spoke on the office phone, barking unnecessarily at the police. Then he paced. His own features were creased. He looked tired. The sun was rising. For the first time in years, there would be no morning chapel. The orphanage was quiet, the kids hiding in their dormitories. Pedro sat hunched in Harold's chair. He stared at his hands, clenching and unclenching them on the desk. She wanted to go to him. Share with her brother what she had learned from Agent Martinez. But it would have to wait.

Then Pedro looked at her. A swift lifting of his head just as Enrique completed another circuit and turned his back to them both. Brother to sister. One quick glance.

It was enough for her to be certain that Pedro already knew about Enrique. How he knew was not important. Because the message in Pedro's gaze was very clear.

She had to be careful. They all did.

Pedro said, "It doesn't add up. Where could Simon have gotten the drugs?"

Sofia remained silent until Pedro tightened his gaze, a silent urging. Sofia said slowly, "I can't believe how dumb we were."

Enrique wheeled about. As though . . . Sofia had the distinct impression that he had been needing for them to speak. Like an actor waiting for his line. He said, "Has anyone checked his room?"

Pedro slowly shook his head. "Not since we returned to the orphanage."

Sofia said to Juan, "Go bring down everything in the guestroom."

Enrique said, "And from the classroom where Simon worked on the device. That is also where he assembled the lanterns, no? Go bring everything he has touched."

When the boy bounded away, Pedro said softly, "Simon played us for fools. Now the whole orphanage is at risk."

"Not necessarily." Enrique patted Sofia's shoulder. "I already have people working on damage control."

She forced herself not to flinch away. "Thank you, Enrique."

"Just do what I say and everything will be fine."

From somewhere deep inside there came the strength to smile. "What would we do without you?"

Juan pattered down the stairs and dumped an armload on the desk. "All the clothes were loaned to him by Harold." Then he was off again, his footsteps racing across the courtyard.

They gathered in tightly. Pedro reached for Harold's book. He opened it at the page marked by Simon's pencil. Sofia realized Simon had worked his way through two-thirds of the book.

Juan's load was heavier this second time. He dumped the apparatus and the carryall and a plastic bag from the electronics store on Harold's desk. Pedro said quietly, "Thank you, Juan. You are a big help. As always."

For once, Juan's smile did not light up the room. "Is it really true, Señor Simon did a bad thing?"

"Very bad," Enrique said, his tone funereal.

Sofia forced herself not to argue, though the tragic disappointment in Juan's face made that even harder still. Enrique was busy stuffing everything on the desk into the duffel. "The police tell me they have the gunman in custody. He fits the description Pedro gave me of the man at the professor's house. You will go down and make an identification, please."

Juan asked, "What will happen to Simon?"

"That is for the authorities." Enrique hefted the duffel and turned for the door. "He will be dealt with in the appropriate manner."

Sofia bit down on her protest.

"Now you must excuse me, my dear. I have a dozen things that cannot wait. A hundred."

Though the effort seemed to rob her legs of strength, she returned his embrace. "Good bye, Enrique. And thank you."

Enrique went to each of them in turn, offering a smooth farewell, even checking in on the slumbering Harold before slipping into the night.

Only when the mayor's car drove away did the voice emerge from the bedroom's shadows. "Somebody come in here and help me up."

Sofia found it piercingly sad to aid the man who had so often in the past been there to help and strengthen her. As they walked into the bedroom, Pedro started, "Harold—"

"Son, I don't have the time or the energy to deal with your worries. Just know that I share them."

"What are you going to do?"

He waited until Sofia had helped him across the office and through the doorway to respond, as though he was intent upon giving them no chance to object. "The same thing I've been doing for thirty years. You're going to drive me to the prison, so I can be there for a young man in his dark hour. Simon needs to be reminded that he is not alone."

Chapter 30

They brought Simon to Ojinaga's main police station, a nondescript building in the valley between the city and Boys' Town. They led him into a windowless back room and chained his wrists to a table. Maybe the Mexican system was different. Maybe he didn't need to be officially booked. Maybe it was normal to lock a foreigner in a holding room for hours on end. The ceiling light buzzed faintly. As though hope and a future were words that belonged to other people. As though he had run away one time too often.

Simon stared at the whitewashed metal door. There was a bitter logic to the situation. As though he had driven two thousand miles and endured a brutal week, just so he could arrive at this point. The fate he had deserved all along.

His mind locked down upon the night Vasquez shared with Simon his breakthrough. The night Vasquez sketched out his great concept on the damp bar napkins. The night he presented to Simon the very real prospect of finding personal definitions for words like *purpose* and *destiny*.

That particular night, trouble had shown up in the form of two very bad men. They arrived about an hour after Vasquez departed. One sat at the stool Vasquez vacated. The other stood to Simon's left. It was their usual approach. They scared Simon. They always had. They were frightening people. It was nothing they said or did. They rarely stayed long and never spoke more than a few words. But they carried with them an aura of danger. That evening two women sidled over, smiling and available. Totally blind to the men's treacherous nature. Or perhaps they were drawn to it. Like moths to a flame. Like Simon.

The men dismissed the ladies with a word, then told Simon to join them in the alley behind the bar. Simon waited for his normal break time, then exited the bar by the rear door. The pair was seated in their Cadillac, waiting patiently, as usual. Simon had been surprised that two men like these would even bother with supplying a small-time dealer like him with a few packets of class-A drugs.

The two men came straight to the point. "That guy who just left the bar."

"Professor Vasquez."

"Him. We want into his lab."

Simon had been utterly shocked. It was the last thing he expected to hear. "Vasquez is a good man."

"Did we ask you about the man's credentials? No we did not."

The other guy spoke for the first time that night. He rarely opened his mouth, which was a good thing because to Simon his voice carried the sibilant promise of ruin. "We're not gonna hurt the prof."

The first guy went on. "The professor's lab connects to the science building's main supply center. They got two things we need: a professional-grade centrifuge and some chemicals we can't get on the open market. We used to be able to, but not anymore. The feds are cracking down."

The other guy turned around. "And this is not a request."

Simon knew this was where it had been headed, ever since he had accepted their first packet of weed. He also knew he had no choice. "I can do that."

"I know you can," the man replied, turning back around. "No muss, no fuss. You open the door, you code the alarm. We go in, we leave. Simple."

Later that night, Simon had done it. But it had not been simple.

The police held him overnight. They pushed hard enough to terrify him with the prospect of prison. They showed him photographs of the duo and tagged him as having met with them that night. In the bar. And in the alley. Revealing in the process that they had been keeping the bar under surveillance. Assuring him that somebody was going down hard.

They then asked if the professor had been in on this. Offering Simon his only out. Which he took. Without an instant's hesitation. And he'd been paying for it ever since.

Simon lowered his forehead to the cold metal table. He yearned for the power to turn back the clock. But he couldn't. He felt as though he had already spent a year trapped inside this dungeon. Not the one where he sat. The one he carried with him everywhere he went.

If only he'd been able to do the right thing. Just that one time. Instead of taking the easy way out. Again. And be gnawed at by guilt ever since. Until he arrived here. In a windowless Mexican holding cell. Until he almost welcomed whatever fate awaited him beyond that metal door.

Finally the lock rattled and the door creaked open. A lone policeman stepped inside, wearing a white shirt and dark trousers. Simon recognized him as Enrique's driver. The man was rapier thin, with a pencil moustache and the cold smile of a killer. He addressed Simon in rapid-fire Spanish.

"Sorry, man. I don't understand the lingo. But you already know that, don't you."

The man responded by holding out his hands, wanting Simon to see how his knuckles were ridged with old scars. His eyes were terrifying. They had no bottom whatsoever.

Simon swallowed hard. "This isn't about getting answers, is it. You already know I don't have any."

The man pulled a leather sap from his pocket and patted it against his palm. The sap made a sickening sound. He spoke a single word, a soft sibilant noise. He started forward, the sap still flicking back and forth.

Then the door opened a second time.

Clearly the man had not expected this. He turned and barked.

Agent Martinez entered the room, her gold badge open and extended. She replied and jerked her head at the door.

The policeman liked that even less. He snarled a response.

Martinez called out. A man stepped into the doorway, a gold badge dangling from his belt. The second agent stepped up alongside Martinez and spoke. He was very quiet. He did not need to be loud to get his message across.

Enrique's driver burned Simon with his glare, then he slipped from the room and was gone. Martinez said something to the other agent, who nodded and followed the officer out. She walked over and unlocked Simon from the table. "I need you to come with me."

"Are we getting out of here?"

"Not yet. But I will make sure you are safe."

"Dr. Clara said I should trust you."

"She is correct. I need to lock your hands behind you again. Stand up and turn around, please."

His legs were so shaky, he had to lean against the table. "That was Enrique's driver."

"I am perfectly aware of who that man is."

"He's gonna come for me the instant you take off."

"Which is why my partner is arranging for you to be placed in solitary. He will stay on duty all night outside your cell."

As she led him from the room, Simon said, "Those drugs they found in the lanterns were planted."

"Those drugs are not the point."

Simon stopped and looked at her. "That's exactly what Vasquez would have said."

"Vasquez. Yes. The professor is certainly part of our puzzle." Martinez gripped his arm and propelled him down the hall. "Come."

"He was murdered."

"Of course he was murdered. And that is also not the point."

Simon felt like his mind had grown wings, flying high and free, liberated by the fact that he was still able to draw an easy breath. "We need to figure out why somebody went to all that trouble. Murdering him. Trashing his place. Luring me down. Trapping me on the highway. And it's all tied to Enrique, isn't it."

"Very good, Simon. These are precisely the questions you should be asking."

"Enrique wants my device as well as the professor's."

"He does not just want it. He has it. He packed up all your belongings and left the orphanage soon after you did."

"He wanted it enough to arrange for me to wind up here and send somebody to do me in."

"In fact, he sent two people. But that must wait a moment. First we must concentrate on the issue at hand."

Simon forced his mind to move beyond the manacles and the station and the beating that was not happening. "We need to know where Enrique took the devices."

"Another good question. And the answer is, that is why I did not arrive sooner."

"You followed him."

"From the orphanage to the technical school." Martinez nodded.

"He's going to try and have somebody else make the machine work. Somebody he controls."

"That is what I am thinking. Enrique waited until now to order his thug to work you over." She led him around a corner. "Which means he has made it work and doesn't need you anymore."

"Impossible," Simon declared flatly.

Martinez pulled him to a halt and turned him to face her. "Explain."

"Vasquez and I have been working on this for nine months. I still don't know how to control the surge problem. Nobody starting from scratch is going to solve that problem in a couple of hours."

Martinez's response was cut off by her partner, who rounded the corner up ahead, called to her, and pointed at his watch. Martinez started them forward. "Then we are missing something."

"You got that right."

"Something vital. It is up to you to find out what Enrique intends."

She led him past the main guard station. Her partner spoke to the duty officer, who unlocked the steel door. Simon realized they were entering the jail proper and decided there was no need to protest. But either he trusted her or he was dead meat.

Simon spotted Enrique's driver. He lounged behind a counter staffed by several bored prison guards. He watched Simon with a flat, unblinking gaze.

Martinez tugged on Simon's arm. "I am going to take you to the main holding cell. This is where you would have been placed after the beating. I want you to take a look around and see if you recognize anyone."

"Mind if I ask why?"

"Of course not. Trust goes two ways, no? It is unlikely that the officer would have killed you himself. There would be too much risk. To soften up a Yanqui drug runner is one thing. Murder, that is another."

Simon swallowed against the queasy feeling. "I told you I didn't—"

"And I have said, Señor Simon, that is not the issue."

He forced himself to steady up. "They planted a murderer in the pen?"

She gave him a look of grim approval. "Let us go and see."

As soon as the long cell came into view, Simon exclaimed, "That's him!"

"Which one?"

"The guy in the leather coat. He's the one who attacked me on the road! And again at the professor's house! And he shot Harold!"

Martinez spoke to the guard, who reached for the prison roster.

Enrique's driver chose that moment to step forward and snarl a warning. The guard hesitated in the process of handing over the book. Martinez's partner stepped between the driver and Martinez. It was impossible for Simon to tell which man possessed the more deadly gaze.

Martinez turned so the guard could see the roster with her. The guard studied the pages, frowned, then spoke to another man seated at the desk in the back of the duty alcove. The second man shrugged. Enrique's driver snarled once more. This time, Martinez's partner snarled back.

Martinez shut the roster and handed it back to the guard,

who was now sweating and speaking rapidly. Martinez said, "It seems there is no record of this man. No name, no reason for his arrest. Nothing."

"Is that normal?"

In reply, Martinez spoke to her partner. The man drew his gun and moved to where he could cover both the bearded man and Enrique's driver. The bearded attacker bounded to his feet and began pacing the cell and shouting angrily. Martinez pulled Simon farther down the hall. She spoke to the perspiring guard, who jerked off another salute, snappy this time.

Martinez positioned Simon by the side wall, placed herself between him and the cell door, and drew her own weapon. The hunter's rage echoed through the concrete chambers. He moved like a bearded tiger, bounding around the cage, lashing the air with his fists and his words.

The prison guard returned with three others. One carried manacles attached to a leather belt. The other two men held Tasers at the ready. They yelled through the bars. Instantly the other prisoners shifted to the very back of the holding cell. The guards entered the cell and locked the door behind them. Martinez cocked her pistol and held it in two hands, her aim swinging back and forth. From Enrique's driver to the prisoner.

The bearded man's rage grew fiercer still as they fitted him into the manacles. Two guards gripped the cuffed man and led him out of the cell and down the hall toward the entrance, followed by Martinez's partner.

Only when they were gone did Martinez speak with the remaining guard, who led them down the hall and unlocked a solid steel door. Martinez holstered her weapon and uncuffed

Simon. "I will remain outside until my partner returns. Then I will transfer the man you see to a more-secure position."

"How long do I have to stay here?"

"As long as it takes for me to arrange the necessary papers. But I will not sleep until it is done."

Simon could think of nothing to say except, "Thank you."

"You are welcome." She started to swing the door shut, then said, "You understand, what I said about needing to work out the puzzle."

"Like you, I won't sleep until it's done."

She liked that enough to smile. "There is a chance that time is against us. Dr. Clara, she insists this is so. She says something very big is happening tomorrow. And your apparatus is important to this secret plan."

"And I'm telling you it won't work."

"Answers, Señor Simon. We need them." As she swung the door shut, her last word was, "Desperately."

Chapter 31

The bunk was nothing more than a cement slab jutting from the wall. A scummy sink dripped constantly. Simon pulled the professor's letter from his pocket, sat on the fetid mattress, reread the words, and felt the past come alive. Vasquez was there in the room with him. Simon could hear his voice speak the letter's final words, "Seek and you shall find. Use the key to open your world. Find God and the true path to your full potential. I love you always."

Simon did not notice he was weeping until he heard the cell door being unlocked, and he found it difficult to bring the newcomer into focus. Harold entered. "Hello, son."

Simon rose slowly to his feet, moving like an old man. He accepted Harold's one-armed embrace as Martinez entered and set down a metal chair. She waited until Harold released Simon, then said, "Ten minutes."

Simon helped Harold ease himself into the chair and said, "The drugs they found. I didn't do it."

"I believe you, son. But that doesn't matter. I'd still be here anyway. You want to tell me about it?"

"About what?"

"Whatever burden that you're just aching to set down."

So he did. The secrets just poured out. The longer he spoke, the more Simon was convinced that Vasquez's final hope would have been for Simon to stop running and face the hardest truth of all. Himself.

When he went quiet and Harold asked if he wanted to pray, Simon knew he had been waiting for this all along. The chance to say, "Yes."

As Harold finished, Martinez rattled the lock and opened the door. She helped Harold rise, then carried the chair back outside. Harold said, "I'm here for you, son. And so is Jesus." Harold pulled a small Bible from his jacket pocket. "This might be helpful."

Chapter 32

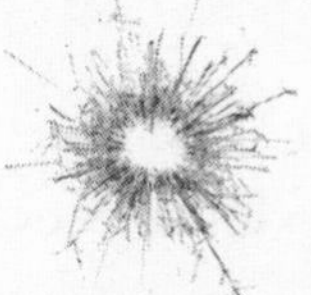

Sofia sat on the veranda outside Harold's office, her arm draped over Pedro's shoulders. She ached with her brother. His pain was hers. As it had been all their lives.

He moaned, "How could I have been so blind?"

She huffed a laugh she did not feel. "You have stolen the words from my own mind."

"The signs were there all along."

"I hope you are wrong, brother. I would hate to think I willfully missed seeing the truth about Enrique."

"I so wanted his promises to be real."

"We all did. It is the myth of Mexican strength. Trust others to be powerful for us." She stroked her brother's back. He was so strong, this one. Sofia felt the love rise up inside her. "I am so proud of you."

"How can you say that? Especially now, when I've allowed myself to play the mayor's fool?"

She knew he did not want a response. Pedro was merely giving voice to his sorrow. He would recover, and soon. He had to. They all needed him to be strong.

Dr. Clara was inside with Harold. Martinez stood by the front gates, talking on her radio. For once, Juan was not in his customary position, at the edge of everything, watching. Instead he had taken on the role of helping around the orphanage, filling in for Harold. He left the dining hall hand in hand with Gabriella.

The little girl was coming along nicely, thanks to Juan and Harold and the other children. Sofia made a mental note that it would soon be time for her to speak with the child, introduce her to Harold's teachings, one young woman to another.

She sought some way to draw her brother out of his remorse and into the present. But the only words that came to mind were, "I can't help but worry about Simon."

Pedro wiped his face. "Martinez assures us he is safe."

"I was talking about us."

Pedro straightened and looked at her. "Us, as in, Simon with the orphanage?" He showed a glimmer of a smile. "Or us, as in you and him?"

She could not meet his gaze. "I, too, have been willfully blind. I tried to argue away the fact that I did not love Enrique. The idea of a partner who could help me fulfill my ambition to assist all our country's orphans was too alluring."

"And Simon?"

"Simon challenges everything I believe in. Even so, I have feelings for him. Genuine, deep, profound." Her heart swelled around the confession. "These feelings challenge my plan to live in sacrifice. Simon knows nothing about sacrifice. He lives for nothing but himself."

Pedro's voice strengthened. "He is changing. We have seen him change."

"But he is still Simon."

"He is also the loneliest man I have ever known. Now that Vasquez is gone, Simon has no one."

"Another orphan." She found it hard to draw a full breath. "In this moment when no one else is there for him, I feel like . . ."

"He needs you."

She studied her brother's face. "Do you really think this?"

His smile grew stronger. "My sister is asking me for advice? Has the world tilted on its axis?"

She bit her lip but could not keep the words from emerging. "That is how it feels to me."

Dr. Clara opened the bedroom door and studied them for a moment. To Sofia it seemed that the doctor's gaze held a haunted quality. "Harold is ready for you."

As Pedro crossed to the door and called to Martinez, Sofia asked, "How is he?"

"Tired. But the wound is healing well." Dr. Clara hesitated, then asked, "You know what I have been doing?"

"Martinez told me some of it." Sofia still had difficulty believing the doctor had been serving the antidrug group in secret. But she had been fooled by so much for so long. "I thought wrong of you. For that I apologize."

"I have done many wrong things."

"For all the right reasons, I'm sure."

"In the daylight, I can say those words and be satisfied." Dr. Clara nodded a greeting as Agent Martinez entered the office. "But at night . . ."

"The tainted life is harder to accept." Harold's voice came softly through the open door. "The justifications for all the wrong actions don't ring true anymore."

The four of them entered the bedroom together. Dr. Clara resumed her seat by Harold's bed. "I just wanted to make the killings stop. I just wanted to help."

"And you did."

"But at what cost? Look at me. I am reviled. Hated. Called a witch to my face by the people I yearn to help. And in the dark hours I think they are right to say what they do."

"You have learned a crucial lesson," Harold said. "Corruption is a virus. You cannot remain just a little bit infected. But you either fight it off, or it takes over."

"It is too late."

"I'm sorry, Clara. But that is just not true." Harold's gaze swiveled to where Sofia stood by the door.

Sofia offered, "Perhaps you and I can discuss this?"

The eyes that turned to her held a desperate hunger. "You will help me?"

"We can start tonight, if you like."

"Now we need to turn our attention to the other matter." Harold eased himself up slightly in the bed. "First, can you tell us how you knew?"

"Suspected," the doctor corrected.

"If we had known for certain, if there had been evidence, we would have arrested Enrique Morales long ago," Martinez said.

Dr. Clara went on, "Investigating criminal activity is much like hunting for an illness. A doctor is trained to scrutinize any number of symptoms and find how they interlink. Gradually a pattern emerges, until a diagnosis was made."

Harold nodded. "And your conclusion was . . . ?"

"The criminals never left. They simply became more hidden."

"That was the first point," Martinez agreed. "And the second was, someone very powerful was behind this masquerade."

"It was only since Armando's murder that we even considered that Enrique might indeed be the puppet master."

"We trusted him too much," Pedro muttered.

"We have every reason to," Martinez replied. "He was masterful at burnishing his good image and using it to hide all manners of evil."

"What tipped you off?"

"Many crimes have been linked to a man only known as Jefe," Clara said.

"He works through a bearded assailant that Simon has identified," Martinez said. "We have a possible link between this attacker and Enrique. And something more. It appears that the cartel run by El Noche is moving into Chihuahua state. They now almost control Juárez. We have two undercover agents inside his organization. They tell us that Ojinaga is to become their new center of operations into the United States."

Sofia felt her body grow cold. "If this is true and Enrique is indeed the culprit you seek . . ."

"It means El Noche is tied to Enrique." Pedro finished for her.

"There are hints of a major undertaking about to take place here." Martinez went on. "Something big enough to bring the cartel's leader himself to our city."

"When?"

"Tomorrow night."

Harold looked from one woman to the other. "What are we going to do about it?"

Martinez looked at Sofia. "I have an idea. But it requires your help."

"Of course."

As Martinez described her plan, Sofia gripped her arms across her middle. It was an action from her childhood, a means of keeping all her emotions and fears trapped inside. Her voice sounded small to her own ears. "I will do this thing."

Chapter 33

The month after Enrique had been elected mayor of Ojinaga, he had transformed a windowless stockroom into a small conference room. The walls now held paintings from his personal collection. A lovely silk carpet adorned the floor. A rosewood table was surrounded by five swivel chairs. He used the main conference chamber for larger meetings. This room was reserved for private discussions, and was swept twice each day for listening devices.

Enrique sat in his customary seat at the head of the table. "I have the professor's apparatus."

The man on the other end of the phone had the most curious voice Enrique had ever heard. El Noche's words sounded like wind through desert-dry cane, a parched rattle that never rose nor fell. "You are certain it works?"

"As positive as I can be without turning it on. Which we cannot do for two reasons. First, each time it has been turned on, the apparatus has shorted out. My technician says it is the most complicated piece of equipment he has ever seen. He could not possibly repair it by tomorrow. But he has checked it thoroughly and assures me that every component is in place and functioning."

"And the Yanqui scientist?"

It was the question Enrique had been dreading. "He is being taken care of."

"Is he dead?"

"Not yet. There have been . . . complications."

"Explain."

"The scientist is in solitary lockdown. Not even the prison guards are permitted into his chamber. My man Carlos, the one who allowed himself to be arrested, has vanished. I assume he is under control of the federals. Everything points to Agent Martinez."

There came the rattling hiss, the man's one expression of rage. "I want you to erase that woman."

Despite himself, Enrique shivered and sweated both. "Of course. It will be done."

"And the Yanqui."

"As soon as he is released." Enrique hesitated, then said, "Perhaps we should postpone."

"That is impossible. Things on the other side of the border are in place. There can be no delay. It is not permitted. Are we clear?"

"Of course, I was simply—"

But the man had already cut the connection. Enrique remained where he was, breathing heavily.

When he emerged from the conference room, he was shocked

to discover Pedro seated in the chair closest to the room's entrance. Pedro almost never came to his office. Their meetings generally took place in the hallways, or outside a restaurant, or before Enrique entered some meeting. Pedro disliked being in the company of power.

"Pedro! How long have you been out here?"

The man looked beyond exhausted. He leaned his head against the wall, just beside the door leading into the conference room. His eyes flickered once, twice, then opened slowly. "Forgive me, Padron. It is these problems involving the orphanage. May I have a word?"

His secretary said, "You are late for the council meeting."

"Two minutes, Padron. Please."

It was so rare for Pedro to ask for anything, Enrique found himself unable to do what was foremost in his mind, which was to determine whether the man had heard anything through the wall. "What is it?"

"I need to take a few days off. Just until Harold is better. Someone must run things at the orphanage. I cannot do that and my job for the city."

"What about your sister?"

"She tells me she is already too busy, between her work and campaigning with you. Your next few days are to be your last swing through Ojinaga, yes? Sofia says you have told her it is crucial that she appear at your side."

"Of course you must do what is required, though we will miss you."

"The doctor tells me Harold should be able to manage by next week."

Enrique remembered, "Harold was to speak at my campaign event this afternoon. Even if he does not speak, have him join me on the podium, yes?"

Pedro shrugged. He fumbled with his hands in the manner of a peasant twisting his hat brim. Enrique detested such signs of submission. Pedro said, "I will pass on your message, Padron."

Agent Martinez did not come for Simon until after dark. He emerged from the station and walked down the street, drinking deep of the cool dry air.

She drove him back to the orphanage. But instead of halting by the main gates, Martinez turned down the alley that ran behind the square. "Wait here."

A few minutes later, Pedro rapped on his window. "Come with me."

Pedro led him up a set of stairs and into an apartment. "This is Sofia's. We will stay here tonight. She is sleeping in the orphanage guestroom."

The place held a sweet fragrance, an invisible presence that surrounded and comforted. "Can I take a shower?"

"Of course. Are you hungry?"

"Starving."

"I will go to the restaurant down the street."

Simon turned the water hot enough to scald and remained there until the shower turned cold. He found more of the simple clothes laid out for him on the bed: T-shirt and drawstring pants. As Simon dressed, Pedro returned with two steaming plates. Over dinner Pedro described how Enrique had fooled them. Simon ate and listened, until exhaustion started rising up like waves.

Pedro must have noticed for he said, "Go and sleep. I will clean up."

"You haven't finished telling me everything."

"I could talk for days and not be finished. Sleep well, my friend."

Simon woke to the first pale light of dawn. He rose from the bed and padded through the living room. Pedro snored softly on the sofa. Simon eased open the balcony door and stepped outside. The air was bitingly cold, but he did not mind. The feeling of liberation, of a freedom far beyond having stepped outside the jail, was exquisite.

Sofia's Bible lay open on the little coffee table. He settled into the balcony's lone chair and picked up the Book. He liked the sense of connection, both to her and to the God he hoped he might someday know as well as she did.

The Book was open to John, the pages filled with her writing. Her script was surprisingly feminine, with carefully looped letters and little hearts drawn beside certain passages. He read several verses, tracing his hand over her notes. Then he raised his eyes to the dawn.

The soft pearl tones beckoned to him. The peaks gleamed with a jewel-like luminescence. The razor edges held the power of divine artwork. It seemed to Simon as though he could read God's script upon the distant stone.

Simon heard Pedro shuffling around inside and knew it was time to move. But first he had to acknowledge the moment. It was fitting that his first solitary prayer be in response to the work and the life he had spent so long running from.

It was just as Harold had said. To be successful, Simon had to accept that he could not do it alone. The challenge, the responsibility, the potential—it was all too much. Unless he accepted help from the divine hand.

Simon bowed his head over the Book in his lap.

Pedro returned after breakfast with a plate for Simon and the news that the police was no longer guarding the orphanage gates, and Harold wanted to speak with him. After eating, Simon followed Pedro across the empty plaza and through the portals. Simon sat by the open window and watched as Pedro helped Harold ease into the chair behind his desk. "You should stay in bed," Sofia scolded.

"Clara said I could get up. Besides which, I've got a speech to write."

Pedro stood over Harold as the orphanage director used his good hand to pull out pen and paper. "You're sure you want to do this?"

"You've known me all your life, son. The only way to stop corruption is to meet it head-on."

"But you've been injured."

"I'm feeling well enough to be impatient," Harold insisted.

Sofia huffed. "You've been impatient your entire life. One small bullet isn't going to change that."

Juan arrived bearing steaming mugs of strong black tea. Simon hated how the kid would not meet his gaze. There was no greater conviction, he decided, than not living up to a good kid's expectations.

Harold must have noticed the silent exchange, for he said, "Juan, look at me. Son, we have all fallen short. You understand these words?"

"Yes, *Abuelo.*"

"Simon is our friend. We accept and we forgive. He is striving toward the light. We will help him onward."

Juan shot Simon a quick glance, lightning fast, but long enough to reveal a world of hurt. And hope. "Yes, Abuelo."

Simon felt the power behind the words crash upon him like a wave. They knew the best and the worst of who he was, they knew what he had done and what he was capable of, and they accepted him. He fought against the tide of emotions and listened as Pedro described what he had overheard Enrique say through the wall.

Pedro concluded, "Enrique said he was certain the devices would do what they wanted. His technicians at the university spent all last night checking them out. He cannot test it because each time the device has been used, it has shorted out. But he is certain they will work."

"I don't understand," Sofia said. "Enrique has both devices, he does not dare test them, and yet he claims they are ready? That makes no sense."

Pedro shrugged. "That is what he said."

"Actually, it makes all the sense in the world," Simon countered.

Sofia said. "Either the device will work or it won't."

"If what I'm thinking is correct, as far as Enrique is concerned, the device works perfectly." Simon turned to Pedro. "Who was Enrique speaking to?"

"I could not hear every word. But it sounded like . . ."

"A bad man."

Pedro sighed. "Very bad."

"Would this bad man be interested in giving free power to the masses?"

"Impossible," Pedro replied flatly. "The cartels have invested heavily in the power company."

"They bribe corrupt members of our government," Sofia confirmed. "They pad contracts and they falsify inspections."

"They would fight anyone giving free electricity like they do other drug cartels," Harold said.

"Tooth and nail," Pedro agreed.

Simon nodded. "Which means this was never about supplying cheap power to Mexico's poor."

"But what else is there?" Sofia demanded.

"The blackout," Simon replied.

Pedro frowned, and started to protest, then he noticed Harold's smile. "You understand this?"

"It's brilliant." He waved his good hand. "Tell them, son."

"The blackout didn't just cut out power," Simon said. "It shut down *everything*. Even the professor's own laptop. Power, phones, everything went down."

Sofia asked, "What difference does that make?"

"What if this effect carried all the way to the border? What if it impacts everything that uses an electrical current? Radar, communication, surveillance, the works?"

"The cartels could come and go at will," Pedro said.

"There have been three blackouts," Simon reminded them. "The first time when Vasquez applied the four frequencies. The second time when he recorded the effect on his laptop. And the third time when we were up by the transformers."

Harold nodded slowly. "Our foes obviously learned from their allies in the border police about problems at the customs station."

"Nobody else put two and two together," Simon agreed. "Not yet, anyway."

Agent Martinez stepped through the open doorway and added, "Which explains why they are so determined to make you vanish."

Consuela settled on the window ledge and listened with grim intent as they summarized their discussion. As he spoke, Simon saw what had before been supposition crystallize into a very real threat. Martinez confirmed this by saying, "Carlos, the man who attacked Simon and shot Harold, has been sprung from federal prison."

Simon felt the tension and fear slice through the room. "How is that possible?"

"Welcome to Mexico," Pedro said.

Sofia asked, "Should we go ahead with our plans?"

"Nothing has changed," Harold insisted quietly.

Martinez looked from face to face, waiting for further objections. But Sofia merely compressed her lips and frowned at the floor by her feet. She said, "Simon needs to relocate, in case they are still hunting for him."

"He can stay in my apartment," Sofia offered.

"I have contacted my allies on the other side of the border," Consuela told him. "They are working on temporary papers. You should be able to travel north tomorrow."

Sofia's head jerked up. She stared at him in mute appeal. Simon had no idea what to say, except, "All right."

Sofia wrapped her arms about her middle and went back to studying the floor by her feet. Pedro watched this exchange, and showed Simon a huge grin.

Martinez motioned towards the entrance. "We should go."

"Just a second, there's something more." Simon turned to Juan. "Did Vasquez leave something for me?"

The boy's eyes went round. "He said I should speak of it only if you asked. And only if you gave me the right . . . I forget the word."

Simon offered, "The right code?"

"Yes! That was it, the code!"

Simon grinned at the abrupt return of the boy's natural ebullience. "Was it 8:12?"

Juan's smile returned full force. "You wait right here!"

Sofia demanded, "Where are you going?"

Juan called over his shoulder, "Uncle Vasquez, he wrote a secret in my Bible!"

Chapter 34

Simon returned to Sofia's apartment and worked on the information he had found in Juan's Bible. In the plaza below, preparations were well underway for Enrique's political rally. Workers strung bunting along the broad stairs rising from the plaza to the church. A podium was erected on the church patio and chairs set in careful rows beneath the trees. Simon worked at the narrow dining table, from where he could see everything and still remain hidden within the apartment's shadows.

Martinez watched him fill one page after another with calculations and asked, "The professor left you a key to making the device work?"

"We'll know when the device gets switched on. The professor never had a chance to test his calculations. But from what I can work through on paper, I'd say yes. He's found the answer."

Martinez glanced out the balcony doors as they tested the loudspeakers strung from the plaza's trees. "Enrique holds the rally here to reach out to the poor and the working class. In this quarter everyone knows and respects Harold."

Simon heard the concern in her voice and asked, "Will he be safe?"

"I've got my own people stationed around the plaza."

Beyond the balcony, workers rimmed the plaza with flags and banner-size posters of their mayor. By the time Simon put away his calculations, Enrique Morales smiled down from everywhere.

Music blared from loudspeakers, and the people came from everywhere except the orphanage. The gates were open, but inside everything remained still. Tightly contained.

The first VIPs arrived, shaking hands as they moved through the crowd. They climbed the stairs just as Enrique's dark-windowed SUV pulled up below Sofia's balcony. Simon remained well back from the open French doors, hidden inside the apartment shadows. Agent Martinez stood where the kitchen cabinets met the living room's rear wall.

Simon watched as a smiling Enrique waved to the crowd and waited while Sofia rose from the SUV. She appeared to have shrunk down inside herself. "I wish she wasn't doing this."

"It is the right thing. We must try to keep Enrique from becoming spooked." Martinez glanced at him. "I wonder why Sofia wanted you to see this."

"She probably wants me to see Harold at his best."

Martinez showed him a rare smile. "Sure. I bet that's it."

Enrique and Sofia climbed the stairs to raucous applause. A portly man with a bright sash draped over his suit shouted into the microphone. Simon asked Martinez, "What's he saying?"

"Blah, blah. Politician speech. Same in every language."

The portly man shouted Enrique's name and the crowd cheered once more. The television cameras panned the crowd, then swooped up to where Enrique held center stage. His voice boomed out, polished and enthusiastic. His smile was magnetic.

"He's talking of how corruption and greed once plagued our region, just like the cartel threatens us now."

"The guy was made for the spotlight," Simon conceded.

"Now he's reminding everybody of what he's done. Cleaning up the streets. Kissing all the babies."

Dr. Clara was seated on the stage next to the portly man. She cheered as loudly as anyone. When the applause quieted and Enrique started talking again, she glanced up at the balcony.

Martinez said, "With the help of the good citizens of Ojinaga, Enrique is promising to bring the same reforms to all of Chihuahua state."

The applause grew louder still. Enrique launched into his next statement, then his gaze fastened on something outside Simon's field of vision, and he faltered. Then the mayor remembered the cameras. He repositioned his smile as he gestured with both hands, waving someone forward.

Harold emerged from the orphanage gates and climbed the church steps. Enrique spoke into the microphone.

"He tells about the shooting," Martinez said. "How such crimes must be stopped. He introduces the people's great friend."

Harold began in his rough-hewn Spanish, which Martinez translated, "I'll be brief and to the point. Corruption is a cancer that slowly but surely destroys. It can annihilate a community, jobs, stability, peace, pride, its very moral fiber."

The bandage that gripped his arm and clenched it to his chest magnified the force of his words. Simon felt himself drawn forward so powerfully, he gripped the chair in front of him just to keep himself from moving to the balcony.

"Corruption has a death grip on our town. But I tell you there is a cure. It is called integrity and honesty. And for this cure to work, it must start at the top." Harold turned and glared at Enrique. "Every individual who is tainted by this cancer must be forced from office. They have no place among us. That is why I am here. Use your vote. Make it happen."

He used his good hand to point at the church behind him. "We stand here in front of our beautiful parish church. Therefore I'd like to close with a prayer." He waited for the people to bow their heads, then said, "God, we ask that You give us leaders who hold to Your standard. We ask that anyone in office who is infected by the cancer of corruption be cut down and stripped of power. We ask this in Jesus' name. Amen."

-

Sofia forced herself to behave as though there was nowhere she would rather be than by Enrique's side. She smiled and chatted gaily with any number of people. She allowed herself to be interviewed twice, once by a regional television news magazine, and then for the national nightly news. She was friendly with people she did not see. She felt Enrique's eyes on her constantly. Measuring. Studying. Wondering.

But it was not until he was leading her back to the SUV that he allowed a trace of his rage to emerge. "What was Harold doing?"

"He is old. He has been shot. Who knows what was behind his words."

His gaze was as tight as his voice. "Was he accusing me?"

"How could he? He has always admired you. He has . . ."

"What? Say it, Sofia."

"Harold's greatest concern is corruption. It is why he has admired you for so long."

"Then why did he not say that?"

"I do not know, Enrique. You should ask him yourself."

The words emerged softly, almost a whisper. "I intend to."

Sofia repressed a tremor of very real fear. "Would you drop me by my office, please?"

"You work too hard." But he leaned forward and gave his driver the directions.

They did not speak again until the SUV pulled up in front of her business. Enrique emerged from the vehicle with her, waited as she unlocked her door, then planted himself in her way. The brooding menace was still there in his gaze. "You know how I feel about you."

"Yes. I know."

"It is time."

She did not respond.

"I will have your answer."

She nodded and smiled the biggest lie of her life. "I am ready, Enrique."

"Yes?" He showed genuine surprise.

"Not here. And first I must tell Harold. It is his right, as my guardian." Her voice almost broke. "My abuelo."

"Very well. When?"

"I have a very important meeting this afternoon and evening. I could meet you later tonight."

His face darkened. "Tonight is impossible. I, too, have commitments."

"I could join you later, if you—"

"No, no. Tonight is . . . family."

"Tomorrow then."

He embraced her. Sofia not only endured it, but returned it. With all the force she had in her, she gripped this strong man and held tight. The repulsion moved through her in waves. She only held tighter still.

Enrique released her and offered his brilliant smile. "I will not sleep a wink all night."

Sofia replied fervently, "That makes two of us."

Chapter 35

Soon after the crowds dispersed, Pedro slipped into the apartment, followed by Martinez's partner. Simon asked, "How is Harold?"

"The talk wore him out and his wound started leaking again," Pedro replied. "He has returned to bed and is resting comfortably."

The downstairs door opened and a light tread raced up the stairs. Sofia embraced each of them in turn, even Simon. It was the first time Simon actually touched her, other than when she had stitched his forehead. Her hug was very quick, a simple enveloping of her arms, there and gone in less than three seconds.

It took far longer for Simon to stop vibrating from the impact of her closeness.

Martinez issued orders in the bites of a practiced field officer. She insisted on everything being done face-to-face. One trusted ally to the next. Pedro left first. Then her partner. Martinez and Sofia spent a few more moments talking softly in Spanish. Simon could see that the federal agent was allowing her doubts and concerns to show. He did not need to ask what was being said. If they wanted him to know, they would tell him.

When he grew hungry, Simon foraged through Sofia's kitchen and made a meal of dark bread and cheese and a salad of fresh greens. He ate standing at the counter, with Juan's Bible open to the book of John. The verse Vasquez had referred to, John chapter 8 verse 12, was circled. The professor had intended this as his final message. The man had gone out as he had lived. By faith alone.

Sofia walked over. "I often stand right here to eat, just as you do now."

"I love the way the mountains glow in the distance."

"As do I. Armando felt the same. He dearly loved those hills." She looked at the page he studied and smiled. "I have to go."

"I know. Be safe."

She touched him once more, a gentle hand upon his arm. The look she offered was liquid and filled with a lifetime's emotions. "Armando would be so proud of you."

Simon was still resonating from her touch when Martinez's phone rang. She checked the readout and grimaced. "Today of all days we have cell-phone service." She answered and spoke briefly, then cut off and said, "Something has come up. I must see to this personally."

"Go."

"You must not leave the apartment. It could be very dangerous for you out there."

"I understand." Simon hesitated, then decided there was

nothing to be gained by expressing his worries. That the hunters were out there. Waiting for him, as they had for Vasquez.

They came for him the hour before sunset. A sense of inevitability accompanied the soft tread, the squeak of a rubber sole, the complaining creak of a loose board. Simon hoped it was Sofia or Pedro, but he knew it was not. Ever since Martinez had spoken about Carlos being sprung from prison. Ever since she had talked about them planning something at the border. Simon had felt them closing in.

Enrique stepped into the room. "I should have known I'd find you here. Where is Sofia?"

"I have no idea."

Enrique turned toward the stairs and motioned. Carlos stepped into view. Same muscular bulk, same shapeless jacket, same maniacal smile. Only the eyes were different. They blazed now. The hatred he carried was a palpable force. It filled the room.

"Perhaps I should let Carlos ask you the questions."

Simon indicated the lone plate and glass. "Sofia hasn't been here since the afternoon. She didn't say where she was going."

"Simple Simon," Enrique sneered. "Able to fool everyone but me."

"And vice versa. I know you hacked Vasquez's e-mail account and had me run off the road. You wanted the apparatus ever since you first realized that was what caused the blackout. Only Vasquez was faster. He knew you'd be coming, so he smashed it to bits. Which meant you had to get me down here."

"And you fixed it and tested it. Just as I planned." Enrique motioned toward the stairs. "And now we must be going. Since you managed to survive the prison, I want you to work the apparatus for me."

"I thought you had your own techies for that."

"They are educated fools. They tell me the device could generate a lethal amount of focused energy."

"They got that right."

"They fear they have repaired it incorrectly. They fear my wrath. As should you."

"And if I refuse?"

Enrique appeared to enjoy the exchange. "Even a failed scientist like you should understand the alternatives. On the one hand, there is Carlos. Shall I have him bring Juan over and demonstrate his talents?"

"No. I'll do what you ask."

"Of course you will. And if you please me, life with me can be very agreeable. I have many ways to show you my appreciation."

"How about a passport?"

"There is only one way you will leave my employment. And you require no papers for that." Enrique jerked his head toward the exit. "*Vámonos*! We have a border to shut down."

Chapter 36

"I should have known there was no emergency and the call was a ruse," Martinez said. "I should have stayed with Simon."

Pedro sat in the rear seat of her fancy SUV, with the woven-leather seats and the chrome vents that glistened in the moonlight. They were parked on a hillside overlooking the city of Ojinaga. Waiting. He replied, "If you had stayed, you might be dead now."

Martinez gave a tight nod. "It was logical that Enrique would be looking for Simon. Especially if there is something big happening tonight that involves this machine of his."

Martinez's partner occupied the front passenger seat. Pedro and Sofia sat behind them holding hands. They had often managed to survive the worst moments by sharing strength. Just like now.

Sofia asked, "Have you informed the border agents?"

"And tell them what, precisely? That there may be a mysterious ray gun that will shut down their entire system?"

"It happened before."

"We have received no confirmation from the American side that the blackouts affected them. And from our own border guards we have only rumors. How could we specifically ask guards on either side without tipping our hand? Because the cartel has observers everywhere. I know this firsthand."

Two more SUVs were parked to either side of them. Three federal agents sat in the one to their right. Four in the one to their left. Hardly an army. Sofia asked, "Do we have enough support?"

"Every one of these agents I can vouch for personally," Martinez replied. "It is far better to move with a small force than risk alerting our foes."

Pedro nodded his agreement. "The question is, where do we go now?"

Martinez snapped on her penlight, revealing the regional map unfolded on her lap. "You are sure there are six transformer stations?"

"The same as last time you asked."

"All within range of the border."

"Again, I do not have any idea how far this device can reach. But close, yes."

Sofia tapped lightly on the window. A faint drumbeat of nerves. "What if Simon planned on this all along?"

The leather of Martinez's seat squeaked as she shifted around. "What are you saying?"

"Vasquez claimed Simon was the smartest man he had ever met. He used a very specific word: *intuitive.* He said Simon had the ability to reach the unseen conclusion." She turned to the agent. "What if he knew they were hunting him?"

"What is the purpose behind letting himself be caught? If he is as smart as you claim, surely he would know what he risked."

Pedro saw the glistening trail cascade down his sister's cheek as she said, "What if this was part of his plan as well? What if he saw this as penance for the wrongs he had done to Vasquez?"

"Harold spoke to him of forgiveness," Pedro protested. "And I did as well."

"But what if he needed an action, something that would give meaning to his sorrow and his guilt? What if he saw himself . . . ?" Her swallow was painful to Pedro's ears. "As a sacrifice?"

"But why?" Martinez demanded. "To what end?"

"You said it yourself. We don't know where to find them." Sofia took in the night-clad vista with a shaky hand. "They could be anywhere. Maybe Simon thinks he can give us a sign."

Pedro turned his face to the window. "I will pray for a sign. From Simon. And from heaven."

Chapter 37

Simon had to admit, the location Enrique had selected was perfect for everyone but him.

The maquiladora did not have a transformer station. It had two. One serviced the new commercial zone. The brightly lit substation sat within a new fence supported by concrete stanchions. It joined the enclosure for the entire commercial zone.

They then turned onto a lesser road, little more than an abandoned trail. It was covered by scrub, and the asphalt underneath had been reduced to rubble. They bounced along for a while, moving parallel to the industrial zone. No one spoke. Finally they came to a monolithic factory, a concrete tomb with empty windows. The smokestacks pointed like broken fingers toward the night sky. Not a single light gleamed.

They parked at one end of the factory lot and walked around the main building. Beyond that was a tumbledown fence, and beyond this was a second substation. It looked like it had not been used in years. But there was still the soft hum of power. Simon assumed the city had left it hoping that someone would restart the factory.

Enrique held a bulky satellite phone. When it buzzed, he listened, spoke tersely, then told Simon, "You have twenty minutes. Less."

"To do what?"

Enrique handed him the canvas carryall that held the professor's device. "Make the machine work, or die. Simple choices for Simple Simon."

Simon started for a dip in the fence. "I need more light."

Enrique turned and spoke to his driver. A few moments later, the SUV pulled up tight to where Simon squatted. The headlights bathed the array of transformers.

Simon didn't need twenty minutes. He could have completed his work in three. But there was nothing to be gained from telling anyone that. So he spent the time checking each of the connectors, jiggling the wires, and adjusting the feeds. He hadn't written down the new frequencies because he didn't need to. They were imbedded in his brain. Right alongside the image of Vasquez. The professor seemed to be standing just outside the reach of the headlights, smiling at him. Urging him on. Counting out the frequencies as he set them into the device's controls.

All the frequencies. The new ones he had obtained from Juan's Bible. *And* the others.

Simon knew Vasquez had intended for the new frequencies to replace the old ones. His final calculations had been aimed at distillation. Reducing the power to a manageable level. Maintaining control.

But Simon was not after control. He wanted mayhem.

Simon was alerted to a coming change when the driver spoke softly to Enrique and pointed into the night.

Tires scrunched over the rough terrain. Enrique swung a flashlight over his head. A second SUV pulled up close to Enrique's. Two thugs emerged from the vehicle, both in suit jackets that looked black in the headlights.

The mayor of Ojinaga underwent a remarkable transformation. He bowed. He became visibly obsequious. Almost fearful. Then he pointed at Simon. For some reason, that simple gesture was enough for the man's fear to transfer across the rubble and the broken fence and latch onto Simon.

"Simple Simon," Enrique called. "Come over here. Now."

When Simon hesitated, Carlos hustled toward him. Simon moved in order to keep a distance between them.

A lone man was seated in the SUV's backseat. As Simon approached, the thugs moved in tight to either side. Close enough to crush him at a word from the old man.

The man possessed the strangest voice Simon had ever heard. If a cadaver was somehow granted the power of speech, it would have sounded like him. He spoke to Enrique, who bowed slightly as he responded. The old man turned toward Simon. "You are a gringo?"

"From Boston," Enrique offered, now speaking English as well.

The old man turned slightly and looked at Enrique, who cringed and went silent. The old man said to Simon, "You are a scientist?"

"Yes."

"Where did you train?"

"MIT."

"I have heard of this place." He pointed with his chin toward the transformers. "You can make this machine work?"

"I think . . . yes."

"The border region is a graveyard of those who tried to be helpful and failed. Do you understand?"

Simon could not entirely mask his own tremors. "Yes."

"Over there you can see the border. It would be helpful if you can cut the power and stop all the electronics from working. If you fail . . . that would not be helpful. Are we clear?"

"Very."

"Good." The old man waved him on. "So go and be helpful."

Chapter 38

Sofia stood beside Pedro on the tallest rise overlooking the border region. The highway was a long ribbon of slowly moving headlights. Four miles away, the border crossing and the Rio Grande bridge formed a brilliant island of light. Beyond that shone the Texas town of Presidio.

Sofia asked, "Anything?"

Pedro dropped his borrowed binoculars to glare at her. "You think I would hide such a thing? Forget to mention it to you?"

"I am only asking."

"You will be the first to know. Believe me."

The agents were stretched out along the rise, all of them studying the terrain. One of the agents spoke softly to Martinez, who replied loud enough for them to hear. "So far, we have nothing."

Sofia said to her brother, "Pray harder."

Simon remained by the apparatus, pretending to make further adjustments while watching as Carlos scaled a rickety ladder attached to the factory's nearest smokestack.

Holding himself in place with one arm, Carlos pulled out a pair of binoculars and scouted the distance. From his position by the transformers, Simon thought he caught a flash from beyond the Rio Grande. There and gone in an instant. In confirmation, Carlos leaned down and waved.

Enrique said, "Make it work. Now."

"Okeydokey."

Enrique glared at him, clearly displeased with anything other than a man who shared his fear. "I don't need to tell you what is at stake. Especially for you."

Pedro exclaimed, "Did you see that?"

Martinez whirled around. "See what?"

"Something by the border. No, it's gone."

"Our side or theirs?"

"At about ten o'clock. Their side."

"You're sure?"

"It was beyond the river." Pedro dropped the glasses. "Maybe I was mistaken."

"No, no. I don't think so."

"It could have been anything. Headlights. A reflection."

"To the west of the American town there is nothing but desert. A light flashing on and off would most likely be a signal."

"Saying what?"

Martinez lifted her binoculars. "Keep looking."

Chapter 39

Simon flipped the switch.

The device took longer than he expected to warm up. Or perhaps it was how his heart beat at triple time.

Enrique shifted impatiently. "Count your breaths, my friend. If you fail, they are numbered."

Simon leaned closer still, craning to hear the hum of power.

"I'm sure one of El Noche's men can loan me a gun. If you fail, I will personally . . ."

Enrique stopped because the headlights flickered. All of them. In a unified vibratory pattern.

Simon heard it then. Unmistakable. "Here we go."

The man in the vehicle spoke. Simon knew it was El Noche. No one else sounded that way. Words emerged like the rattle of old bones.

One of the thugs whistled sharply. A single note.

Carlos looked down. The thug waved his hand.

Carlos turned and flashed a light at the border.

Enrique demanded, "How long?"

"It's happening."

"I need to know *precisely*."

Simon had to say something. He could feel the man's latent rage, the natural desire to reach out and strike someone, anyone, him. "Almost there."

Which he hoped fervently was true.

Pedro hissed, "Something's happening."

Martinez and her partner moved in unison. "Where?"

Pedro dropped his glasses and pointed at the border. "The lights at the station just flickered. And on the bridge."

"That's not . . ." Martinez's eyes widened. "I see it too! But how is that possible? They have their own generator."

"I told you. Simon's device affects all power in the region. Everything from laptops to car batteries."

Sofia moved like a tigress protecting her young. "Will you two stop talking about what does not matter? *Look for Simon*!"

The machine's humming noise continued to rise as it fed off the transformer system. The headlights brightened immensely. They became so intense, they hurt Simon's eyes. One of the thugs rasped out a curse. The old man still seated in the vehicle shielded his eyes.

Then the secondary effect took hold.

The cars went black. As did all the flashlights. And the phones. Everything.

The only illumination came from a faint trace of lightning that flickered at ground level. Encircling the device at its heart.

Carlos yelled from the ladder and pointed.

In the distance, the lights along the border fence began going out.

"It works! It works!" Enrique was almost dancing.

The massive island of lights to either side of the border bridge went dark. The old man in the car laughed.

"Now you will see why your device could not be permitted to fail," Enrique said. "The night winds are almost always from the south. Feel? Strong enough to carry a dark balloon. There, see? It rises from the earth!"

And it did. A massive silhouette carved from the stars, big as a floating castle. It drifted steadily northward, silent and massive. Simon asked, "How much?"

"The cargo?" Enrique's laugh carried a manic edge. "Six tons!"

And then the night took a ragged turn for the worse.

All of Martinez's agents were staring and pointing. The night was totally dark, as though some massive beast had eaten away every vestige of civilization. The river ran silver and smooth. A dog barked. Then another. But nothing moved. The highway was silent. The border bridge was simply a dark line drawn across the Rio Grande.

Then one of the officers shouted and pointed into the distance. A monolith rose into the night sky. It was the largest hot-air balloon Pedro had ever seen. The giant ball cut a swath from the stars. It had to be a good three miles away, perhaps as much as five.

Martinez nudged him. "Keep looking."

Pedro lifted his binoculars. Searching the darkness between them and the border. Hunting. Hunting hard.

Still, it was Sofia who first noticed it. "I see something."

Then Martinez said, "I see it too."

"But it's so faint."

"What difference does it make? A light is a light."

Martinez and her partner called softly. The other agents moved swiftly. They had come prepared. There was no telling what they had thought of Martinez's instructions to bring mountain bikes. But they had done as she had ordered. They opened the rear gates and pulled out six bicycles. There was soft argument between them. Martinez pointed at Pedro, insisting that he come along.

Sofia said, "The light! It's growing!"

Martinez looked over. "We must hurry."

Her partner squinted into the distance. "What is it I see?"

"Later!" She hoisted herself onto the saddle. "Move out!"

Chapter 40

The entire scenario changed for Simon in the space of about three breaths.

The ground-level lightning gathered and magnified. The effects were heightened by the utter absence of any other illumination. The humming resonated at every level of the audible range and far beyond, both high- and low-end vibratory patterns. Simon knew because his entire body felt like a tuning fork. Even his bones rang to the symphony of rising power.

The electricity gathered around the apparatus until the device itself became invisible. To Simon it looked as though the machine had entered a shimmering chrysalis. The effect grew in strength, both the brilliance of the light and the sound.

Then it became painful. Both auditory and visual effects reached the point where they began to sear the senses.

Enrique shrieked, "Make it *stop*."

Simon sensed the mayor was waving a pistol in his general direction. But it did not matter. Nothing did, except observing. Being the scientist. The professional analyst who designed a controlled experiment and carefully assessed the results.

Which, Simon had to admit, were totally awesome.

The lightning gathered until the ground between the transformers and the device was *carpeted* in power. The tapestry of energy was no longer content to remain where it was. It began to rise, a swirling pillar of blue and purple and gold lightning, an inverse whirlpool, forming a column that rose and grew and intensified.

The pillar of fire rose to join with the sky.

Simon lifted his hands to heaven. "For Vasquez!"

The police did not come with sirens. They came screaming.

If Simon's life had not been on the line, he would have found it hilarious.

They bounded and leapt over the rough terrain. Pedro pedaled out front, yelling louder than any of them. Which was nuts. The guy didn't even have a weapon. Maybe that was why he shouted until his voice broke. It was the only thing he had to throw.

Some of the cops had clearly not been on a bike in a long while. They puffed and they wiggled, struggling to find enough air to get up the rise, much less take aim.

Then the pillar of fire vanished. A blinding force one moment, nothing the next. The humming stopped as well.

Two seconds later, the power returned. The headlights snapped on. Radios crackled. The border crossing came back to life. In the distance rose the faint *whoop-whoop* of an automatic alarm.

The first gunshot came from overhead.

A stone by Simon's left leg pinged. Martinez's partner proved a modern-day gunslinger. He spun his bike through a tight wheelie and drew his weapon, all in one smooth motion, and fired a single shot.

Carlos yelled hoarsely and dropped from the ladder.

One of the thugs fired his weapon. Both of El Noche's guards were instantly trapped in a hail of bullets.

The old man snarled something that did not need translation as Martinez dragged him from the car. Then Simon's attention was caught by a flittering shadow. He was up and racing before he was fully aware that the shadow belonged to Enrique.

Simon tackled him at the point where the earth met the pavement. They fell in a heap. Enrique rolled and came up with a stone in his hand. He rasped, "Good-bye, Simon."

Then out of the shadows raced another figure. One transformed from a soft-eyed town manager to a snarling foe.

Enrique did not stand a chance.

Chapter 41

Six days later, they buried Armando Vasquez. A small cemetery stood by the city's oldest church, in a historic setting north of town. Strings were pulled, and space made for Ojinaga's friend.

The city and the state reeled from an endless string of revelations. The police had been shamed into admitting they had covered up Armando's murder. Fingers pointed straight at Ojinaga's former mayor. Enrique Morales was jailed pending trial, and not even his family's wealth and power could get him bail.

The gravesite service was a small affair. Of the orphanage children, only Juan attended. Too many of them held painful memories attached to funerals, and so the night before Harold held a candlelit remembrance in the orphanage chapel, full of laughter and song and only a few tears.

The day was hot, the sky empty. Simon was one of the pallbearers, along with Pedro and Juan and Agent Martinez's partner. Harold walked behind them, his good hand resting upon the coffin's bronze cross.

The cemetery was rimmed by ancient cottonwoods and looked out over the farming valley to the desert peaks beyond. Simon helped them lower the coffin into the waiting grave, then accepted the Bible from Harold and gave the first reading. As Harold spoke a farewell for them all, Simon held the key in his hand and prayed Armando would consider this a fitting end.

A week later, Simon sat in the dining hall. The light through the side window was soft in the manner of the long hour after sunset. The sky he could see was glorious, a gentle wash of rose and gold and palest blue. A pair of birds circled in and out of his field of vision, writing a winged script upon the dusk.

Pedro bustled in. "Have I missed anything?"

"It starts now!" Juan pointed at the empty place beside him. "Hurry!"

All the kids were there. Sofia sat with Gabriella on one side and Simon on the other. Sofia held both their hands. Simon looked down at the long fingers intertwined with his own. Here was the strongest evidence of all that the change was not just real, but ongoing. Pedro glanced at Simon from across the room and smiled a heartfelt benediction.

They occupied the second table from the kitchen. Above the opening where the food emerged, a television was screwed into the wall. Simon had never seen it on before. The kids all treated this as a party. Which they should. Great tubs of ice cream glistened on the pantry counter. The tables were filled with empty bowls and well-licked spoons and happy chatter.

The regional news went through its opening spiel. The kids all hushed one another with giggles until Juan called for silence. As the newscaster spoke, the orphanage came into view. Everyone in the room cheered. Simon loudest of all.

Sofia translated for Simon. "The newscaster, she is talking about free unlimited energy. Available for everyone. Some call it an impossible dream. But some say the dream is almost within reach. All because of scientific research that was accomplished here. By a local professor of physics and a visiting American scientist."

Simon's photograph appeared on the screen beside the newscaster. The cheers grew so loud, the newscaster could no longer be heard. Juan and Pedro's protests could do nothing to stifle the glee.

When the program went to commercial, Sofia turned to him. "Can I borrow you for a moment?"

"Or a lifetime," he said.

Sofia hesitated in the act of rising. But she recovered well enough and said simply, "A moment will do." Then she added two words that brightened the evening immensely. "For now."

The kids giggled and pointed and made kissy sounds as they left. Simon turned and lifted his free hand in a fist and scowled at them, which of course only resulted in more laughter. Even from Pedro.

Sofia pulled him across the courtyard and into the girl's dorm. The last time Simon had been there was to place the solar lantern on Gabriella's bedside table. Sofia pulled him down the central aisle and stopped before a bed beneath one of the three windows.

"This bed was mine."

The most vulnerable moment of a strong woman's life. The place she had become reborn to hope. Here. Simon thought it was the most beautiful way of revealing herself she could have ever made.

"I have something to give you." Then Sofia stopped because the phone rang in Harold's empty office, and Juan popped from the doorway and scampered across the courtyard. "Juan! Shame on you!"

The boy just laughed as he raced into Harold's office. Simon heard him answer, "Three Keys!" Then, "Everyone! It is Dr. Harold!"

That morning the orphanage director had traveled to Juárez with Consuela Martinez and Dr. Clara. A church group had asked for their assistance in establishing a new orphanage.

Sofia hesitated, clearly torn between what she intended to say and wanting to hear Harold's news. So Simon made the decision for her and led them out of the dorm and across the courtyard.

The kids crammed into the office and the hall. Sofia and Simon joined those outside the window in time to hear Harold announce, "I think I've found the spot for our next orphanage!"

"This is amazing news," Pedro shouted over the din. "And the bank tells us the first payment from the tech fund has arrived."

"So much money!" Juan confirmed.

Harold waited through the joyful chatter, then went on. "This means I'll need to be away for a while longer. So now is the time, Pedro."

"For what?"

"For you to take over Three Keys."

All the kids turned and beamed at him. Pedro's mouth worked for a moment, then he managed weakly, "Dr. Harold . . . what?"

"You've earned it. Commit your ways to the Lord and your plans will be achieved."

Sofia smiled at her brother, then stepped away from the window and the children. She tugged on Simon's hand. "Come."

Pedro said, "You have no idea what this means to me. I will work very hard. You will see."

"I know that, son. I have every confidence in you. Now tell me, how is Simon?"

"Making progress every day. And right now I think he is working on his fourth goal."

"Which goal is that?"

"The one he did not write down. My sister."

Harold's laugh was captured by all the children. "I think unlimited energy is easier than that!"

"It is too noisy here to talk, much less think." Sofia pulled on Simon's hand. "Come with me. Please."

She led him out the courtyard gates and into the plaza fronting the church. The bunting was still up, rattling softly in the night breeze. She drew him to the church steps and sat down next to him. "Something has finally come for you."

She reached into her purse and came out with a new United States passport. Simon took it and breathed a soft, "Oh, wow."

"You're finally free. You can go back home whenever you want."

Simon slipped the passport into his shirt pocket, next to the small Bible Harold had given him. "What if I've found a new home?"

Sofia studied him, somber, almost afraid. "You would do that?"

"It's on my list of dreams."

"What?"

He rose high enough to pull the crumpled paper from his pocket. "I've been working on it since, you know, the night." He handed it over. "Only Pedro got the order wrong."

Sofia unfolded the page and flattened it on her leg. Studying intently.

"You weren't fourth on the list," Simon said. "You were first."

Sofia reached into her purse and pulled out a pen. She clicked it and slowly crossed her name off the list. "Mission accomplished."